Hammour Ziada was b
He has worked as a civil soc
currently a journalist based i
novels and two collections of

The Longing of the Dervish won the Naguib Mahfouz Medal for Literature in 2014 and was shortlisted for the International Prize for Arabic Fiction in 2015.

Translator of the winning novel in the Independent Foreign Fiction Prize and winner of the Saif Ghobash–Banipal Prize for Arabic Literary Translation, **Jonathan Wright** was formerly the Reuters bureau chief in Cairo. He has translated Alaa Al-Aswany, Youssef Ziedan, and Hassan Blassim. He lives in London, UK.

The Longing of the Dervish

Hammour Ziada

Translated by
Jonathan Wright

hoopoe
AN IMPRINT OF AUC PRESS

Cover image from *Fire and Sword in The Sudan: A Personal Narrative of Fighting and Serving the Dervishes 1879–1895*, by Colonel Sir R. Slatin Pasha (London, 1899). Courtesy of the Rare Books and Special Collections Library at the American University in Cairo.

First published in 2016 by
Hoopoe
113 Sharia Kasr el Aini, Cairo, Egypt
420 Fifth Avenue, New York, 10018
www.hoopoefiction.com

Hoopoe is an imprint of the American University in Cairo Press
www.aucpress.com

Exclusive distribution outside Egypt and North America by I.B.Tauris & Co Ltd., 6 Salem Road, London, W4 2BU

Dar el Kutub No. 26101/15
ISBN 978 977 416 788 1

Dar el Kutub Cataloging-in-Publication Data

Ziada, Hammour
    The Longing of the Dervish / Hammour Ziada.—Cairo: The American
University in Cairo Press, 2016.
    p. cm.
    ISBN 978 977 416 788 1
    1. Arabic Fiction –Translation into English
    2. Arabic Fiction
    I. Title
    892.73

1 2 3 4 5   20 19 18 17 16

Designed by Adam el-Sehemy
Printed in the United States of America

To she who . . .

Any longing that diminishes through meeting is not to be relied on.
—Ibn Arabi

One

1

"I'm not frightened of dying. I'm frightened I won't see you again."

2

Fire and smoke everywhere.

Fire and smoke in his heart.

The Mahdi's city had fallen.

The holy city of Omdurman had been pounded by the shells of the infidels.

The Hour had come.

It was what Bakhit had spent seven years waiting for.

Now he would be free.

You brutes, I'm coming.

3

As soon as the shackles were off his legs, Bakhit Mandil jumped to his feet.

The prisoners who were still around him congratulated each other. One clapped his hand on Bakhit's shoulder and shouted, "At last! Freedom, Bakhit!"

Freedom had come to them with the warships and cavalry of the invaders. It was September 1898 and the Egyptian army had entered the country. The Mahdist state was defeated.

But Bakhit didn't feel he was free. Bad blood and revenge stood between him and freedom.

He pushed his way through the crowd to get out of the prison. He felt weak. He hadn't eaten for eight days. He hadn't drunk anything for three. But he couldn't stay a moment longer.

The city had fallen two days earlier. In prison they had heard the news that the Khalifa and his commanders had fled. The Egyptians had entered Omdurman. A group of Christians and Egyptians had come to the prison and released some important people that they knew, but left the others.

Two days with no guards and with no one asking after them. It looked like those outside had forgotten them completely. They could hear the sporadic sound of shelling. They were in their shackles on the floor where the warders had left them before running away. Some were in the little cells, some in the prison courtyard in the sun. Bakhit was in one of the cells. There were about seventy people in a room that shouldn't have held five. The air was thick and heavy. They were breathing in the air that the others breathed out. Some of them wept for joy; others wept for fear of dying forgotten in the cell because the warders had run off and the new rulers were ignoring them. But Bakhit knew he wouldn't die there. He had put up with prison for seven years waiting for this moment. He wouldn't die till he had herded his enemies to their deaths like sacrificial lambs. He would go to Hawa with them in his power.

He stumbled out into the street.

Fire and smoke everywhere.

The city had been open to pillage and the black soldiers were still looting the houses.

He heard women screaming, and sergeants were walking around shouting that the time for pillage was over.

He slipped warily into the violence and the madness, looking for Merisila's house. Soldiers stopped him and searched him several times. Some soldiers attacked him to rob him but then realized he was poorer than a mangy dog. They beat him up and let him go. He walked through the streets of a city he didn't recognize, asking the way from passersby. Omdurman was greatly changed. He had seen it two weeks earlier when he was last taken out on work duty. Now it seemed that years had passed between that time and the mad scene into which he had stumbled. There were dead bodies in the streets, swollen and surrounded by swarms of black flies. The putrid stench made the stunned city retch. The doors of the houses had been forced open. The roads were dirty and full of potholes. The smell of gunpowder was everywhere. To add insult, the dome of the Mahdi's tomb had been badly damaged.

He asked a passerby if he knew the house he was looking for. He received a surprised look and terse directions.

He walked past the arsenal, alongside the market, under the empty gallows. Then he turned west. He walked like a child who has just passed the crawling stage. He could feel where the iron shackles had cut into his legs. He was reeling but his determination held him upright. If he had succumbed to weakness he would have died years ago, but a man with a debt to love never dies.

He followed the directions of passersby.

When he stood at Merisila's door he wasn't sure he would find her. But he was certain that the safest place he could now seek shelter was under her roof. He pushed his way inside. Blinking, he noticed there were bodies piled up whose identities he couldn't make out. He heard his name. As he fell he saw Merisila rushing toward him. He collapsed on the ground, panting. He was sweating and bleeding, yet full of determination.

Merisila hugged his head and screamed. She thought he had come to die on her doorstep.

But he looked up at her and said in anguish: "It's time for revenge, Merisila. Death to those who killed her. Death, Merisila. I am death."

Merisila slapped her face. She sobbed and beat her chest with her hands like an angry mother.

"Damn that Christian woman! Damn that Christian woman! You poor wretch, Bakhit," she said.

"If I adopted your religion and abandoned the religion of the Mahdiya, would that make you happy?" asked Bakhit.

Theodora laughed. "You're joking!"

"I wanted to see you laugh. I'll change my religion to please you when you next get angry with me."

Merisila had never liked Theodora. She thought she was wholly evil. A white devil that took possession of Bakhit at sunset.

With help from other women, Merisila dragged Bakhit to the matting enclosure in the courtyard. She laid him on the ground and examined his legs. The iron shackles had worn the flesh to the bone. His flesh was septic and oozing pus. His body was hot with fever.

He would have been dead if it wasn't for the vow he had made.

The shackles with their two iron rings had left marks in his flesh. He had been going out on work assignments in Omdurman with the shackles on his feet. With every step the shackles sank into his flesh. Bakhit had walked for months, and the shackles were years deep.

For days Merisila poured ghee into his wounds. She stripped him down every morning and rubbed his body with oil. She gave him a mixture of ghee, garlic, honey, and dates to drink.

He didn't moan or try to escape the pain by fainting. The pain inside protected him from any other pain.

He lay on his back looking at the matting roof under which he had taken shelter. His body was naked and visible to the women Merisila had hidden in her house. He could hear them whispering and then suddenly laughing. His body glistened like an olive when Merisila washed it with oil. She turned him over and he writhed. She ran her oiled hands over his naked body, back and front. She wrapped the wounds on his legs in cloth after cleaning away the pus and packing the wounds with ghee and salt.

Merisila's house was just a mud wall with one room and two enclosures in the courtyard.

When the women found out that their menfolk, after going out with their spears to meet the enemy, would not be coming back, they had rushed in panic to Merisila to seek refuge. They knew what the soldiers would do if they won. Many women had come to Omdurman from towns that had been defeated. They begged in the street or were forced to go to the public treasury for alms. Their bodies were at the mercy of the victors.

Even women who hated Merisila knew that safety lay with her.

If anyone was now so busy helping others that she wouldn't save herself, it was Merisila, who was twenty years old and from a family of slaves. She sold home-brewed beer secretly, told fortunes with seashells, arranged love trysts and marriages, helped fugitives, and traded in necklaces, chains, and secret potions to make people fall in love, to bring people together or separate them, to help men get hard erections and tighten up women's vaginas. The whole city knew she had saved seven women from the gallows in the marketplace and had humiliated the standard-bearer of one of the commanders in front of the mosque and within sight of the Khalifa. Love was her trade, magic ran in her family, and she had the valor of a mounted tribal warrior.

Merisila had taken in women seeking shelter. She had helped women escape when they wanted to escape. She had tended to women who were overcome with sadness. Mysteriously, she provided food for dozens of women, some of whom she knew and others whom she was seeing for the first time.

When Bakhit Mandil came to her she immediately cleared out one of the shelters and put him in it alone. She nursed him tenaciously, fighting off the death and the weakness that was in him. He heard her crushing garlic to make the potion for him, muttering anxiously, "You're not going to die on me, you dirty slave, you mindless bastard. I won't let you die."

She was sniffling noisily and the women wondered whether she was about to cry.

"You're weak, lying there like dead on the ground. You can't stand up. Your wounds are infected with maggots. What for? You really are a sorry slave! I'll nurse you back to health, to kill you later, you mule."

She rushed the mixture over to Bakhit. She lifted his head for him to drink it, and insulted him as she did so. "Drink, you idiot, drink. Merisila won't let you die."

Bakhit's eyes lit up, but his mouth was full of the sticky liquid and he couldn't answer.

He wasn't angry or frightened. He was in the right place. He had to put himself in Merisila's hands, and she would look after him.

After that he started to strive for the goal for which he had survived the years that had passed.

Out of sight of the other women, when he felt Merisila's tears falling on his face and running down his beardless cheek and into his mouth, mixing with the potion he was drinking, he felt he had been saved from all his old problems.

When he tasted her tears, as bitter as desert rain, he felt at peace with the world.

Leave yourself in Merisila's hands; you're safe now.

4

Bakhit didn't know how many days had passed, and he didn't care.

What did counting time mean when he had told himself that time had come to an end when Hawa was gone?

He stayed with Merisila till he could feel his body once again. He gained strength as if reborn. The marks of the shackles on his legs hadn't disappeared but the wounds had healed, thanks to the black woman's magic.

He willingly put up with her insults and abuse. He wasn't embarrassed that the other women were looking at his nakedness. He wasn't curious about the shouts from the city and the sound of bullets in the distance or nearby.

He had a dream. His dream stretched out endlessly. It recurred persistently when he was awake and in his sleep. There were six people he knew by name and he had a score to settle with them.

On the day he recovered and stood up naked under the matting roof, Sudanese soldiers broke into the house.

Merisila brought him a jelaba and he put it on. He sat up on the mattress for the first time and ate his meal. He told Merisila in a whisper what he wanted from her. She was the only person who could accomplish what he wanted in a city that was trembling like an old woman's hand. He gave her two assignments that were equally difficult, but Merisila didn't complain that they were too much trouble. She complained that he was mad and obsessed with a delusion. Ever since he had met Merisila, he had never cared about her opinion. But he valued her efficiency.

When the soldiers came into the house, he was eating gruel that she had made specially for him without allowing the other women to see it. The soldiers were black like him, wearing military uniforms and fezzes, with rifles and powder belts across their chests. The women screamed and the house was in an uproar. The soldier in charge announced their purpose.

"We're looking for men," he said. "The government has imposed a corvée on all able-bodied men."

Merisila wasn't impressed. She was antagonistic and stood in his way. Her head hardly reached his chest but he looked insignificant compared with her.

"If you were a man you'd get past me and search the house!" she shouted.

The sergeant was taken aback. He looked at his soldiers, then back at Merisila, who was seething like a cauldron. "I know you," she continued before he had a chance to speak. "You're Farajallah, the fugitive slave of the chief butcher. You're him, you wretch. And now you come charging into people's houses, proudly wearing the Christians' stripes?"

"We only want to take the men," the humiliated sergeant replied. "If you tell me this is the only man here," he continued, pointing at Bakhit Mandil, "then we won't need to search the house. We'll just take him off to work. We're taking everyone."

Bakhit stepped toward him, upset that Merisila was protecting him like a hen guarding her chick.

"Apart from me, there aren't any men here. I'll come with you," he said.

Merisila spat on the ground, just missing the sergeant's boot. She rushed into her room, and came back with nine amulets that she wrapped around Bakhit's arm. Nine large amulets that would protect him from ghouls, magic, envy, and prying eyes. In a whisper that she made sure the sergeant could hear, she said, "Don't be frightened of his fancy uniform. It's just Farajallah, the slave of the chief butcher in the market. He was the worst slave that ever lived there. Then he ran away a year ago. They thought he'd drowned in the Nile. If only he had! If he takes it into his head to order you around, remind him who he is. His back is covered with scars from his masters' whippings."

When Bakhit went out into the road with the soldiers, he found they had rounded up dozens of other men: Arabs, blacks, mulattos, slaves, and freemen. Sergeant Farajallah pushed him gently into line. "What a woman!" the sergeant said, trying to reassert his authority. "If it wasn't for my orders, I'd teach her a lesson."

Bakhit smiled guilelessly as the sergeant moved away. "If it wasn't for orders, she would've eaten you up on the spot, Farajallah," he said.

5

The years in prison had taken a heavy toll on him.

Those who had the misfortune to be in the Sayir prison in Omdurman had to buy their own food and drink. The prison didn't provide food for the inmates. All it provided was torture. For reasons unknown to anyone else, the warders would pick a few prisoners and flog them, or assign them futile tasks, or put them in sacks with scorpions and make bets on who would die and who would survive. Whenever the warders came through to check them, the prisoners felt that fate was walking among them looking for prey. Some of them couldn't take the torture and died. The warders might hand the bodies over to their families, or dump them behind the prison to swell up and rot there. Nothing was certain. The only truth was that the torture might start at any moment.

In the prison there were Europeans, Egyptians, military commanders who had fallen out of favor with the Khalifa, political rivals, and poor wretches who never stopped crying and who were there for reasons that no one knew.

The prison was a big compound near the river, with a wall of unbaked brick. Inside there were small cells, mostly without windows. During the day the prisoners were allowed to sit in the courtyard, but they spent the night crammed together in the cells, piled on top of each other.

The wealthy prisoners, and there were many, had people to bring them food and drink through a long chain of bribes. But lowly creatures such as Bakhit Mandil had to fend for themselves. They were taken out to the city to look for work that would earn them some money. They went out in shackles, guarded by warders who took a cut of what they earned. The warders made sure they were present when the prisoners struck agreements with their employers, so they would know how much the prisoners were going to be paid and could calculate their share.

Bakhit Mandil had worked in these streets often in the previous seven years.

He went out in a chain gang, walking slowly because of the shackles on his legs. He took care not to fall over. The warders took them along the city streets. The prison and a number of important government buildings lay behind a large stone wall. Years earlier, Bakhit had helped build this wall, which surrounded the Dome district in the city center. The warders took them out through the northern gate in the wall. They went past the Bayt al-Mal, the treasury, and the houses where the clerks, the Egyptians, and people from old Khartoum lived. The procession veered east and walked parallel to the river. Sometimes they turned south to go back into the dome district and sometimes they went west into the market. The procession didn't have a fixed itinerary. The idea was that people should see them and come and ask for workers they could hire.

There was a difference between the work he had done then and this corvée work.

The streets had lost their color. The sparkle had faded. A sullen mood had settled over the workers. One injustice begets another. Maybe they were used to the old injustice. But today they were on the threshold of a new injustice and didn't know what it would mean for them.

The soldiers ordered them to fill in the holes in the streets and clean up all the rubbish.

They picked up the dead bodies and the guts spilled out. Bakhit and some others lifted one body and a leg came off in his hand.

Bakhit and five others were assigned to some streets close to the arsenal. As they worked, the Sudanese soldiers came and went. Once or twice they saw a European officer on a horse. "Is that red man Egyptian?" one of the workers asked in amazement.

Bakhit looked at the officer, listened carefully, and replied, "He's English. They're everywhere these days."

His colleagues looked at him in puzzlement.

"Like Gordon," he explained.

They knew what he meant. Everyone remembered the English pasha who had been sent by Cairo some years earlier to fight the Mahdi. The Mahdi's soldiers killed him in his uniform on the steps of the palace in Khartoum.

A pasha with red skin. Full of delusions. He had come to the city at the darkest of times. He had allowed the slave trade, after previously banning it. He had tried to win over the Mahdi, then threatened him. He had tried to tempt him with a governorship. He had written letters to him. He had tried to improve morale in a city that was consumed by despair. He had stood on the palace balcony scanning the horizon with a telescope in the expectation of relief. Two warships had arrived to help but he was already dead and the artillery fire forced them back.

"Would you like to make some money with me?" one of the workers whispered to Bakhit.

Bakhit took a good look at him. He was of medium height, about the same age as him, with a noticeably large head and cloudy eyes.

"Tell me more," he said.

"At the end of this street is the arsenal. There must be weapons and gunpowder there worth stealing," the man replied.

Bakhit looked toward the end of the street. He could see soldiers around the arsenal, holding weapons and watching them.

"Haven't you seen all those guards?" Bakhit asked.

The worker looked around to make sure their colleagues couldn't hear. "I know one of the clerks who work inside," he said. "He'll help us get past them. With his help we can take some of the gunpowder and the weapons and smuggle them over the wall to the river."

The idea stirred Bakhit's spirit of adventure, but he kept his enthusiasm firmly under control. "That's rather too risky for me," he said. "I've just come out of prison. I don't want to go back to prison when the Egyptians are in charge."

The workman shook his head in surprise and slipped off to find another partner. Bakhit was familiar with this relentless enthusiasm for taking advantage of opportunities, but he wasn't interested in all that. He intended to make do with whatever he was paid for his work at the end of the day. He was staying with Merisila so he didn't need more money. If he took any ill-considered or unnecessary step he could end up further from his objective.

As he worked he thought about his next steps. He had asked Merisila for the information he wanted. But he also needed a weapon and some money. He wasn't going to steal them. That could endanger his whole mission. He had to save his earnings little by little like a busy ant.

He wasn't in a hurry. There was no time frame for his mission; it could take an eternity.

6

The city of Omdurman had begun as a small village for fishermen on the west bank of the Nile opposite Khartoum, the capital the Turks had built. When the Mahdi took Khartoum in 1885, he came to Omdurman and made it his base for a while.

The Mahdi wandered around on his camel until it knelt at the spot where God wanted the Mahdi to build himself a house. That was where he was buried when he died, and a dome was built over his tomb.

Little houses sprang up everywhere, built of mud, straw, and animal skins, and with time they were dressed with red brick and stone.

The city expanded along the river. In the heart of it stood the Mahdi's dome and to the west of the dome the great mosque. To the south stood the houses of the Khalifa and his relatives, their guards, and people from the west of the country. To the north stood the houses of people from the Nile valley in the north of Sudan.

In the middle there was the Bayt al-Mal, or treasury, the Bayt al-Amana, where ammunition was stored, and the Sayir prison where Bakhit had been held.

On the night years ago when Bakhit was thrown into the prison, it had been summertime.

They threw him down in front of the warders. He was bleeding profusely and shaking in trepidation, unsure whether to believe what was happening to him. He could still remember the taste of the beer he had been drinking that night.

The warders wanted to whip him but they couldn't find anywhere on his body to do it. His body was swollen and bleeding. You could hardly make out his features. They put him in a small, windowless stone cell and locked the door. It stank of putrid, festering wounds and was as hot as a furnace.

They threw him on top of other people who were lying on the ground. The people were startled and they shouted out, insulting Bakhit and the warders. The cell was as dark as the world of the blind. Bakhit was wearing only a pair of torn trousers that hardly covered his legs. He could feel the bodies beneath him moving aside to make space for him on the ground. He was drunk with fear and the remains of the beer. His urine came out hot beneath him. He heard someone cursing in the distance but he didn't care. He kept forcing his urine out in a stream that mixed with his blood. Someone kicked him in his side and cursed him when he noticed that his foot was covered in blood.

Toward dawn he started to cry.

He sobbed out loud. After that he never cried again throughout his imprisonment. He seemed to have vented all his grief in that one cry. He crawled in what he thought was the direction of the wall and tried to vomit up the beer in his stomach. The other inmates moved away, but they came closer again when they saw that he couldn't bring anything up. The only alcohol left inside him was the alcohol in his veins but the grief would burn inside him for the rest of his life. He spat, then leaned back against the wall. The cell was hellishly hot. He heard the dawn call to prayer from the mosque nearby and the sound of metal gates moving aside to let people through to pray.

He didn't move. The other prisoners asked him what crime he had committed. He didn't answer. All of the others volunteered the charges against them:

"I killed three people."

"They picked me up because I was late in paying a debt."

"I've been sentenced to five years for smuggling grain from the east."

"I'm innocent."

"I ran away from my master and the Mahdi's army caught me and locked me up here. I don't know till when."

"I'm serving three months because I smoked tobacco."

"I stole a donkey from the butchers' market."

So many of them were competing to say what crimes they had committed that Bakhit's brain was overwhelmed. The whole world existed in this little room.

They were interrupted when daylight appeared, along with the warders. They took hold of him, put six heavy shackles on his feet, and tied his hands with a heavy chain that they pulled tight around his neck. He resisted and they flogged him. Some of the people around him also got whipped by mistake. They shouted and moved away. When they had finished with him, they inspected the other prisoners. They found that one of them was dead, so they dragged him outside and shut the door. The other prisoners, sweaty and frightened, moved closer again. Again they asked him what his crime was.

"My crime was love," he said. His voice betrayed the loneliness he felt.

There was a moment of stunned silence, and then they started to laugh cautiously. "They accused a man of love? You poor wretch," one of them said.

Bakhit Mandil wasn't interested in explaining.

In his sadness he kept apart from the other prisoners, who had been taken out to the courtyard. Humbled, he cowered at the base of the wall and wallowed in his sorrows.

He didn't have the strength to talk. He wanted to think over every moment of the previous day so that he wouldn't forget. He wanted to etch those moments onto his body like tattoos.

In silence he set about burning the memories and delusions into his skin. They would stay with him as long as he lived.

7

It was a day that seemed like a thousand years.

A day when he reassessed all of his previous life.

He relived past happiness. He suffered sorrows he hadn't thought existed.

Then he arrived at a truth by which and for which he had lived.

He would take revenge.

He would take revenge and he would die for her sake.

He would give her a sparrow once again.

Nothing would stop him seeking revenge. He wouldn't succumb to sadness. He wouldn't torment himself with guilt. Instead he would keep the anger alive in his heart. He didn't know how long he would stay in prison but the day he came out there would be enough anger in his heart for him to exact revenge like an expert.

He defined his fantastical objective.

He decided to eat and drink only hatred. Until the day he came out.

He didn't know at the time that he would have to wait seven years for that day.

The next day he realized he would have to work to eat. But he was withdrawn and wasn't interested in going out. He pottered around the courtyard in his shackles.

Whenever he moved, the chains made an unpleasant metallic sound. The rhythm of his steps could be tracked by the clanking of the chains.

Some of the prisoners were kind to him and offered him some of the little food they had.

One of them gave him a piece of cloth, which he used as a fan on hot nights.

"You need it more than me because you're new," he said. "My body's gotten used to this inferno. You'll need it to fan yourself. The air here is trapped, like us in our chains. It's stifling and it can't move. You have to move it with this piece of cloth to get a breeze," he explained.

He walked around the courtyard looking at the other prisoners with his generous new friend, who was called Jawhar and was also a slave who no longer had a master.

Jawhar was thinner than Bakhit, but taller—taller than anyone Bakhit had ever known. On his cheeks he had thin scar lines. He had a few small hairs under his chin, but not what one would call a beard. He was talkative and friendly. They took shelter in what little shade there was. Jawhar pointed to a secluded room and said, "That's the chamber of wonders. There are three Egyptians there. Two of them are civil servants and the third is a soldier they caught spying in Berber. There's a man with them who claims to be Jesus the son of Mary, and the fifth man is a Christian sheikh. All of them except Jesus pay the warders a riyal a day to keep that room for themselves."

He showed him the warders' rooms and told him about Touma, the wife of one of the warders. She provided services to the prisoners in exchange for small gifts.

"Services?"

"She'll smuggle a letter in from a woman or pass on requests. She'll bring you a mug of beer. Maybe for a riyal she'll let you touch her bottom," Jawhar said. "Her bottom's worth a riyal, or more," he continued. "It's amazing, like the dome."

Bakhit had no interest in women right now. The woman who had stolen his heart wasn't here. She was gone, and with her everything he desired in women.

"I hear your crime was love," Jawhar said with interest. "What's that about?"

Bakhit didn't answer.

"Did you kill the husband of the woman you loved?"

He didn't answer.

"They caught you in the house of a married woman?"

He didn't answer.

Jawhar didn't insist. He moved on to other subjects.

Within a few days Bakhit was familiar with all the details of the prison: its history, stories about it, the balance of power between the prison governor and the warders, the customs and sorrows of the prisoners. Jawhar told him everything, however insignificant. He became his constant companion. Sometimes fortune smiled on them and the warders put them in the same cell for the night. But mainly they put them apart. The prisoners were put into the cells at random. They were herded like sheep and locked up till morning. The warders put handcuffs back on some of them, counted the living, and dragged off the dead. They collected their bribes and then locked the doors.

Bakhit spent the night with handcuffs on, but they were taken off in the morning and then he shuffled around with just the shackles on his legs.

On the day he completed his first month he went out with a chain gang for the first time.

The warder dragged him by the neck and pushed him into a long line of prisoners that was shambling out. He was amazed by how quiet the streets were. Although he was inured to suffering he had thought the city would be weeping and the streets dressed in mourning clothes. How come the Nile was still in its place? The dome hadn't collapsed and the mosque hadn't flown away. He couldn't imagine Omdurman without the dome. He hadn't known Omdurman without it. But he knew that the sadness was his sadness. He realized how alone he was in this world. Perhaps others were crying, but he was the sad one. Perhaps there were people around him, but he was alone.

Someone picked out Bakhit, Jawhar, and a third prisoner when they were close to the neighborhood inhabited by the Kinana tribe. The man took them to his house to finish off a well he was digging. Bakhit wanted to chat because his heart was burdened with old wounds. He insisted on going down the well with Jawhar while the third prisoner stayed at the top to carry away the soil. As he filled the bucket time and time again he told his friend his story. Jawhar cried as Bakhit spoke, and tried to keep himself distracted by digging. But the streaks of tears, mixed with mud, were visible on his cheeks. Bakhit told him about Hawa. His love. How she had shunned him at first and had then become favorably disposed toward him. The birds he had given her. The desire that he found hard to bear. Her notebook and the way she poured her innermost thoughts into it in ink. He told him stories that were confused and fragmentary, in which the only common thread was his love for her. But they touched Jawhar and made him cry. Bakhit made Jawhar feel his pain. He said nothing critical of Hawa and took full responsibility himself. Among his fantasies he included some facts. But what are facts other than what we remember? Our memories are our reality and fantasies what really happened. That day ended but the stories didn't end. Jawhar tried to arrange to be locked up in the same cell as Bakhit but the warder had other ideas and it was the warder's will that prevailed. Even a bribe didn't work. Jawhar went off sadly and full of curiosity to another cell, leaving Bakhit and the rest of his stories in another cell.

They didn't put shackles on his hands that night because he gave some of his earnings to the warders. He squeezed in among the other prisoners. He heard someone complaining that he was near the shit hole. Some of the people moved around in the darkness. Someone shouted out, asking the people near the wooden door to move aside to let the moonlight in through a large crack in the wood. A moment later the light came in, pale and faint. Some of it fell on Bakhit's face and some lit the way for the grumblers to change places. Before the light was blocked once again, Bakhit Mandil heard someone saying, "Is that you? What a coincidence!"

He didn't know who the man was talking to, but he could feel him creeping closer.

"You're Bakhit. You worked at the soap factory. Have you forgotten me in just a few days?" the man eventually said.

Bakhit squirmed in his place. That filthy voice.

"I haven't forgotten you. But I can't see you," he said.

The voice laughed. Bakhit was thinking how disgusting the man was.

"In this tomb I wouldn't have seen you either if it wasn't for the light that came in just now," the man said.

The man was close by now, right next to him.

"Who are you?"

"I'm Younis Wad Jaber."

"Younis."

"Yes, Younis."

"Younis the soldier in the Mahdi's army?"

"Now you remember."

Bakhit felt Theodora's presence as a halo of light.

There was an uproar among the prisoners and they started shouting. Some of them tried to push Bakhit. Some were hitting him. But he didn't back off.

"For God's sake! You're going to kill him."

Yes, Bakhit wanted to kill Younis.

The shouting got so loud that the door opened and the warders attacked. They hit Bakhit hard but he wouldn't let go of Younis's neck. When the light streamed in through the open door and filled the room, Bakhit could see Younis's flushed face. His eye sockets were inflamed and his tongue was hanging out of his mouth. He was gasping loudly and Bakhit's hands were tightening around his neck. Someone hit Bakhit on the side of the neck and he loosened his grip. Another blow, and everything went murky. But he hung on. He dug his fingernails in to hurt his enemy more. But the violent blows to his neck didn't give him time to kill him.

As he collapsed, hardly conscious, he saw Hawa looking at him through the open door. She was white, framed by silver light.

Her face was sad.

9

When the doors of the cells were opened in the morning, Jawhar ran out looking for his friend.

Overnight the news had spread like magic through the whole prison. All the cells knew that Bakhit Mandil had tried to kill a new prisoner. Jawhar paid a bribe to see Bakhit at the pillar he was tied to. The guard took him to within a few feet of Bakhit and made him stop there. Jawhar wanted to rush to his friend's side but the guard held him back.

"I agreed you could look at him. If you want a closer look, you have to pay more," the guard said.

Jawhar didn't have anything to pay him with, so he had to make do with looking at him from a distance.

Bakhit was tied to a large wooden post on the eastern side of the prison courtyard. His back was streaming with blood. His trousers, already torn, were now in shreds. His feet were not touching the ground. Two heavy, rust-colored chains were wrapped around his wrists and his neck. Jawhar could see the blood dripping from Bakhit's toes and seeping into the ground.

Saddened, Jawhar turned back.

He rushed around the cells collecting leftover food and then started looking for Younis. He asked the prisoners where he was and they pointed to where he was hiding in the shade in a remote cell. He was sitting alone, recovering from the shock. Jawhar offered him some food. For those who were new to prison, the novelty distracted them from making arrangements to eat in the first few days. He tried to be friendly by making conversation and he allayed Younis's apprehensions. Jawhar was a smooth talker. Bakhit Mandil would learn from him how to wrap his listeners around his little finger.

"Welcome to Sayir Prison," he said. "It's not common for a new prisoner to go through what you had to go through, but what happened has its advantages. It's made you famous. Fame in prison has its benefits if you use it well."

Younis stuffed his mouth with food and nodded. Jawhar steered the conversation warily toward what had happened. He told Younis details he had invented about Bakhit Mandil's unexpected attack on him. He deliberately hurt him by saying Younis had screamed and begged for mercy.

Younis shook. "Lies! That's all lies! If I'd wanted to, I could have killed him."

"That's not what they're saying."

"That filthy criminal took me by surprise, but I'll kill him," said Younis.

"Kill him for what he did yesterday or because of some old grievance?"

"I've known that bastard a long time."

Jawhar had picked up a scent. "How come?" he asked.

Younis asked for a drink and Jawhar hurried off to fetch him some water. On his way back he went past Touma. He told her to visit Bakhit and secretly give him a drink. He promised to give her his wages for the coming week. When he had second thoughts about this generosity, he consoled himself. "He who loves is at the mercy of the wise," he said to himself.

He went back to Younis and found him surrounded by other prisoners from the Mahdi's army. He slipped in among them grumpily. It was no longer the right time for stories.

He found out that the prisoners were old acquaintances of Younis's who had served with him in the army. They were urging him to take revenge. In the commotion they didn't recognize him, but he knew that one of them would remember he was friends with Bakhit, because he and Bakhit hadn't been apart for two weeks. If that happened, he wouldn't be able to escape. He slipped away, having heard enough.

He spent the day watching his friend from a distance in case the Jihadiya, the Mahdi's old soldiers, tried to do him harm. He saw Touma sneak up to him to give him a little something to drink. The day passed peacefully until Jawhar was stuffed into a cell. The next day he tried all kinds of ruses to avoid going out with a chain gang. He kept watching his friend, guarding him. When it was too hot in the sun, he moved to a piece of shade where he could still see Bakhit. A guard passed by and Jawhar asked him how long they would be keeping Bakhit there. The guard shrugged his shoulders and said he didn't know.

Probably no one knew. He would stay tied up there till someone in authority noticed him and ordered them to take him down. Until then no guard would dare to go anywhere near him. And if the Jihadiya soldiers got their hands on him, he was so insignificant that he wouldn't count if he was killed. They would throw his body into the wasteland between the prison wall and the river, where it would swell and rot.

Younis Wad Jaber came across Jawhar on the fourth day of Jawhar's vigil over Bakhit. He was swaggering around with two Jihadiya men when he caught sight of him. He left his companions and went up to Jawhar. Greeting him with a friendly smile, he sat down next to him and thanked him for the favor he had done him. Younis said he'd been looking for him, to add him to a group of friends he had known before he was imprisoned. Jawhar thanked him and asked him about the friends.

"They're people from the Jihadiya," said Younis. "We fought the infidels together with the Mahdi."

"So what brings you here if you're from the Mahdi's army?"

Younis laughed.

"There are lots of people from the Jihadiya here. Didn't you know? In my case, it was greed that brought me here," he said.

He didn't explain further, but Jawhar guessed that he was one of the soldiers who had embezzled the money they had been given for safekeeping and who had ended up in front of the chief judge, who ordered them dismissed and imprisoned.

In the unfinished story of Bakhit Mandil, there was clearly a "someone else" who had made Bakhit jealous. That someone was from the Jihadiya. Bakhit only called him "the other man" and never spoke his name. Could he be Younis?

The answers to these questions all lay with his friend Bakhit, who was tied up some distance away. He couldn't help but ask Younis directly. "Are you planning to take revenge on him?" he asked.

Younis looked toward the man who had attacked him, suspended there like a dry cadaver. "Not now," he said. "My colleagues are pressing me to take revenge, but I wouldn't kill a dead man. If he survives being tied to the post, then I'll have to kill him. If not, I'll forgive him."

Jawhar read honesty in Younis's eyes, though it seemed to have a cunning edge. He was relieved, but not so confident that he gave up watching. He decided to err on the side of safety and stay on guard until God intervened one way or another. He didn't have long to wait.

That evening, as they were being squeezed into the cells, Jawhar saw the guards taking Bakhit down from the pillar and dragging him to the chamber of wonders in the distance. He didn't understand why, but he was relieved that maybe fate had finally been kind to his wretched friend.

10

He's surrounded by clouds.

That white stuff could only be clouds.

The only things in the world are the post he's tied to and the white stuff that swirls around him and clings together like tufts of cloud.

Hawa, Theodora, appears to him from somewhere in the distance. She carries the sun in her hands and his body glows with warmth. She courses through him like a dream. Tall and slender as usual.

She's white.

One day he had said to her, "You're as white as daylight."

Her eyes are mischievous and project an enduring sadness. Her charming nose. Her lips as he always desired them.

Absence has not changed her.

Perplexing, just like life.

As painful as life.

And as fickle as the river.

She's wrapped in a robe of sunlight.

She hovers around him. Can she see him? Is she speaking to him, or is she ignoring him?

How hard hope is when you're waiting for something uncertain.

The two of them alone in a world of tiny pieces of clouds. But he's worried she's ignoring him.

He tries to call her, but he's lost his voice.

He sees her looking at the blood that has gathered under his feet. He knows there's a blood-red pool there but he can't bend his head to see it. His body is tied to the top of the post with a chain, which is digging into his flesh.

Maybe she pities him because of his suffering and his wounds.

But then she moves on to some other scene.

She passes him like a fleeting light. All he had from her was one glance, but what a prize!

He tries to capture the glance by shutting his eyes on it. She can move on if she wants, he thinks, because I have her image here.

But to his distress he finds that the image of her he thought he had captured by closing his eyes soon fades.

"Don't go!" he says.

But she abandons him and moves on.

11

The Egyptian army that had invaded the city included people of various ethnic origins. The bulk of the soldiers were Egyptian, along with some squadrons of Sudanese troops, who were harsher toward their fellow countrymen, and some English and European commanders.

They laid the city waste as if trampling on an ants' nest. Then they spread through the city and used the remaining local men to repair it.

At the end of the day, Bakhit went back to Merisila's house, heavy with fatigue and frustration.

He had been surprised to find that the forced labor he had done was unpaid. The government was using the men to repair the damage done when it attacked, but it wasn't going to pay them any money. When he asked for his pay, he saw a flash of malicious pleasure on the face of Farajallah the soldier.

"There is no pay. This is a corvée," he said.

"What does that mean?"

"It means a corvée. You work for nothing."

He thought Farajallah was tricking him, so he asked one of the officers.

The officer said, "You're working for your country. Would you ask your country for money?"

He didn't understand what *your country* meant and why he shouldn't ask it for money. But he realized that Farajallah wasn't tricking him.

He went back to Merisila, exhausted.

She scolded him like an anxious mother. She cursed Farajallah, the Egyptians, the Christians, and the Khalifa's soldiers. She slapped a woman who dared ask her to calm down. She examined Bakhit carefully to make sure he had come home safe and sound. She played down the question of pay. Without asking why he needed it, she reassured him.

"Money can be arranged," she said.

She led him to his enclosure and brought him a little food. He ate. She smelled him and said: "You need washing. You smell like a wet chicken."

"I'll go to the river tomorrow."

She looked into his eyes. He knew she was desirable and nubile. The way she looked at him might have won over someone other than Bakhit, but he was dead before he even met her. With her, he was safe.

"What have you done about my request?" he asked her.

She threw a closed bag into his lap.

"That's one of your requests," she said. "But the information will take time."

He took hold of the bag, amazed that she had managed to obtain it within a day. He asked her how she had achieved this miracle.

"It wasn't difficult," she said. "Your description was accurate. I found the place and I found where you had put it. There was nothing there to give anyone any reason to look for it, so no one had touched it since you slipped it in."

He opened the bag and was hit by the smell of musk.

He put his hand in to feel what was inside. An old leather amulet. A piece of cloth. A rusty sliver of metal. A brass kohl stick, delicately engraved. Her little notebook. A bundle of old papers and letters. A dagger and a necklace that his Egyptian master had given him.

Merisila was looking at the things with surprise. When he put the empty amulet around his neck, she said, "What are those things?"

He picked up the piece of cloth. It gave him a glimpse into the past. The feel of it reminded him of stories, little incidents and details.

Merisila knew the answer before she even asked.

"This is all that's left of her," he said.

She wanted to curse him, to insult him, but her tongue wouldn't do her bidding.

Her heart was saddened and her thoughts were wet with tears.

She could hear the distant noise of the city—shouting and laughter borne on the wind. Muffled banging. The chugging of steamboats on the river. Was that a dog howling somewhere? Fall evenings were so oppressive. Merisila's life went on in front of her.

Despite all the resentment she had shown, what she really felt was something like envy. Despite all the people around her now and all the people she had known in her life, she felt alone. The piece of cloth in Bakhit's hand was safer than her against the uncertainties of life.

"Merisila?

"Don't speak to me."

"Merisila?"

"Don't say my name."

"Merisila?"

"Go away!" she shouted. "Go and chase your ghosts. You've nothing to do with me." Then she ran off, away from him and away from her weakness.

Two

1

BAKHIT COULDN'T SLEEP.

He tossed and turned in his hiding place close to Abu Haraz and tried to make himself feel sleepy. *"Say: 'Who will keep you safe by night and by day from God the Merciful?' Yet they avoid remembrance of their Lord,"* he muttered, from the Chapter of the Prophets in the Quran, but he still couldn't sleep.

He didn't know they were after him, his tireless pursuers. He didn't know he was someone's quarry, just as much as he was the hunter.

He was thinking about the people he was pursuing, and he didn't know that the people pursuing him were only a few days away.

They were looking for him in earnest to take their revenge on him.

He remembered his last victim.

Sheikh Ibrahim Wad al-Shawwak.

The way he looked when he cracked and fell like the trunk of an acacia tree.

Sheikh Ibrahim Wad al-Shawwak, killed by Bakhit a few days earlier, was born in a village in the Dongola area of northern Sudan around 1826. As a child he had moved with his family to Khartoum at the time when Khurshid Pasha was trying to attract people to the new capital of the country by expanding it, building new buildings and setting up gardens. His father, Abdallah Wad al-Shawwak, had made a considerable amount of money working with the boss of the boatmen of North African origin, Sheikh Abdel-Salam, transporting stone to the new city from the abandoned city of Soba. The Dongolan immigrant had experience that was useful to Sheikh Abdel-Salam, so he took him on as partner and made sure he didn't need to work for anyone else. If his relatives ever criticized him for promoting Abdallah, he would say: "Wad al-Shawwak never refuses to work. He's tireless. He doesn't even know what being tired means. Like all the people of Dongola he's a devil in human clothing."

Sheikh Abdel-Salam had such respect for Abdallah Wad al-Shawwak that he married him to one of his relatives out of gratitude for his loyalty. The main beneficiary of the marriage was Ibrahim Wad al-Shawwak, who years later married the niece of his father's wife and through her inherited a massive fortune from her father.

Ibrahim Wad al-Shawwak grew up in Khartoum, initially with the North African community. When he was a young man he went around with the sons of the Circassians and the Greeks, from whom he learned the basics of business and how to make a living. He developed an instinct for making money and a strong sense of which way the wind was blowing. He was like a seer of profit. None of his deals went wrong, and profit followed in his wake like a faithful servant. When he married al-Nawwar, the daughter of al-Hajj Qasim, a grain merchant of North African origin, he could claim to have reached the peak of wealth. But he did his most profitable business when Khartoum was under siege and, in the mistaken belief that Cairo would soon relieve the city, most of the rich—slave traders and dealers in ivory, ebony, skins, and grain, as well as the upper classes, the sheikhs, the ulema, and the notables—supported General Gordon, the English governor-general who ended up slain on the palace steps.

Sheikh Ibrahim Wad al-Shawwak wasn't deceived by Gordon's speeches or statements, in which he said that relief and the defeat of the rebel dervishes were imminent. He sent secret messages to the rebel commander in chief, Abdel-Rahman Wad al-Nujoumi, declaring his allegiance to the Mahdi. Along with his allegiance he sent money and gifts to the besieging army, as well as a thorough report on the food situation in the hard-pressed city and a detailed listing of the wealth and the attitudes of the city's rich, including his in-laws, the sons of al-Hajj Qasim. His messages soon reached the Mahdi in Abu Seid and were appreciated and praised. In return, a few months later Sheikh Ibrahim obtained high status and a favored position with the Mahdi's successor, the Khalifa. He boasted that he was one of the few people who had gone with the Khalifa to see the Mahdi's dead body before the news that he had ascended into heaven was announced.

Over the next thirteen years Sheikh Ibrahim's star rose as high as was possible for a Khartoum merchant whose family came from Dongola. When the Khalifa sent the army to invade Egypt, Sheikh Ibrahim spent an inordinate amount of money on the army and reinforced it with dozens of slaves that he bought. He wasn't shaken by the power struggle between the Khalifa on one side and his Dongolan tribe, the Arabs, and the sharifs on the other. He helped to support the Jihadiya forces in all their campaigns. He ensured his son a place in the group around Othman Sheikheddin, the expected heir of his father the Khalifa.

The world whose faith he followed was indebted to him, but he only believed in making a profit in this world through usury.

With his usual instinct for gain, he sensed the anxiety before the invasion. He smuggled some of his money out of Omdurman. He bought orchards and houses in several remote southern towns where he might settle if anything happened that forced him to flee.

On the day of the battle, when the Khalifa's entourage was on its way out of the wounded city and ten thousand fighters had been killed in two hours, Ibrahim Wad al-Shawwak's convoy, led by his commercial agent, Hassan al-Jerifawi, was just a few hours short of al-Musallamiya, far south of Khartoum.

As soon as he had settled there, he started sending envoys to the invading Egyptian army with instructions to make contact with former prisoners who had spent some time under the oppression of Omdurman and had then fled to Egypt, only to come back as conquerors to the city where they had suffered as prisoners. He soon had friendly relations with several commanders, who gave him promises to protect his property and his businesses, as far as they could, until he came back to the capital, but they advised him to postpone his return until things had settled down and they could tell their friends from their enemies with certainty. In return, he ceded to these commanders some of his orchards and some of the money hidden in Omdurman, and sent them a report on the whereabouts of money and arms hidden by officers who had fled or been killed.

He stayed in al-Musallamiya waiting for a messenger to come and tell him it was safe to return. He kept himself busy expanding his commercial operations in the local market. Although he was over seventy years old, his passion for making money never abated. He began every day in the hope of making a profitable deal, but he had received no news from his son and no messenger brought him glad tidings.

On the last day of his life he set out for the market with his agent. They were talking about what was happening in the country. The cunning old sheikh said, "The Egyptians won't leave. The Mahdist movement is finished. They have lots of weapons, very many weapons. People don't like them but they hate the Khalifa. It's the age of the Christians. They're powerful and well educated. Omdurman was an amazing city but it's finished. The Egyptians and the Christians have moved people back to Khartoum. They've rebuilt the old governor's office and made laws about everything. We'll have to get used to it."

His agent, Hassan al-Jerifawi, listened and nodded. If he had known it would be his last conversation with the sheikh, he would have said many things, but he didn't know that. So he nodded in agreement when the sheikh said, "If we have to wear Christian hats and change the color of our skin, we'll do it. The Mahdist movement's finished, my boy. That's the will of God."

It was painful to hear, but Hassan pretended to agree. He then turned back to deal with some goods that were waiting in the storerooms to be carried to market. At the end of the street he heard screams.

. Bakhit had been squatting by the wall, covering his face with his dirty turban, his hand resting on his only sword. The agent nodded in agreement, then left the sheikh and walked on. Ibrahim Wad al-Shawwak came closer to where Bakhit was sitting. A short old man in his seventies, wearing a cotton cloak and shirt and trousers, and on his head a turban that smelled of oil.

He was smiling as if his whole life lay ahead of him.

Sheikh Ibrahim's eyes drilled into his adversary, who had been looking for him for months. Sheikh Ibrahim was the fourth of the six.

Here he is, Hawa.

Here he is, and power and influence no longer protect him from me.

Bakhit stood up slowly. The whole world was desolate. The sky shouted at him to proceed.

Hawa, you are the world.

What was I before I met you and where have I ended up? I dreamed I was strong. I dreamed I had some influence. If only I could wipe all the sadness from your eyes and make the sun shine in your smile.

"Can you see that star? I'll go up on the roof, then fly to it. I'll grab it and steal a ray of moonlight and make you an anklet you can wear around your leg."

She laughed, then pretended to be angry.

He went up to his adversary, dragging his sword behind him in the dust. He lifted the sword and shouted, "There is no god but God!"

A streak of blood whipped through the air, tracing a dark-red line on the wall.

Sheikh Ibrahim Wad al-Shawwak didn't have time to be surprised. He had been walking along, full of life and dreams for the future, when the sword struck.

Bakhit raised the sword and brought it down on the sheikh's chest. Then he swung his arm again and brought the sword down on his stomach. He struck him eight times before he ran the sword into his chest. When he pulled the sword out Sheikh Ibrahim collapsed in a pool of blood.

Bakhit heard the shouts. He looked back and saw them coming. He lifted his jelaba and rushed away, leaving the sheikh dead and Hassan al-Jerifawi vowing revenge.

In his hideout near Abu Haraz, unaware of the people pursuing him, he heard his horse whinny. He turned over warily.

He remembered Merisila.

When he revealed his plan to her she made no comment. She just stood up and left. She came back carrying a rag wrapped around some Majidi riyals, some Abu Tira riyals, and some Egyptian piasters. She poured them into his hands and said, "This will help you do what you want."

He turned the coins over in his hand. He looked at the eagle design on the Abu Tira riyals. He wished he could refuse to take them, but without Merisila's help he would be lost in darkness.

"These are your savings," he said.

"Who would I save money for? I don't need it. I just didn't know what to spend it on. Take it and carry out your crazy plan."

When the city woke up in the morning, Merisila came to him, pulling Farajallah the soldier by the arm. She said Farajallah could supply him with a Remington rifle and a sword at a reasonable price. Farajallah was terrified. He was looking around him and he spoke in a whisper.

"I know someone who hasn't handed in the weapons he looted. I can put you in touch with him," he said.

"Stop lying, you eunuch," said Merisila. "You're the one who's hiding the weapons."

The soldier looked around in fear. "I'm no looter. I just happen to know someone who is. He's a poor guy so I didn't report him. This is a crime but it's not like hiding weapons. If the government finds out someone's hiding firearms, they'll be severely punished."

"And how much does this poor man want for the rifle and the sword and a reasonable amount of gunpowder?" asked Bakhit.

Farajallah bargained with him on behalf of the notional third person, and they reached a mutual agreement.

The horse whinnied louder.

Farajallah brought the rifle, the sword, and the gunpowder, and Merisila provided clothes and fabric she had obtained from some women she knew.

Despite his objections Merisila accompanied him to Hawa's grave and then to the outskirts of the city. As they walked in the dark, Bakhit realized that she was attractive, as desirable as sin.

She smelled pleasant and her body was nicely oiled. There was something unsaid between them, a silence that spoke volumes.

When he looked at her, she said, "I know."

She hadn't looked up at him, but she knew he was looking at her.

"It's out of my hands," he replied.

She didn't answer. They shared an intimate silence till they parted.

*

Why was the horse neighing? He sat up to have a look. He made out a white figure crouching on the ground. He jumped up, on the offensive. Drawing his sword, he stepped toward the sheikh, who was sitting by his horse. There were bandits everywhere these days. He advanced warily in case his target noticed. He ran into cold air as he drew near, a cold as pleasant as a dream. It was pitch black but the man crouching by his horse shone like the moon. When he stood over the man he felt at peace with the world. He didn't raise his sword. He stood there, yielding to the sense of euphoria that came over him.

The light that fills my veins.

What does a human being ever have in this world, other than love?

Take me to you.

Don't abandon me.

Who was the ingrate who claimed that the woman you love can die?

He smelled musk filling the world around him.

She looked up at him. She was white. Her eyes were mischievous and projected an enduring sadness. Her charming nose. Her lips as he had always desired them. Absence had not changed her. Perplexing, just like life. As painful as life. And as fickle as the river. Wrapped in light like the moon.

"Are you here?"

"I'm here, Bakhit."

"Oh Hawa, I've missed you."

She stood up straight. Tall and slim as usual. Her body was always lithe, defying the misery of the world around her.

He loved her Arabic. She spoke it fluently with a Sudanese accent, but a little childishly. She pronounced the letter jeem soft, with charming cuteness. She spoke rapidly and breezily, as if the words were spilling out of her.

36

During his seven years in prison she often visited him. She crossed the yard at night to stand by the door of the cell where he was sleeping. She put her eye to the cracks in the door and looked at him. He crawled till he was against the other side of the door. He had long conversations with her. She teased him and flirted. Sometimes she was angry, sometimes silent. She told stories and joked. He could smell the musk from her chestnut hair.

Who was the ingrate who claimed that the woman you love can die?

Merisila didn't know about these visits, but she did indulge in wild speculation about Hawa. "That Christian girl is a devil. If we opened her grave, we'd find it empty. She probably walks in the wilderness in the moonlight to lure travelers and carry them off to the mythical land of Saqatlaqat."

Nothing he said could undermine Merisila's certainty.

"I know more about this than other people," she said. "Have you forgotten whose daughter I am? My uncle was abducted by the djinn, and it was with magic like that that my mother brought me into the world. You're like my mother. Madness will finish you off. You'll die. You need to be chained to the Mahdi's tomb until you recover."

He and Hawa were walking over soft sand. There was no moon but their shadows overlapped on the ground.

"I didn't bring you a present that would make you happy," he said.

She smiled in silence.

He told her what he'd done. He told her what he planned to do.

"Don't do it, Bakhit. Please," she said.

"I can't not do it, Hawa. That's what I owe you."

"It won't make me happy. You'll die for nothing."

He didn't care.

"I'll die trying to make you happy."

"Nothing you do can make me happy. Unfortunately that's out of your hands."

He scowled and dismissed what she said. She always wanted him to be safe, not worried about her. She was always urging him not to hold her captive with his concern.

"Live your own life, Bakhit. Live it for yourself. Please, for my sake."

"What kind of life could I live when I feel indebted to you?" he replied.

"You're not indebted to me."

"I am indebted for the happiness I've known with you."

They walked on. The whole world stretched out in front of them.

"I had hoped to make you happy," she said. "But all I've given you is sadness."

"I've been happy," he said stubbornly. "I'll die trying to repay my debt to you. I will make you happy."

"As usual, it's too late. The time has passed. Nothing can make me happy now."

Why was he fated always to arrive when it was too late?

Her sorrows were always one step ahead of him.

Whenever he walked toward her, her sorrows took her away at a gallop. If he ran toward her, her sorrows spread their wings and flew off with her.

Between them there always stood a gap of ardent sadness, and the horse of his love stumbled in that sadness.

"I'm going now."

"Don't go. Wait," he said.

"I have to go."

He heard his horse neighing. They had left it a whole life-time behind them, but now it sounded close. Had the earth turned and brought them back to where they started?

He stopped involuntarily and she walked on.

"Hawa!"

She looked at him. "You know, I don't like the name Hawa, except from you," she said. Her words took flight like a flock of turtledoves disturbed by a hunter. In his confusion, he didn't know what to say.

"And from you I like it more than my real name," she added, as she plunged into the void and disappeared.

2

"From which country inhabited by angels do you come?"

3

Theodora wasn't from Sudan.

She was from a faraway country, and in that faraway country she was a stranger from a country even farther away.

Theodora was born in Alexandria, at the far end of Lower Egypt. Her parents had come from over the sea.

She had never seen Greece, her parents' country. Her father, Andreas Eleftherios, emigrated to Egypt after the military rebellion against King Otto of Greece in 1862.

He was a conservative man who believed in the sanctity of the throne and was offended by the rebellion, which forced the king to abdicate. He never understood the political storms that gave parliament more powers at the expense of the king. For two or three years after the change he tried to adapt to the new reality and what he was told was freedom. But he failed, and he dragged his pretty wife, Laskarina Eleftherios, and their two sons off to Egypt, determined never to return.

On the far shore of the Mediterranean he planted roots. He worked in the European-run postal service and settled down. Theodora was born to him at a time when he was content that he had achieved what he wanted, happy with his little family, his work, and his post-office uniform.

The girl inherited her height and chestnut hair from him. Otherwise she looked like her mother. She had amber eyes the

39

size of lakes and her nose was pleasantly long. Her lips were wild and often made her father anxious for her.

He spoiled her, along with his sons and his wife. The city on the sea also spoiled them. His anxiety for her chastity did not abate. It was Laskarina who suggested dedicating Theodora to the Lord. Despite his conservatism, Andreas Eleftherios was not a pious Greek Orthodox, but he liked the idea. He wasn't sure that the Lord could protect her chastity forever if she stayed on at their house behind the Mohamed Ali Club. So he would take her to the Lord, to His house.

"That way the Lord won't forget her," he said to his wife.

4

"What brought you to this country?" Bakhit Mandil asked Theodora out of curiosity.

She smiled sadly. "The Lord decreed it."

He turned to her in shock and snapped, "Don't speak like the Christians. If you say things like that you could end up on the gallows in the marketplace."

She looked toward the gallows he was pointing to.

"Why have they replaced beheadings with hangings?" she asked absentmindedly.

He didn't understand her temperament. She skipped from one subject to another like a wild gazelle grazing. He brushed some persistent flies off his lips. They were sitting in the vegetable market, close to Idris al-Nubawi's stall.

"I don't know," he said. "I asked Saadallah, the butcher who used to carry out death sentences, and he didn't know. He said it was an order from the Khalifa."

She nodded. "But if they tried to hang me, you'd save me, wouldn't you, Bakhit?" she suddenly added.

"I'd do the undoable to protect you," he said with enthusiasm.

"Why?"

"What?"

"Why would you do the undoable to protect me?"

He shivered and was lost for words. She was waiting for his answer, her head bowed, staring sadly at the ground.

"Because I care," he said.

"You're my black brother."

He didn't know if any brother could feel for his sister what he felt toward her, but he didn't object.

She suddenly went back to the question she had avoided. She wasn't in the habit of talking about her past.

"I came to serve the Lord and spread His word," she said.

He imagined her being part of something like the Jihadiya, the Mahdi's army, which carried the Mahdi's banners to spread the word of God. He had gone to Egypt under one of those banners, but the banner was captured and he was taken prisoner.

"They chose me to accompany a missionary delegation to serve the Greek community in Khartoum. It was a joint Orthodox–Catholic mission," she continued. She could see from his eyes that he didn't understand. "The Catholics and the Orthodox are like the schools of law that you have. You know—the Hanafis, the Malikis, the Shafiis, and the Hanbalis?" she said, trying to explain.

"No," he replied. "The Mahdist movement is God's religion."

She tilted her head and didn't argue.

"The Catholics went west to the city of El Obada and we stayed in Khartoum."

"El Obeid."

"What?"

He laughed. "The city of El Obeid, not El Obada," he said.

She scowled as if angry. "Don't laugh at my mistakes," she said.

"I don't laugh at your mistakes."

"Yes, you do."

He smiled affectionately and looked deep into her big amber eyes. She had a beguiling childishness despite her sadness.

Her chestnut hair rebelled against her headscarf and rippled like brilliant daylight. How could she trap daylight under a covering made of cloth?

Her suffering and her enslavement only made her more alluring.

She seemed to have been created sad. Sadness gave her grandeur and allure. And when she laughed she looked guilty, as though she had committed a sin. Her laugh was a flash of light that had slipped through a crack in the stone walls of her sadness.

"I'll kill your master and make you free."

"You have a kind heart. If the sheikh dies, his son will inherit me, or the Treasury will take me," she said.

"No," he said defiantly. "When my master died in Khartoum, no one inherited me and they didn't take me to the treasury."

He knew that his master didn't have any heirs. They had all died when the Mahdi's troops entered Khartoum and slaves like him were left free to wander around, unattached. His freedom fell into his lap sometime between the death of General Gordon on the east bank of the Nile and the beginning of the Khalifa's rule on the west bank. While power was shifting from the Turkish-built city of Khartoum to Omdurman, the Mahdi's patch of land, lowly creatures such as him slipped through the cracks and no one missed them.

He and Theodora were not in the same situation. He knew that, but he lied to give her hope.

He found himself free in a new country. It was born, so he was born. Both of them were creatures of the moment, so he decided to be like the country. To create himself. He would learn how to be free.

He threw himself into life. He tried out every trade. He walked across Omdurman, from one end to the other. The bigger the city grew the more deeply rooted his freedom became. Like the city, he was hungry in a way he hadn't expected. The people he had worked with at the beginning died, followed by the people he worked for later. He saw death swaggering around him. He expected it to take him unawares. He decided to escape. He wasn't going to wait for death. He would run away from it. He had a strong desire to live. He calculated that he was five years old—his five years as a free man, that is.

He wouldn't die.

So he picked up his spear and went off with the army to invade Egypt. He chose war.

So that he could live.

5

It was Father Pavlos who made an effort to convince Andreas Eleftherios that Theodora should accompany him to Sudan.

The Greek postal worker was uneasy. "I didn't take her to the Lord for Him to take her from me, but rather to protect her for me," he told the priest.

"The Lord possesses us all, Mr. Eleftherios," said Father Pavlos, "and the assignment won't be dangerous. We'll stay in Khartoum two years. Your fellow Greeks there need guidance and ministration, and the mission needs a school. Theodora will work at the school. The governor of Sudan, Mohamed Raouf Pasha, is a friend of mine. We'll be there under his patronage. And Khartoum is a beautiful city."

"No good comes from those barbarians."

"Most of the inhabitants of Khartoum are Europeans and Egyptians and a few friendly local people. Life there is no different from life in any European city. It has the same virtues and the same flaws. Khartoum is a little Europe."

Laskarina helped Father Pavlos persuade Andreas. She reminded him that some of his cousins had been living in Khartoum for many years.

The Greeks were the largest foreign community in Khartoum. They traded in groceries, readymade clothes, tableware, meat, and vegetables. They lent money and arranged money transfers.

Andreas wasn't arguing with the intention of refusing, because in the end he couldn't go against the wishes of Father Pavlos. He was arguing just to feel reassured. He still had qualms about the plan, but he agreed.

He looked at his daughter sitting in the corner. He counted himself luckier than he deserved to be for having produced this angel. She was so quiet she was hardly there. A saintly serenity surrounded her. Like the icons in church. Even her face, despite the prettiness she had inherited from her mother, was a touch reminiscent of pictures of women martyrs.

Her mother must have spoken with the tongue of the Lord when she suggested dedicating Theodora to the Church. The light of serving the Lord suited her. Her father didn't know what thoughts were going through her pretty head or what things she left unsaid, but he was happy with the ecclesiastical splendor that surrounded her.

Khartoum was not the end of the world. His angel with the chestnut hair would be fine. At least that's what hope tricked him into believing.

"Very well, Theodora, you're going to Khartoum," he said.

Three

BAKHIT CROSSED TO THE EAST bank of the Nile.

The information that Merisila had gathered over the months was as accurate as the reports by the Christians' spies. She had managed to find out the precise location of each of his targets. He found the first four of them where she told him they would be, and now he was on his way to the fifth. His quarry, Taher Jibril, had moved eight months earlier to the town of Abu Haraz, north of where the River Rahad meets the Blue Nile. He had gone there from Gedaref to melt into the population of the town.

He would meet his death as the others before him had met death. Bakhit had hesitated slightly a few weeks earlier, after killing Mousa al-Kalas. After that killing Bakhit felt that he belonged in this world. Maybe it was the right place for him after all. His heart had softened toward humanity. He was frightened. The way he thought about people was confused. But he soon came back to his usual world. Her world. That world where there was only him and Hawa. He might smell Merisila there. Hawa might see that he was thinking about Merisila. She would be jealous that Merisila had an honored place in his heart, but she would tell him she didn't care. He had the right to love another woman. She would press him, insincerely, to fall in love, to marry a girl who was black like him and belonged to his world. But how could a dervish turn his back on his fellow mystics? It was with them that he communed with God and merged with the Absolute. Then his world would become a reality, rising from the world of phantasms and sensations through the stages that lead to the Unique Essence.

I won't leave Paradise, as our forefather Adam did.

He looked up at the sky. He saw a group of vultures circling, hovering low and squawking, then swooping down behind a distant hillock.

He thought it might be carrion. The desert was full of ostriches. Perhaps it was a quarry of some sort.

Bakhit steered his horse toward the hillock. He went down into a valley and rose again. He stopped on the hillock and looked.

The vultures were tearing into four bodies lying in the sun. He hurried on and took his rifle. He fired a shot and the scavengers around the bodies dispersed. He fired another shot and the birds screamed and took off. He was worried they might attack him. But they just made a loud noise and flew into the distance.

He cantered down toward the bodies.

He heard Hawa shouting at him. "What are you doing? They're dead," she said.

"I'm looking for plunder that the people who killed them might have overlooked," he said apologetically.

"But they're dead. Are you going to rob them?" he heard her saying in disgust.

He didn't comment. You don't understand this cruel world, Hawa, he thought. He reached the first body. A man completely dried out by the sun. His flesh torn by the vultures. The man was wearing a dirty cloak, patched with strips of cotton of many colors. Along with the damage the vultures had done Bakhit could make out bullet wounds. He searched the body quickly. The killers hadn't left anything. Even his feet were bare. He moved on to the second body. Nothing. Just like the first one. But the vultures had been kinder to this one. They had only eaten a part of his cheek and torn flesh from two fingers. When he moved the third body, he found a small leather bag underneath. It was the same color as the sand. Maybe that was why the killers hadn't noticed it. He opened it and found some riyals inside. He searched the fourth body but didn't find anything. But he saw the marks of shackles on the man's dry skin. He smiled.

Here was another man who had been a guest at Sayir Prison. If it hadn't been for what the vultures and the sun had done to his face, Bakhit might have recognized him. They were a lucky few, the people who hadn't spent time in Sayir in recent years. Inside the prison he had met many more people; he had met most of the people he had known outside.

Bakhit climbed the hill. He decided to make camp for a while. He poured some sand on the bodies, as a kind of burial. Then he pounded some of the jerked meat he had bought from a village and lit a fire to cook it.

While he was eating, he heard Hawa asking him, "What's a revenge killing like, Bakhit?"

He wiped his lips with the back of his hand.

"Like life." He paused a moment and then explained: "You feel powerful, full of life. You fly. Your body feels so light you can almost float in the air. It's like wine of a kind that no man has ever made and no tongue has ever tasted. The ecstasy of it carries me to the stars. It carries me to you."

"Is it nicer than love?"

Bakhit shuddered. "It is love."

When he'd finished eating, he took out his dagger and put it against his chest. He closed his eyes. He could smell Hawa's refreshing scent. "O Mahdi of God!" he shouted in invocation, and plunged the dagger into his chest.

2

In her notebook he read:

> Don't love too intensely, or else you'll suffer intensely. Don't fall in love. That way you'll come out safe. Nothing gained and nothing lost.

3

Taher Jibril was a name many people knew in Omdurman.

He was a fighter in the Mulazmin forces under the command of Othman Sheikheddin, the son of the Khalifa. He had come to Omdurman as an immigrant after the Mahdi ascended to heaven. He succeeded by demonstrating true loyalty. He outdid those who had joined the Mahdi movement earlier. He wasn't rich and he wasn't famous for his intelligence, but he was known for his loyalty. As soon as he received an order from his commander he followed it single-mindedly. His motto and his defense was the Quranic verse: "*O you who believe, obey God and the Prophet and those of you who are in authority.*" The city said of him that once when he was preparing for jihad one of his friends said, "May God keep you safe," and Taher Jibril complained about him to the sharia judge, saying that the Mahdi didn't seek safety for his followers but ordered them to fight or be martyred.

When the Battle of Omdurman took place and all the followers of the Mahdist movement fled the Mahdi's city, which had been polluted by invaders, Taher went to the town of Gedaref, where his third wife was living. He sought refuge with her family and they took him in. He stayed with them for a month, but then they grew tired of the disagreements between their daughter and his other two wives, and they told him the other two wives had to go, but he could stay if he chose to. He lost his temper and divorced their daughter. With his other two wives and his children, he moved to Abu Haraz. He stayed there in the expectation that he would soon move on. He walked from house to mosque and back in the expectation that God would call him for some mission. He spent eight months on the alert, and then God did arrange for something to happen to him.

4

Bakhit Mandil came into the town thrown over his horse. He was wearing a dirty cloak, patched with strips of cotton of many colors, full of holes and covered in large bloodstains. He had dust and sand on his face and head, like someone who'd come back to life from the grave. People were amazed to see him. He spoke only to repeat one name.

The people took him off the horse under a tree and carried him to a nearby house. People gathered from all directions, drawn by curiosity. No one was able to examine him closely. Whenever they touched him or made too much noise around him, he flew into a rage, had convulsions, and started calling out the one name that was the only thing he said: "Taher Jibril."

Some people remembered that they knew a man by that name, and several of them offered to go looking for him. They found him in the mosque reading the Quran. Unaware that he would be dead two days later, Taher came running, surprised that the injured man was asking for him. He stood over Bakhit and tried to make sense of it all. When he failed to persuade him to say anything, as others had failed, he announced he was going to move Bakhit into his house.

Bakhit was carried off groaning. The wounds in his chest hurt even more because of the way they were holding him. They carried him a while and then put him on a wooden bed in Taher Jibril's house.

He kept gasping and repeating the name Taher, sometimes incoherently and sometimes as a scream.

The people observing him concluded that the shock of his injuries had driven him mad. They grew bored of watching his ravings and left him. He could hear them in the courtyard sharing their conclusions. The one who was most uncertain was Taher Jibril.

Bakhit ranted and raved for the rest of the day. Night fell and Taher Jibril sneaked into his room every now and then to find him still shouting and mumbling his name. Bakhit concentrated on his mission and didn't fall asleep. He was anxious to play his role properly and was worried that a moment of carelessness might expose his deception.

Toward dawn his screams began to subside. When he heard Taher getting ready for morning prayers, he began to call out. "Water," he said.

Taher came into the room after a while. Bakhit opened his eyes to see him, but it was still dark. All he could make out was his massive frame. It was like the first time he had seen him. "Water," he repeated in a daze.

Taher Jibril hurried to fetch him some water and Bakhit drank a large amount. He was really thirsty. He drank deeply, then stretched out on the bed. He closed his eyes and acted as if dead.

Taher tried to rouse him several times. "*There is no power or strength save in God*," he said, and left.

Bakhit heard the muezzin calling the dawn prayers. He smiled in the darkness and decided to get a little sleep.

He woke at noon when a hand touched his chest. Opening his eyes, he saw Taher Jibril in daylight for the first time. He was just as he had imagined him.

As massive as the gates in the walls of Omdurman. In his late thirties, dark-skinned, with a little snub nose. He didn't have a beard but his mustache drooped to his chin. He was wearing a jelaba, loose trousers underneath, and leather sandals. On his large head he wore an embroidered skullcap with a tassel hanging down. He had the energy of someone who would never die, but he was going to die the next day.

When he smiled in Bakhit's face, his eyes narrowed and his regular teeth were visible.

"Thank God you're better," he said.

"I want Taher Jibril," Bakhit replied, pretending to be stupid.

"I'm Taher Jibril," he said. "Are you well?"

Bakhit closed his eyes in relief.

"At last I've found you," he said.

"And who are you?" Taher asked him anxiously.

But Bakhit didn't reply, as if he held him responsible for an unforgivable offense. He pretended to be asleep. He breathed regularly and heavily. It was too early to lure his quarry into the trap.

He pretended to be asleep until he really did doze off. He woke up to a faint clatter and saw Taher putting a bowl of food next to him. He got up languidly and Taher hurried to help him. He groaned when his chest wound was stretched. Looking at the bowl, he found it was full of gruel. He thanked Taher. He ate and then drank plenty of cornmeal brew to regain the strength he was pretending to have lost. Then his quarry brought in some water for him and he washed himself where he was.

When the afternoon was almost over he was ready to talk. He gave up his pretense of being exhausted and put on a tough look. Taher sat close to him on the bed. The small room, built of fired brick and with a high wooden ceiling, brought them close.

"Can anyone hear us?" Bakhit asked.

"The people outside are waiting to hear news of you," he replied.

"Send them away. I've come with a secret that no one but you should hear."

Taher hesitated.

"I've come to you in God's cause," Bakhit explained.

Taher stood up and went out. Bakhit heard him telling the people to leave and promising to meet them in the mosque.

A dead man making an appointment.

Little did he know.

I am death, you pagan. All appointments end with me.

"I come to you as a messenger from El Obeid. The Ansar are gathering, and the Khalifa mentioned you by name."

Taher gasped for joy. "My master the Khalifa!" he said.

"The commanders praised you to him, so he asked for you."

Taher trembled in delight at the good news.

"Some thieves prevented me reaching you earlier. We don't have time to wait now. Can you leave with me in secret, after sunset?"

"Nothing could hold me back when it comes to answering the call of the Khalifa."

"Where's my horse?" asked Bakhit.

"I'll bring it. I have my own horse and some provisions. We'll set off when you're strong enough."

"Just like you, I could never ignore the call of the Khalifa. Bring the two horses and we'll set off at sunset. Bring some flour and oil and dates and water. Not too much because I hid some of my supplies under a solitary thorn tree to the east of the town and I have some companions a few days' journey away who have everything we need."

"Are there many of us?"

"Enough to crush the infidels," Bakhit replied.

Taher sprang into action with the fervor of a believer. Paradise and the Lord of Creation had called him. The Khalifa had remembered him. He prepared some clothes for Bakhit that he thought would fit, but when Bakhit tried them on he disappeared inside them. He put them aside and went back to his tattered cloak. He did take a turban, which he wrapped around his head, leaving one end dangling on his left shoulder. He waited a short while till Taher Jibril came back ready.

"I told my wives I was traveling," he said apologetically. "I advised them to go and see a neighbor of mine if there's anything they need. That doesn't mean it's no longer a secret that we're leaving, does it?"

"No. But we'd better move fast before they spread the news, as women do," said Bakhit.

A few minutes after sunset Bakhit and his companion Taher left town under the tender cover of darkness. Taher led Bakhit through empty lanes. Bakhit was going through Abu Haraz for the first time. The crows perched on the roofs watched him leave, never to return. The only people they met were some women who crossed the street in alarm. Bakhit wrapped the loose end of his turban across his face, leaving only his lively eyes exposed.

When they had left the houses behind them, Bakhit asked, "Which way to the thorn tree I spoke to you about?"

"We're on our way to it, my friend and bringer of good news."

They traveled for two hours under the stars and a moon that was fighting to break through the clouds. Bakhit saw the outline of the thorn tree looming in front of them. They reached the trunk. He dismounted, holding the horse's halter in his fist. He bent down and scraped the ground with his free hand.

Backing away in alarm, he shouted, "By the Mahdi of God!"

Taher started and cried, "What is it?"

Bakhit stepped back nervously and said, "Get off and take a look. God protect us!"

Taher jumped off his horse and rushed to the trunk of the tree. He bent down over the spot where Bakhit had been scraping, but couldn't see anything. He put his hand out cautiously to feel around. Nothing. He looked up in surprise. "There's nothing there. What's wrong with you?" he shouted at his companion.

"You've fallen for it, you dog!" he heard Bakhit shout back.

Then Bakhit struck. He couldn't make out anything for the darkness and the shock. He pinned Taher down with his body, but was hit on his face and head until he started bleeding.

Bakhit took hold of Taher's head and slammed it against the trunk of the tree several times. Taher growled. He tried to lift his opponent, who was crouched on top of him, but his legs weren't strong enough. He collapsed, crying, "Don't kill me! Don't kill me!"

His face sank into the sand.

5

I am death.

Nothing can deter me.

Don't you know who I am?

6

When Taher Jibril woke up, the sun was burning his skin.

He tried to sit up but he found he had been tied up. His hands had been tied behind his back with his turban, and his feet were bound too. He was naked except for a short pair of drawers. He looked around as much as he could. He had been thrown into a sandy wadi between two hills. In front of him there was something that looked like an improvised sandy grave from which a foot protruded, as dry as a crust of bread.

"Anyone there?" he shouted.

No one answered. The sweat was running down his face. He kicked his feet and raised some dust. He tried in vain to sit up. He called again. The heat of the sun sapped his strength. "Anyone there?" he shouted fearfully.

He sensed movement behind him, and shook for fear someone might attack him again, but Bakhit came around him and stopped in front of him. All he could see were Bakhit's flat feet, cracked like dry mud. He looked up but the sun made him look aside.

"Who are you?" he said.

Bakhit took hold of his hair and pulled him up on his knees, then sat in front of him.

"Do you recognize me?" he asked.

"I don't. Who are you?"

Bakhit scowled. "Do you remember Hawa?" he asked.

Taher didn't know what the man meant. He shook his head nervously. He couldn't think what reply might secure his release.

Bakhit reminded him: "Abdel-Gayoum, the son of Sheikh Ibrahim Wad al-Shawwak, and Naim, the son of al-Hajj Taha the guide?" he said.

The trace of a memory flickered in the eyes of the captive giant.

"It was the night of the twenty-seventh day of Rajab. Do you remember?"

"The infidel woman?"

"Hawa!" shouted Bakhit.

Bakhit dug his fingernails into Taher's face and shouted: "You killed her! You killed her, you dog!"

Taher howled in terror. Bakhit was throttling him and screaming her name. But Bakhit held back, unwilling to kill him immediately. He was in a frenzy, frothing at the mouth.

Just like that night when Naim told him what had happened.

He had been in Idris al-Nubawi's house, drinking beer. He was angry with Hawa and the decision she had taken to escape. He was cursing her and cursing Younis Wad Jaber, the soldier in the Jihadiya. He was drunk for a day and two nights. Crying that he had betrayed her by failing to save her. Naim came into the room without him noticing. When Naim told him casually what had happened, Bakhit flew into a rage. That night the city shook, and the stars cried out with him.

You sky, I'm going to smash all the constellations.

I'll pick up the planets and throw them at Earth.

Taher Jibril fell on his face, weeping and stunned. Bakhit sat next to him, breathless and angry.

As he wept, Taher was muttering something Bakhit couldn't make out. Taher lifted his face from the ground. Soil spilled from his mouth as he spoke.

"*So what happens when misfortune befalls them because of what they have done? Then they come to you, swearing by God and saying, 'We only wanted to do good and bring about harmony*,'" he said, quoting the Quran.

He repeated the verse incessantly. The words came out mixed with his tears. Bakhit didn't feel sorry for him. What good would a verse from the Quran do today?

Bakhit tugged on his massive mustache and Taher Jibril turned to face him.

Bakhit put his face close to Taher's and said cruelly, "Did you think you could kill with impunity, you murderer?"

Taher Jibril remembered the incident well now. He knew he would pay the price that night.

There was no escape.

Four

1

BAKHIT GAVE TAHER JIBRIL A powerful punch. Taher fell on his back in convulsions. Bakhit put his foot on his neck and shouted, "Murderer!"

Fear flashed in Taher Jibril's eyes like lightning in a thunderstorm. His eyes were swollen and wet with tears.

"May God forgive me, may God forgive me," he said.

Bakhit gave him a painful kick.

"May God never forgive you. You're a murderer," he said through his teeth.

There is no mercy for a bloodstained murderer. Blood can be appeased only by blood. Murderers are not given a chance to repent. Those who violate the sanctity of human life can only be punished.

Bakhit made a cut in Taher's throat and the two of them slumped to the ground. Bakhit then cut off Taher's fingers with the sword. One after the other. "For God's sake, take as much of me as you like!" Taher shouted. Taher's blood ran till it soaked the ground. He was still ranting incessantly, begging for forgiveness and speaking with difficulty. He lost consciousness for a while and then came around. He turned pale. His body trembled. His words were mixed up and incoherent.

Bakhit threw him to the ground and sat close to him, out of breath. He poured hot sand on his wounds, and when Taher started to groan like a camel, he cut his throat.

He left the body in its place in a pool of sticky blood, lying facedown on the sand. Ten fingers were dispersed around it. He saddled the horses and was about to leave when they surrounded him. He made to draw his sword but their spears were already at his neck.

As he let his arms fall limp in surrender, he heard someone say, "I swore to God and my master I wouldn't let you escape. If you're thinking of running away, then let me tell you, I am Fate and Fate never lets its prey escape."

2

They bound Bakhit's hands with a chain and tied a rope of coarse fiber around his feet.

They threw him under the thorn tree and went down to examine his victim. He heard their shrieks of shock. What he had done was brutal. Even he wouldn't have had the stomach to do what he had done if it hadn't been for Hawa's sake. When he'd seen executions at the gallows in the marketplace, he'd turned away like a little rabbit. He ran from the brutality of the world to the warmth of her presence. But today he was born again, a new creature.

They climbed back up to where he was.

Hassan al-Jerifawi stood in front of him and looked at him.

The man who had killed his boss and patron, face to face, in front of him.

A streak of blood whipped through the air, tracing a dark red line on the wall.

Sheikh Ibrahim Wad al-Shawwak didn't have time to be surprised. He had been walking along, full of life and dreams for the future, when the sword struck.

Bakhit raised the sword and brought it down on the sheikh's chest. Then he swung his arm again and brought the sword down on his stomach. He struck him eight times before he ran the sword into his chest. When he pulled the sword out Sheikh Ibrahim collapsed in a pool of blood.

The chase had finally come to an end. His hands, stained with Sheikh Ibrahim's blood, were in chains.

Hassan al-Jerifawi had pursued the killer relentlessly for months.

Since the day Sheikh Ibrahim fell he had been under oath not to rest till he had taken revenge.

When Bakhit butchered Sheikh Ibrahim, Hassan al-Jerifawi had hurried back to his master in panic. People gathered around the body, while the killer took advantage of the crowd's confusion and escaped.

"Catch him!" some of them shouted.

People ran after him but Bakhit ran ahead and slipped off.

Al-Musallamiya was devastated, as if this were the first death in history.

The old merchant had done favors to everyone in town. He was courteous and easygoing, and regularly attended communal prayers. Why would he have been murdered in the street? He was mourned by men and women, the poor, the wealthy, and the elite. Even the walls of the city and the dusty streets seemed to be mourning his death.

Hassan al-Jerifawi was full of rage, and when Sheikh Ibrahim was placed in his grave, wrapped in shrouds of affection, Hassan stood up and swore revenge.

He gathered some slaves, hired a guide to follow the tracks, and went out looking for Bakhit Mandil. He followed him into towns and spent the night in villages. All they had to go on were the tracks that the guide read on the face of the earth and in the passing of the clouds.

And now their mission of revenge had put the killer at their mercy.

One of them insulted him. Bakhit looked around at them. Nine fierce-looking armed men. In their eyes there was an unmistakable thirst for his blood.

One of them took hold of his hair and lifted his head up. "What's your name, slave?" he asked.

Bakhit answered defiantly.

Hassan came up and sat in front of him. "We're going to ask you some questions. You'd better answer, for your own good," he said.

One of them tore his jelaba from behind. Hassan looked up to see who was behind Bakhit. There were some minutes of calm and then the whip landed on his back, tearing into his flesh to show him what to expect if he refused to answer.

"Why did you attack Sheikh Ibrahim?"

"I killed him, as he was meant to be killed."

Hassan wanted to humiliate Bakhit. "Your attack was a failure and we saved him from death. He will live to punish you," he said.

Bakhit smiled scornfully. "I struck him with a blow that would have smashed a mountain to pieces, you Arab."

Hassan didn't contest the point.

"Where did you think you were escaping to? You kill important people and you think you can escape?"

The men exchanged looks and smiled tensely at each other. One of them said, "The slave's mad."

Hassan rested his hand on the ground and leaned toward him. Hassan's breath stung him.

"Who sent you?" he asked.

"No one sent me."

"So who incited you to do this deed?"

Should he mention her? Should he tell them something they wouldn't understand?

He looked defiantly into the eyes of Hassan al-Jerifawi and in them read complete understanding. Hassan's eyes were like his. They had the same uncertainty and longing.

He would tell him his story.

"Let's kill him here," one of them said.

Several others agreed, but Hassan rebuked them.

"It's not up to us. We'll take him back to al-Musallamiya and leave it to the government to decide what to do with him. Or to Abdel-Gayoum the sheikh's son, if he comes."

Bakhit repeated the name Abdel-Gayoum with a smile. Hassan looked at him inquisitively.

"You'll have to wait a long time for him," said Bakhit.

Bakhit wasn't frightened. He was annoyed. He had one man left. He hadn't caught up with Younis yet. He had missed a chance to kill him a few years ago in prison. And now he had fallen into the hands of the people pursuing him before he could catch Younis.

"There's no point in moving him," one of them said. "There's no mercy for murderers. Let's kill him now."

There's no mercy for murderers. Hassan al-Jerifawi knew that well. The two years he had spent wrestling with his guilt knew that. Ever since he had drawn his sword in Metemma. The women screaming. The children trampled under the hooves of the galloping horses. The banners flying in the sky over the town. The ghosts of the battle had haunted him and he had escaped them by busying himself working as an agent for Sheikh Ibrahim.

Hassan had left the east and gone back to Omdurman, decorated with the dust of jihad, as contented as a believer lolling in Paradise. No amount of worship is as meritorious as an hour holding the line in battle. *"God loves those who fight in his cause in a line of battle as if they are a solid structure,"* as the Quran says. But Omdurman was a sad place, somber and beset with troubles. The city staggered around blindly when it tried to walk and slumped when it sat. It was ravaged by fear.

Hassan wondered what had happened to the city that the Mahdi had founded and chosen as his burial place. The torch of faith no longer blazed there. Hassan didn't like the city. He hated it despite himself, and was impatient to leave. There was the same oppression he had hated in Karkouj. But he was afraid to admit this to himself. If he doubted the rightness of the things

61

he saw, he would lose his faith. Speaking of the Khalifa who would succeed him, had not the Mahdi said, "All his deeds and rulings have a sound basis because he has been granted wisdom and the authority to resolve disputes, even if he rules that one of you must be killed or that your property must be confiscated. Do not oppose him, because God has given him authority over you, to cleanse you and purge you of the filth of the world, so that your hearts will be pure and you can approach your Lord. And if anyone is critical of him, even within himself, then for sure that person will forfeit this life and the afterlife, which is a serious loss, and he will be in danger of meeting a bad end, God forbid."

He tried hard to make his heart deny what his eyes saw and dismiss what his ears heard. When he walked past the gallows in the marketplace, he said to his skeptical self: "The Khalifa has a right to deal with those who disobey."

His sheikh, Salman Wad Hamad al-Duwaihi, had advised him to follow his heart, but his heart was not at ease. It cried out to him to flee. He sought God's pardon and imagined sending his excuses to his sheikh, but he did not flee.

And now he had a murderer in his power and did not know what to do with him.

3

"Unlucky man! In the service of God you will shed blood. You will emerge guilty but the hand of God will receive you and comfort you," Hassan's sheikh had predicted.

4

Years earlier, when Hassan's mother took him to Sheikh Salman Wad Hamad al-Duwaihi, she asked him for only one thing. "Sir, for my only son I seek from you a life as long as the course of the Nile," she said.

She left him under the sheikh's tutelage and went. He had been gifted to God. The sheikh showered him with affection. Hassan set out on the path of a boy seeking Paradise.

"Everything has been preordained by God," the sheikh told his mother, "and Fate has already traced the course of the river."

In the sheikh's school Hassan al-Jerifawi picked up a wooden board to write on and sat among the boys from poor families. He rocked back and forth as he recited from the Quran: *"And those who lived before them were also deceitful, so God destroyed their building from the foundations and the ceiling fell in on them and they had no idea what had struck them."*

Sheikh Salman smiled and little angels fluttered around his mouth. "This is the hardest verse in the Quran to recite. If you can do it, you're a really clever boy. Whoever does it well, I'll give them a stick of sugar in their weekly rations," he told them.

Hassan was a hardworking boy. His enthusiasm never flagged. He was the first to turn up for Quran lessons. When he wrote on his board, his handwriting was good and well shaped. When he went to sleep, he saw the prophet Khidr. He was a stocky man with a face like the full moon. He gave off a pungent smell of musk. He led him by the hand in a Sufi procession, stopped him at the Nile, and showed him some red soil in his hand. He wiped it on Hassan's gown. Hassan woke up ecstatic. Whenever he saw Khidr he told Sheikh Salman, who smiled and stroked his head.

"May God have mercy on you, my boy," the sheikh said.

His classmates resented the kindly attention that Sheikh Salman gave Hassan. When Hassan sat down to memorize the Quran, they would hit him from behind. He would turn around but he couldn't tell who was doing it. They would all be busy with their writing boards. He went on reading, and would be hit again. Then he'd shout out and attack everyone behind him. He knocked over three of them and laid into them, biting and punching. The boys ganged up on him, pretending to be pulling the fight apart, but in secret they were hitting him too. One of them would pull his short jelaba and tear it at the back, while another stuck his finger in his bottom. They kicked his leg and made him fall over. They dragged him through the dirt, while pretending to shield him from his opponents and chanting, "Bless the Prophet. Don't hit, don't hit."

They dragged him along the ground to the edge of the courtyard, threw him down next to the garbage heap, and ran back.

His eyes filled with tears. He resolved to take revenge. But Sheikh Salman brushed the dirt off him and poured balm into his wounds.

"Those who vent their anger, my boy, end up ruined," the sheikh said with a smile.

The sheikh gave him a new jelaba. Hassan was delighted with it and felt proud, and the poor boys hated him even more.

5

One day he was looking for his writing board and couldn't find it. His suspicions led him to look through his classmates' things. He found it under the animal skin that one of them, named Hassouna, slept on.

He picked up the board and told Hassouna, "You're a thief."

"I'm not a thief," Hassouna answered rudely. "In the *Mukhtasar*, Khalil says: 'A lucky find is property that is liable to get lost, whether a dog, a horse, or a donkey,' and under certain conditions the finder can keep such things. I found a board and I took it."

"You knew it was my board."

Hassouna shrugged his shoulders dismissively. "You're a dog and a donkey and the son of a horse, so your property is a lucky find, as Khalil says."

Hassouna hit him on the head with the board, cracking Hassan's head and breaking the board. The boys started fighting noisily.

When he went out with the boys to the Dinder River to fetch water, he walked behind them alone, carrying a clay jar. He watched, to catch Hassouna off guard. He hadn't planned it but the anger inside him suddenly boiled over. As Hassouna bent over the water, Hassan jumped onto his back and pushed him down into the river. The boy screamed.

"The Prophet will turn against you!" he said.

Hassan grabbed Hassouna's head and pushed it under the water. The other boys hit Hassan and tried in vain to pull him off Hassouna. But Hassan's resolve was like Mount Sigdi, an unshakable block of hard red granite. Hassouna breathed out underwater and air bubbles surfaced. The boy gurgled in Hassan's grip. When Hassouna was certain he was dead and the boys thought that Hassan had killed him and so had given up hope, they saw the dove.

The white dove appeared from nowhere and landed on Hassan's head. It stood there confidently as if it were sitting on its nest. It cooed and then flew off to where it had come from. With it flew Hassan's anger and resolve. In his heart he found peace of mind and tranquility. He let go of his opponent and collapsed next to him. He sat down with water up to his chest, panting and confused. Hassouna raised his head and took a deep breath. The poor boys stood in amazement. When Hassouna found his voice, he shouted: "You're a murderer! You're a criminal!"

Then he stood up and staggered off, leaving Hassan in confusion.

Sheikh Salman forced him to stay home.

"It's best you stay here," he said.

Hassan was crying from a sense of injustice, and he complained to the sheikh.

"There's no good in people, my boy, and you're naughty," the sheikh told him. "You're better off here than living with the poor."

Hassan wiped away his tears and said expectantly, "Will you honor me by letting me serve you, sir?"

Sheikh Salman embraced him tenderly. "You are my servant and my son. You can find an example in my master the Prophet and Zaid ibn Haritha," he said.

The sheikh took him into the inner quarters of his house and treated him as the male child he had not been blessed with. He taught him how to live in solitude.

"The Almighty Lord said, '*No good comes from much of their secret deliberations*,'" said the sheikh. "My son, people are in fact really bad, so be wary of them."

Sheikh Salman was a jewel among men. He combined learning and action, indifference to the world, and aversion to other people. He hadn't slept the whole night through for forty years. He performed his prayers again and again until the morning. He never sought help from anyone in authority or accepted a salary.

"The gateways of rulers are the gateways to hell," he told his poor followers, "and the Turks' money is the devil's coin."

He had a donkey that Hassan used in Karkouj Market to carry goods for merchants for a fee. His wife and his daughters wove palm fronds into bowls that they sold. That earned him some piasters that he spent on the household and his pupils. The only wealth he had was a sheep that he tied to the door of his house.

Hassan al-Jerifawi grew up with his master's donkey, which went to Karkouj Market with him every day. He pulled it behind him for the mile between the school and the town. The merchants in the market respected Sheikh Salman's donkey because it shared in its master's merit. They singled out the donkey, and with it Hassan, for easy tasks that paid well, and if the donkey urinated in front of a shop the shopkeeper was pleased, thinking it brought good luck.

The donkey carried peppers, fennel, and coriander for the merchants. Hassan walked alongside because for a whole three years he had repeatedly forgotten to ask the sheikh for permission to ride it. He was worried that if he did so he would be abusing the sheikh's trust. He kept telling himself he would ask the next day, and then forgot about it and only remembered when he got tired on the way to Karkouj.

He received twice the usual fee for carrying goods and turned down offers of food. He only drank water because there could be no suspicion that there was anything haram about that. Water was something that Muslims shared. He impressed the merchants with his piety and they doubled the amount they paid.

Things turned bad whenever government troops came to market. They imposed taxes on the merchants' goods and a poll tax of sixty piasters for every adult male. On the sheikh's donkey Hassan had to carry women who wanted to visit the tomb of Sheikh Mohamed Hejazi, the patron saint of Karkouj. He attached the donkey to a cart and carried them reluctantly, averting his eyes and answering their questions tersely. Hassan kept his distance from them as much as he could. Sheikh Salman's counsel saved young Hassan from temptation: "Jerifawi, women are a blessing. Jerifawi, women are a curse. Love your wife, for she is your delight. Beware of women, for they are the ruin of true religion."

The woman he wanted to marry was Fatma, Sheikh Salman's daughter. But she was a girl no more than nine years old. She took from her father his tenderness toward Hassan. She had memorized the Quran as far as the twenty-seventh chapter and when she recited the angels came down in the form of specks of light. She brought him food and asked him about matters of Islamic law and Khalil's commentary. He had every hope of becoming engaged to her. Month after month the pleasure of hoping gave him the strength to be patient.

When she turned eleven, he plucked up the courage to mention her to the sheikh. The sheikh promised to be good to Hassan and was very receptive to the idea, so his happiness in this world was complete and he asked God for happiness in the afterlife.

6

Hassan and the sheikh were sitting together one night around a lantern.

Sheikh Salman wrapped himself in a woolen shawl to stop the cold creeping in.

"I used to be neighbors with Sheikh Abdel-Mahmoud," he told Hassan. "One night I heard someone reciting the Quran but I couldn't see who it was. He was reading the passage that goes, '*O David! We made you a vicegerent on earth: so judge between men fairly and do not follow your desires, for they will lead you astray from the path of God, and those who stray from the path of God will be severely punished for forgetting the Day of Reckoning.*' And God sent me a revelation. Ever since then, whenever I'm asked about some matter, I can see it as clear as the sun.

"Hassan, if a man is honest with the Lord, the Lord will teach him and show him the light. Hassan, if you're selfless you'll have access to true knowledge."

"Father, sir, ask God to grant me entry to Paradise," Hassan said.

"But Hassan, the way to Paradise is submission," the sheikh replied. "God will plant the light in your heart. Don't dismiss it. If God speaks, don't say no."

"Sheikh, people say: 'Understand in order to obey.'"

"Hassan, the poor say: 'Obey in order to survive.'"

Hassan sought learning: "Father, sir, does a person have any control over his fate?"

"Hassan, if a person tells the truth the Lord will give him control over his own life and the lives of others." He continued: "The scholar Sheikh Awouda Shakkal al-Qarih asked a man from Dongola to give him a hundred piasters for the poor and said he would give the man a hundred years of life in return. In his meanness the man replied, 'Our fates are written in heaven and it's too late to change them. I'll save my piasters and give you eleven piasters for the poor.' And the sheikh said, 'And I'll give you eleven years of life.' And the man died on the spot for being miserly."

When the government troops attacked, they seized Hassan in the market and said to him, "Pay your tax."

"This is the donkey of my master, Sheikh Salman al-Duwaihi," Hassan told them.

Driven by greed, they searched the shops and the houses. A Turk pulled him by the collar and hit him with his whip.

"You barbarian, you son of a dog!" he said. "Everyone has to give the government its due."

They took Hassan's earnings for the day. He went home sad, with his lip bleeding. He complained of the injustice to the sheikh, and the sheikh consoled him.

"God will soon bring relief," he said.

Hassan sat cross-legged on the ground, so angry he was almost crying.

"They humiliated people," he said.

"My boy, God helps those who help Him. The Sufi master Ibn Arabi said: 'If the matter appears at the junction of the two seas and the secret is evident to those who have eyes, the Prophet's namesake will stand up, with the namesake of the holy man on his right-hand side, and that will come about when the letter kha disappears from the alphabet.'"

The sheikh sent Hassan to the woods to collect firewood. He vented his anger on the trees. He hit them with the ax many times. When he reached home his anger had abated. He thought only about the unfairness. If people were humiliated and lost faith they had a case. Where is your justice, Lord? The Turks were tyrants. The help that you promised, O Lord. Nothing was treated with such contempt as Islam these days. Would no relief come?

Hassan asked God for protection. With faith he warded off his devil. He put his load down at the door to the house. He did his ablutions, then picked up his firewood and went inside.

Fatma was weaving in the courtyard. He looked away but loved the feeling of being close to her. She had started covering her hair and was almost ready for marriage. The sheikh's promise still stood and the marriage was inevitable. She was the apple of his eye and would ensure he remained true to his faith. His heart longed for her. Then he felt a sudden pain in his shoulder. He panicked and dropped his load. The pain was so intense that he screamed. Fatma was startled. He pulled his gown off his shoulder and a scorpion fell out.

He tried to stamp on it but missed. Fatma screamed and Sheikh Salman rushed in.

"It's a scorpion, father! A scorpion!"

Sheikh Salman asked God for protection from his anger and took Hassan into another room. He took off his jelaba and told Fatma to fetch the poison stone. Placing the stone on the sting, he recited the scorpion spell over him.

At night when his fever was high, Hassan told the sheikh he wanted to state his last wishes, with Sheikh Salman as his executor.

"Don't worry," said the sheikh.

"I'm dying, sheikh, so let me state my last wishes," Hassan said in resignation.

"Don't let the pain frighten you, my boy. You won't die here."

Three days later he was still alive. He overcame the fever and survived the hallucinations. The poison left his body and he ate some gruel that Fatma had prepared.

"You saved me from death, Sheikh," he told the sheikh.

"You were in such a hurry to die, my boy. Whenever you had an attack, I thought it was the end."

He recovered his strength and enjoyed days of being nursed by Fatma. And when it was the celebration of the Prophet's birthday, Sheikh Salman came with good news.

"My boy, we're marrying you to Fatma, so get yourself ready," he said.

7

Fatma. Fatma.

His sweetheart was a good woman.

He felt as if he hadn't lived before. Can one know how pleasant life is if one isn't married?

How did sleeping alone on his rough mat compare with the warm embrace of his beloved? For twenty years he hadn't known that such a thing existed in the world.

Fatma let her hair hang loose on her shoulders, covered with a shiny silk shawl. She smelled of perfume and sandalwood.

Oh darling Fatma. You put his heart at ease. He found comfort in your affection and compassion.

His wedding present to her was a Quran he had copied with his own hand and ten piasters he had worked hard to save. The poor people celebrated his wedding with Sufi dances and poems of praise.

When he went into the bridal chamber, their voices rang in his ears:

"O Leila, lady of Paradise,

The defense against Hell.

The man who's in love with you longed for you and went mad.

Visit him because night has fallen."

"Time to pray, master," she said.

"Time to pray, my dear," he answered joyfully.

They performed two ritual prostrations, and then didn't pray again for the next forty days. Newlyweds don't need to pray. They have angels hovering over them and protecting them for forty days and nights. When he reached out to her, she said, "Master, my promise."

He listened to her.

"You have taken me righteously, and if a woman obeys her husband, she will go to Paradise. The best way to obey is to help others to be obedient. So, master, don't let me stand between you and the approval of your Lord. Don't let me tempt you away from obeying God. If you ever think I'm a distraction from your religious obligations, then consider me divorced."

He promised her that. He got up and blew out the lantern. He groped his way in the dark till he fell on her warm body. He kissed her cheek and made beautiful love to her.

8

Man, nearness is when your heart is in My hand, and farness is when your heart is between My hands.

Man, aim and seek or else you will not stand firm, and when you aim and seek, then say, "O Lord, by Thee I aim and by Thee I seek and by Thee I stand firm."

Man, you have seen Me in every heart, so guide every heart to Me, not to the mention of My name, so that I can address it and it will see the right way. Guide it only to Me, for if you do not guide it to Me, you will be guiding it astray and it will be lost to Me and then I will demand you retrieve it.

Abu Abdallah al-Niffari, Address no. 54

9

Injustice is the stuff of life.

As time passed, Hassan grew sadder and sadder when he came back from his work in Karkouj Market. He shared his concerns with his wife and she tried to comfort him. He asked the sheikh, who promised him that God's help was at hand. But his heart was not at ease.

The Turks ruled iniquitously. They openly extorted money from ordinary people. They flogged respectable people and humiliated the powerful. The previous week they had stopped his donkey and stolen the money the women were taking as offerings to the tomb of Sheikh Hejazi. He had stood there cowering till the government troops finished their extortion. One of them patted him on the cheek playfully and laughed. He wept in silence at the affront to his manliness. He learned from the women that the Turks had given the chief merchant three hundred lashes in the marketplace because he hadn't stood up when the soldiers went past.

"Are the Turks Muslims?" he asked the sheikh.

"The caliph, the sultan of the Muslims, is one of them," he replied. "But it's what you do that makes you Muslim. It's not just a label."

"They behave like infidels, my father, my sheikh," said Hassan.

"Everything happens by God's command—things past and things to come. Once God gives His command, they can't make something happen one hour later or one hour earlier."

Sheikh Dafaallah al-Majthoub came to visit Sheikh Salman, and Sheikh Salman's school celebrated the visit of the holy man. People came from all quarters seeking baraka, or blessings. The school was packed with hundreds of people and the women made trilling noises when Sheikh Dafaallah stood up and sprinkled water from his ablutions on the crowd.

"Sir, life has become miserable because of oppression," Hassan told Sheikh Dafaallah.

"Everything happens by God's command—things past and things to come. Once God gives His command, they can't make something happen one hour later or one hour earlier," he replied.

"So when will God get rid of the people oppressing us?" he asked sadly.

Sheikh Dafaallah smiled.

"Who knows? It may be soon. How would you feel about joining an army to help God in the future?"

"Nothing would be more welcome than martyrdom," Hassan replied.

"Be patient, my boy, because you may walk under the banner of God and then do something bad."

Hassan objected. "I wouldn't do anything that would involve making the Lord angry," he said.

"Be wary of faith, my boy," said Sheikh Dafaallah, "because sometimes it can be as destructive as lack of faith." He smiled. "Slaughter the sheep and in return I'll give you a male child of your own, instead of you having girls," he said jokingly.

Sheikh Salman brushed off the idea, saying, "For a sheep I wouldn't take from you a boy that the Lord hasn't bestowed on me. If I had told the Lord I was intent on a boy, He wouldn't have rebuffed me. But I behave properly with Him, like a good subject, and I accept whatever He provides me with, and He has given me Hassan as a substitute son."

"Then slaughter the sheep out of hospitality," said Sheikh Dafaallah.

"I'm not going to slaughter the sheep unless the Lord commands me to, Dafaallah. And having you as our guest is sustenance enough for us poor people."

Sheikh Salman then gave orders that the people should be fed, and Hassan asked in surprise, "Where will we find enough food to feed all these people?"

Sheikh Salman answered cheerfully: "We say as Sheikh al-Hamim said long ago: 'I spent the evening as the guest of God in my empty house. A host has an obligation to be generous to his guests.'"

Sheikh Dafaallah smiled and asked, "How much food do you have?"

"A little millet. It may be enough for five, but certainly not enough for six."

"Cook it and bring it," said Sheikh Dafaallah.

Hassan went into the women's quarters and told them to prepare the food. He waited in puzzlement but told himself that holy men didn't say things without good reason. An hour later he took the pot of food and went into the room where the sheikhs were. Sheikh Dafaallah dipped his hand into the hot food. Hassan was about to warn him but a look from Sheikh Salman prevented him. He thought the sheikh was reassuring him, as if to say, "Watch what happens." Sheikh Dafaallah muttered something inaudible, and then told Hassan to take the food around to the other people. After everyone had eaten, the pot was still at least half full. There was no one left who hadn't eaten, and everyone was full. He took the rest of the food back to the two sheikhs.

"My boy, there's faith in your heart but you don't recognize it," Sheikh Dafaallah said.

That day Hassan learned to obey his heart. He came to believe that the light was there, except for those who refused to see it.

Sheikh Dafaallah took Hassan's hand in his gracious palm and looked into his eyes. The sheikh looked uncertain and then turned to Sheikh Salman, who nodded in agreement.

"Do you know what it means?" Sheikh Dafaallah asked him.

"I know," said Sheikh Salman.

"So let God's will be done."

Hassan was about to ask a question, but he held back. Holy men only reveal what God allows them to reveal. The sheikhs both knew secrets about him that he didn't know. He made do with the happiness that he felt, from being close to Sheikh Salman al-Duwaihi and from the affection of his beloved Fatma. He was offended by Turkish oppression but God would not leave his people unaided.

He tossed and turned at night, listening for the fluttering of angel wings from his sheikh's far-off room. All night long, they bring down news of heaven and take prayers up from earth. He reached out to embrace Fatma. She was resting her head on his chest. He kissed her oiled hair. He asked God for justice. Then he went to sleep to dream of the prophet Khidr.

10

A year after the visit of Sheikh Dafaallah the holy man, Fatma still wasn't pregnant. But Hassan wasn't worried. She looked sad but he tried to reassure her.

"Maybe it's a good thing," he said. "What would a child do in a world disfigured by injustice? It's good to be patient."

But she wasn't consoled. She asked her father to say prayers. He nodded to acknowledge the request but didn't say anything.

11

Hassan stood in for the sheikh and taught the pupils.

They sat in front of him writing out the Quran on their boards by dipping date pits in ink. As soon as they had memorized one section, they erased it and wrote out the next one. The classes began after morning prayers. When they had performed the noon prayers, he sent them off to the river to fetch water. Then he went to market with the sheikh's donkey and whatever the women had woven. He came back after sunset, exhausted and with layers of sadness in his heart.

He met Hassouna, his old enemy. He smiled at him and embraced him. Time had changed him. He was now stout, with plenty of fat. Hassouna asked him how he was and Hassan told him what he had been doing.

"Who would have thought you would become a sheikh?" Hassouna said.

"God assigns us our livelihoods," he replied.

"Not at all. It's because of Sheikh Salman's baraka, which favored you rather than us."

Hassan asked him how the market and the merchants were. Business was obviously poor and hardship was rife.

"There's no cash in the till," Hassouna said. "The Turks take everything and people are in dire straits."

"Is there no prospect of relief?"

"After prayers on Friday there was a disturbance in the mosque in the marketplace. People went out into the street shouting, 'O eternal God, be kind to us in our misfortunes.' The poor are powerless, and even the men of the world, the merchants, are helpless." Hassouna then asked Hassan about his wife: "Has she given you any children?"

"Not yet."

"Take a second wife."

Fatma was his beloved. He wouldn't hurt her by doing that. And if God gave him a boy the Turks would whip him. So why be so eager for one?

"It's God's command that decides, Hassouna," Hassan replied.

Hassouna looked into his face and smiled.

"You're strange, old friend. A part of you wants one thing, but another part of you submits to something else."

How truly his quarrelsome colleague had spoken! He could tell at a glance what was going on in Hassan's mind. But Hassan wasn't in a hurry.

He resigned himself to God's will and waited.

12

Hassan had a sleepless night.

When he tried to sleep, a coldness came over him and made him shiver. He got up and prayed in the hope that he would calm down. He felt that the heavens were planning something. When he'd finished praying he heard his wife breathing irregularly. He called to her in the darkness.

"Fatma!"

"Yes, master."

She was as restless as he was and couldn't sleep.

"What a night!" he said.

It was summer and the air was still. He could hear the donkey braying. He sought God's protection. Going to the window, he looked at the sky. He could see lines of shooting stars. He took a deep breath.

"*There is no god but God*," he said.

Fatma got up and came to his side to look. The shooting stars were falling everywhere, stoning the devils. He recited the verse of the Quran: "*And we do not know whether evil is intended for those on earth or whether their Lord intended good for them.*"

He looked out toward Sheikh Salman's room and could see that it was swathed in white light. He went back to bed, stifled by the darkness.

"Light the lamp, Fatma," he said.

He could hear her moving in the dark and after a moment the flame shone. In the dancing light he could see that Fatma's forehead was running with sweat. He pulled her toward him and wiped the sweat off with his hand. He kissed her to comfort her. He ran his hand down her naked back and her body shivered.

"Is it the fever?" he asked her.

"In my heart, master," she answered in a trembling voice, "not in my body."

When he heard the call to prayer he imagined the whole of creation was calling. He trembled when he heard the muezzin say "Allahu akbar." He went out to pray and stood in the front line behind the sheikh. The poor people, in their humility, also felt that something extraordinary was astir. When the prayers were over, Sheikh Salman sat in silence with his back to his pupils. Some of them left while others stayed. When the sun came up Sheikh Salman stood. He took Hassan by the hand and started walking.

"Slaughter the sheep, Hassan," he said.

Hassan was upset.

"Why, sir?" he asked.

"Slaughter the sheep, Hassan."

The sheikh left him in the courtyard and went into his room. Hassan turned to the main door. He untied the sheep and took it to the corner close to the kitchen. He fetched a knife, put it to the sheep's neck and, with the animal facing Mecca, mumbled, "In the name of God, Allahu akbar."

The sheep was silent throughout. It did not bleat or move. He severed its neck and left it for the blood to drain. Then he dragged it to a wooden joist. He hung it up and made a hole in its leg. Putting his mouth to the hole, he blew into it till the skin was inflated. With the knife he made a cut in the sheep's belly. He skinned it and cut the meat into pieces. The women came and carried the meat to the kitchen. By breakfast time the meat was cooked and there was plenty of broth. He went into the sheikh's room to ask him what to do next and the sheikh told him to share the broth and the meat with the poor.

"And you, sir?"

"Just bring me some of the hock and some bread."

He chose the best portion of the hock and took it to the sheikh, who told him to invite in anyone he found outside. Hassan stood in the doorway and saw five poor people. He invited them in and they came in and sat eating with the sheikh. The sheikh pointed to a place and said, "Sit down, Hassan, and eat."

Obeying the sheikh's order, he sat among the others who were eating and took a piece of meat. Before he put it into his mouth, the sheikh spoke.

"God's command has come," he said. "Woe to the unjust. Blessings on the poor who believe."

The guests stopped eating and looked at the sheikh in wonder. Sheikh Salman Wad Hamad al-Duwaihi picked up the roast hock and said: "This sheep tells me that the Mahdi of Allah has appeared."

Five

Nevertheless I have somewhat against you, because you have
left your first love.

Revelation of St. John the Divine, 2:4

2

Theodora Eleftherios left the town of Suez on the first day
of 1881.

She was accompanied by Father Pavlos, another nun, and
a large Catholic delegation. Their ship sailed through the Red
Sea for three days. Theodora was delighted with the voyage.
She felt she was sailing toward approval from the Lord. She
felt free for the first time in her life. When the Lord approves
of you, He grants you freedom. She was no longer subject
to her father's fears that some man might try to seduce her.
Even when she had appeared in church in Alexandria, some
of them clearly found her attractive.

When her father had given her to the convent, he thought
he was protecting her out of love for her, and in the convent
the other nuns knew how to reinforce her sense of sin.

"Man is the son of God, Theodora. But he has made the
Lord sad that He created him. The things that we love are
pure evil, because man has a natural inclination to love sin,"
said the nuns.

On the ship, in the same cabin, Sister Dorothea shared her enthusiasm for serving the Lord in Sudan, the land of the barbarians. She shared her sadness at the sins of man, the sons of God.

But on the ship, in the same cabin, Theodora hid from Sister Dorothea the memory of Georgios, who had kissed her on the lips when she was only thirteen years old and left her trembling till it was time for mass.

Their families were happily celebrating the new year in the Mohamed Ali Club when Georgios took her unawares and forced his kisses upon her. Her mother, Laskarina, sensed the change in her and spoke to her about men—their tricks, their lies, and their physical desires.

Theodora concluded that the trembling she felt was the work of the devil. Two years later, in the convent, she came to believe that she had been defiled.

Her soul felt laden with guilt, but her heart still danced at the memory of the sin.

How lost mankind was, between the Lord and the pleasures of the senses.

She hid the memory of the pleasure under her nun's habit and spent two years in the convent, the prisoner of her sin.

Now, as she sailed south from Suez to Sudan, she looked forward to freedom.

When he kissed her, Georgios had said, "Your lips are the wine of devils."

Bakhit Mandil, on a similarly dark night, would ask her, "From which kind of marble did the angels sculpt you?"

And in her heart were the words of Saint Theresa of Avila in her autobiography: "The pain was so great that it made me moan; and yet so surpassing was the sweetness of this excessive pain that I could not wish to be rid of it. The soul is satisfied now with nothing less than God."

She ran away from all this to serve the Lord in Khartoum, where her services were needed by the Orthodox sinners who traded in groceries, readymade clothes, tableware, meat, and vegetables. Only among these people in the land of the barbarians could she become a saint.

In Alexandria she was a captive of the Lord for her sin, but she won her freedom to become a servant of the Lord in Khartoum.

And her soul was satisfied now with nothing less than God.

3

Over the three days of the voyage she became friends with Sister Dorothea.

She had met her for the first time in Suez when Father Pavlos introduced her. Dorothea came from noisy Cairo, the city of the Khedive. She was about the same age: seventeen. And she was the same dazzling white, like a burst of morning light. But Dorothea, unlike Theodora, had a knowledge of politics. She knew about the turmoil in Egypt, the plots that were being hatched in palaces, and the struggles between politicians. And unlike Theodora, she was as cheerful as a lark. Like Theodora, she saw herself as Egyptian and thanked the Lord for creating her white. She felt sorry for those who had the misfortune to be black. She hadn't been isolated from the people of Egypt like Theodora. Her family hadn't kept her in a cocoon, and she had had plenty of friends. Dorothea was full of praise for Egyptians, to Theodora's surprise. She told Egyptian stories and jokes, to Theodora's amazement. She laughed heartily, unrestrained by a sense of sin, to Theodora's puzzlement. They ended up thinking about the country where they were heading, and fell silent. It was a dark spot about which they knew nothing worth mentioning.

They turned to Father Pavlos, who sat with the Catholic priests. With him was Bishop Comboni and Fathers Joseph Ohrwalder, Franz Pimezzoni, and Johann Dichtl. They always wore dazzling-white robes with large crosses on their chests. The girls asked Father Pavlos about Khartoum.

He told them that the city had been founded by Khurshid Pasha fifty years earlier as a capital to replace Wad Madani. It was where the Nile began, he said, as mentioned in the Book of Isaiah: "Pass through your land like the Nile, daughter of Tarshish. There is nothing to hold you back any more."

Theodora knew the Nile but Father Pavlos told her that the Nile in Khartoum was different from the river she was familiar with.

"It's a wild river, as virgin as it was created by the hand of the Lord. It's impetuous and vigorous. It hasn't been tamed by engineering works like the Nile in Egypt.

"Do the blacks smell as horrible as they look?" Theodora asked him with interest.

Father Pavlos reminded her of the story of the sons of Noah.

"Noah said his son Ham would be a slave to his brothers, and that Ham's descendants would be slaves to his brothers' descendants," the priest said. "But we are bringing the word of God to them, and the more we love them, the more God will love us."

In the cabin that night, Dorothea said, "They smell horrible and rotten, like rotten fruit. And their sweat is poisonous. They don't have the magic or the kindness of the Egyptians," she added dreamily.

Dorothea had seen some of them as soldiers in Cairo.

Theodora's mother, Laskarina, had read her letters from relatives and acquaintances in Khartoum to show her what she should expect.

"They are treacherous by nature. Savages. But they are like farm animals. You will be the shepherd to the Lord's black sheep."

Where else would the Lord be if not in this frightening country?

Father Pavlos put her mind at rest whenever she showed fear.

"Khartoum, where we are heading, is a little Europe," he said.

4

They landed at the port of Suakin on the fourth day.

It was the biggest and oldest town on the western shore of the Red Sea. Theodora went for a walk with her companions and was amazed. It was an old Arab town, with buildings that were close to how she imagined *The Thousand and One Nights*. Houses of two or three stories, built of coral taken from the seabed. Wooden balconies overlooked the narrow streets. Maybe Shahrazad was asleep behind one of them, dreaming.

They walked through the streets among a medley of peoples. There were Turks, many Egyptians, and Europeans who seemed to be adventurers.

But the local people were black and their skin was rough.

The air was humid, salty, and slightly chilly. The sky was heavy with clouds, louring over the houses threateningly.

The governor of the town received them with honor. He put them up at the guesthouse close to the government offices, and the Turkish and European elite in the town welcomed them. They saw them as an addition to the civilizing mission that was chipping away at the hard stone of the country's barbarity.

Theodora loved to stand on the upper floor, behind the carved wooden windows, watching the blacks passing by like energetic beetles roaming the streets.

There were men who wore only a strip of cotton without trousers and walked barefoot. Their wild coarse hair gave off the smell of castor oil. She saw women in the guesthouse kitchen with plaited hair, wearing bracelets, anklets, and necklaces. The sun was bright in the tropical town despite the heavy clouds, but in her prejudice Theodora saw the black skin of the people as inauspicious.

She prayed to the Lord that He would not try her heart through pride.

She believed they were the lost black sheep of the Lord, but the shepherd had to be humble. So she kept herself busy, trying to overcome the homesickness she felt. She was amazed to see the black women hovering around her and Dorothea and the other nuns, admiring their fair hair and long, clean tunics.

Theodora thought they didn't smell bad, just strange.

She accepted the women's invitation into the kitchen and saw them warily tipping a third of what they had cooked onto the ground. She asked them why and they told her they were giving the food to the djinn as an offering so that they wouldn't spoil the food for the people who were going to eat it. Father Pavlos said, "The local people say Suakin was built by King Solomon, whom Muslims call a prophet."

Solomon, the son of David, defeated the rebellious djinn and sent them in chains to this place. He gave orders to the obedient djinn that were his troops and they built an impregnable town with guards on the walls. Solomon imprisoned the rebellious djinn in the town and called it Sawajin, from the Arabic word meaning 'prisons.'

"When the people outnumbered the djinn, they changed the name to Suakin," Father Pavlos said.

He told her that King Solomon had a son by the Queen of Sheba and was worried his enemies would harm his son, whom they named Sheba. So he sent the son to Sudan and built a city there in his name. People later changed the name to Soba.

The people of Suakin are frightened of cats, which they consider to be djinn. They don't pour away boiling water in case it harms creatures that they can't see. At sunset they refuse to move until it's dark everywhere, so that they don't get in the way of the djinn when they emerge from hiding.

Theodora remembered all this and wrote it in her first letter to her mother. She asked her mother how she had been, so far from her in the past days. She sent greetings to her two brothers and kisses of respect for her father's rough, pudgy hand. She told her mother she missed her and that she was happy that they had almost arrived in Khartoum, where she would serve the Lord.

Dorothea looked up and watched her writing enthusiastically. "Since when did you miss them so much that you're sending a letter?" she asked in surprise.

"My mother told me to write whenever I had a chance."

Dorothea laughed.

"Of course, because you're their spoiled only daughter. The apple of your mother's eye. But I'm the third of six girls, with four brothers," she said.

She sat up in bed, having decided to chat with Theodora rather than go to sleep.

"My middle brother is in love with an Egyptian girl whose father works in the palace. She's as pretty as a picture, but she's Muslim. She doesn't care much about that but Muslims, as you know, get angry about such things. Her mother is a snobbish Turk but she's happy with her daughter's relationship with my brother. She thinks he's better than the Egyptians. My mother says my brother's going to convert to Islam so that he can marry her."

"He's going to abandon the religion of Christ for the sake of a girl?"

"It's love, Theodora. But that's not the problem. My father's the problem."

Dorothea's father was a doctor with a modest reputation in khedival Cairo, but he was proud of his status and his religion.

"My father won't agree unless he thinks the marriage will enhance his position," she said.

Theodora listened to the story and unconsciously added it to the stock of news in the letter she was writing.

Dorothea put her feet down from the bed, stood up, and walked around the big room. She looked up at the wooden ceiling. She went to the window and looked out over the sleeping town.

"Do you think this country needs us?" she mused.

Theodora glanced at her friend's back, and her fingertips played with the small silver cross that hung around her neck.

"Everyone needs the word of the Lord," she said.

"If Khartoum is anything like this town, I'll be dead before anyone benefits from the word of the Lord."

"Father Pavlos says Khartoum is different."

Dorothea looked out to the black horizon. She could hardly make anything out. But the smell of salt reached her, laden with images. She looked north in the hope of seeing the tomb of Sheikh Barghout, whom the sailors hailed when they sailed past, but she couldn't see it.

"Two years in this country is quite a long time," Dorothea said.

"It will pass quickly," Theodora said confidently. "And when we go back to Egypt, we'll have lots of memories and stories we can tell everyone."

"I already miss Egypt," Dorothea said.

Theodora gave a brief chuckle and said, "You don't seem to have quite left it yet."

Dorothea turned to reply to her friend's remark. "Maybe I caught that from you," she said.

She looked at Theodora's letter, which lay in front of her. "I have an idea," she said. "Write to your family all the time, and when you go back put your letters together in a book."

"A book about what?"

"A book of your letters from Sudan. Imagine: the letters of a teacher in Sudan. It would be wonderful."

Theodora frowned. "That's not something that well-brought-up girls should do. And anyway, who would read such a book in Egypt?" she said.

Dorothea pranced around the room, delighted with her idea. "Don't write it for Egypt. You're good at English, aren't you? Write it in English and have it published in London. It would be a great book."

"You're crazy. Women don't write books," said Theodora.

Dorothea went back to her bed.

"I'm not mad," she said. "You're the mad one. If I had the patience to write letters, I would do it myself."

She thought for a moment, then added sadly, "But maybe my idea wouldn't really work, because this country's not very exciting. It doesn't seem to have anything that would interest readers. Maybe if we'd gone to Abyssinia."

"Abyssinia? Dorothea!"

"Yes."

"Maybe it would be best to go to sleep. Our caravan's going to start out early, and with your imagination we'll never even get to Khartoum."

Dorothea grumbled in protest. Theodora folded up her letter, stood, and put out the lamp. Darkness flooded the room like a scream. She walked cautiously toward her bed in the darkness. She could hear her friend saying a prayer and was grateful she had given up and decided to sleep. But as she was pulling the cover over her, she heard Dorothea say, "When I prayed to the Lord I asked Him to make something exciting happen in our two years here, so that your book will be interesting."

5

In the world you shall have tribulation: but be of good cheer;
I have overcome the world.

John 16:33

6

Theodora was living a dream.

She left at dawn in a caravan of camels, accompanied by the sound of the call to prayer from Suakin's two mosques.

She felt like Shahrazad leaving the Baghdad of *The Thousand and One Nights*, swaying on top of a Bishari camel with a light step and a soft back and a ring in its nose. Her small silver cross swung across her firm breasts. The desert watched them go. Daylight emerged from the heart of the earth and climbed up the sky.

It was a caravan of twenty-one camels—ridden by the missionaries, three servants, Issa the caravan leader, and two guides—and five horses for the guards. The horses were leaving the mists that came from the sea off Suakin to venture into the sand hills of the desert behind the town.

The caravan leader and the guides were bareheaded, with long, oiled hair. Each was wrapped in a single piece of faded cloth. One of the guides had a spear and a leather shield. The five guards were very black. Their commander wore a blue jelaba, sandals, and a Turkish fez with a long tassel. The others had short tunics that ended just below the knee and sharp swords at their belts.

Theodora looked at them from on top of her camel and thought she was like an Abbasid princess traveling between Baghdad and Mosul. Maybe she was the daughter of a caliph and they were taking her as a bride to marry a great king. She had never seen a desert like this one, but she had read about them in books. It was grander than all her imaginings.

They traveled for hours, flanked by one of the mounted guards. Theodora took a quick look at him. A strongly built young man with a firm body and eyes as black as kohl. He had a round head and short curly hair. She noticed small scars under his eyes. He might have been two or three years older than her. But he was self-confident and full of energy, and he was in his own country. Unlike her, a white Greek-Egyptian. A city girl who had never seen such a vast emptiness, except for the Mediterranean off the coast in Alexandria. She turned to Dorothea, who was hanging on to her own camel nearby, and she saw that she was equally impressed and maybe dreaming the same dream.

A large rabbit started from under her camel. She caught a glimpse of it kicking up dust before it suddenly disappeared. The guard called to her from his horse. "That's a wild rabbit," he said. "There are lots of them in the desert and we'll come across them all along the way."

Theodora bowed her head and hung on to the pommel of the saddle.

"Are there many other animals here?" she asked.

The guard laughed. Unlike the other local people she had heard, he spoke in an accent that wasn't difficult to understand. He used many Egyptian words and some Turkish pronunciation.

"It's desert. You'll find lots of animals in it. You'll see hyenas, wild cows, and gazelles," he said.

She was very excited. How marvelous the Lord's creation was, she thought.

When they camped the commander gave orders to two of his guards and they rode off into the distance. The commander came up to the missionaries, who were exhausted from the first day's travel. He gave them a toothless smile and spoke with pride, beating his hand on his chest. Theodora didn't understand what he was saying. She asked Father Pavlos, who shrugged his shoulders in bewilderment.

"He says that the guards who went off were his sons," said Father Johann.

"People here pride themselves on having lots of children," said Father Pavlos. "The more children you have and the more they help you, the greater the cause for pride."

Dorothea whispered: "My father would be proud as a peacock in a country like this."

When the women wanted to relieve themselves, they walked away from the encampment in a group and hid in the dogbane bushes. Theodora was afraid because darkness was falling and she could feel the chill of the desert night nipping at her legs.

"Would you believe it? We're taking a poo in the desert!" Dorothea called out.

She could hear one of the Catholic nuns mumbling in protest, but Dorothea didn't care.

"Do you think there's a chance the djinn will see us here and fall in love with us? They say that in this country there are djinn lurking in every shadow."

"The Lord preserve you, Dorothea," said Theodora.

They finished one after another and gathered together again for the return journey. There were seven Catholic nuns. Three of them had gray hair and had been alive for eternity. One of them was the same age as Theodora and Dorothea, and the other three were in between. For three of them, it wasn't their first visit to Sudan, so everything they passed was banal and ordinary, with nothing impressive about it.

Theodora's whole body was trembling with pain. Her thighs were throbbing and she hardly had the strength to stand up. When they reached the camp they found the guards had pitched nine tents. The two guards who had left earlier came back carrying a gazelle that was bleeding but still alive. One of them was the guard who had spoken to Theodora. She went up to him to ask what had happened. He told her proudly they had caught the gazelle for them to eat. She was speechless. He was telling her proudly how they hunted gazelles.

"We drive them into the open, then chase one of them. We keep heading them off until one of them is exhausted from running. When it falls we drive a sword into its leg so that it can't run any farther."

She looked at the trembling gazelle. Its eyes were bulging with terror. Its throat was throbbing and she could see its little heart beating despite the fading light.

She went back sadly to her companions, so tired she could hardly walk. Father Pavlos showed her to her tent. "Dorothea and Hortensia will be with you," he said.

Hortensia was the Catholic nun who was the same age as them. She was from Austria. Throughout the voyage on the steamer Theodora had felt she was snobbish and unpleasant.

She went into the black tent, which was made of wool, and found it empty. She took off her headscarf and let her chestnut hair down. It fell on her neck and shoulders. She took off her leather boots and threw her stockings aside. Her toes wriggled with pleasure at being free. She threw herself down on the ground without a care in the world because the exertion had sapped her strength.

She closed her eyes. What a joy to be exhausted doing the Lord's work.

The daughter of Greek post-office worker Andreas Eleftherios, born and brought up in a pampered lifestyle on the shores of the Mediterranean, was now relieving herself in the Sudanese desert and sleeping on the ground. Our Father, which art in Heaven, give us strength. The brown-haired girl who sang in the church choir was exhausted from riding a Bishari camel on the way from Suakin to Berber.

All the girls in the church choir were young virgins. But none of them were as beautiful as Theodora.

She would leave their house behind the Mohamed Ali Club, walk to the beginning of the street, and then turn to go east, parallel with the shoreline. She came to the church within a few minutes. She went in and felt at home. Here the Lord waited for her to earn His grace by service to the church. Father Pavlos loved her and cared for her as if she were his own daughter. She didn't tell him, or her father, that on her walk every day she had to deal with shopkeepers, cart drivers, itinerant fruit sellers, gentlemen, and fishermen, along with the sea breeze. The men pestered her with supposedly flirtatious remarks, but she did not look up from the ground. She only looked at where her feet fell. When she was about to turn off the seafront, she took a last loving look at the Mediterranean waves that she adored. For a moment she caught sight of the foam as the waves swept toward her. She heard the boom of the sea calling her name. She smiled coyly, then turned her back on it. Life was nice and pleasant; if only the Devil hadn't tainted her with sin.

Dorothea came into the tent, wild as the wind.

"Come quickly! They're going to slaughter the gazelle," she said.

Theodora jumped up in alarm. She picked up her head-scarf and threw it on any old how. She ran barefoot behind Dorothea. The sand was cold. She could feel it under her feet like wet clods. Darkness lay across the world, but the servants had lit several fires that warded it off. The fires flickered around the encampment. Theodora found Father Pavlos, Father Johann, and one of the Catholic nuns watching the slaughter of the gazelle. The guard, her traveling companion who was so proud of himself, put his bare foot on the gazelle's legs to hold it in place on the ground. The gazelle's four legs were locked together under his foot. With his left hand he took hold of the frightened animal's jaw and lifted it up to expose the neck. The light flashed in its big eyes.

"It's crying!" exclaimed Theodora.

Tears gathered in the gazelle's eyes. It made a sound like a groan of a mother with a broken heart. It kicked its legs helplessly, and its executioner trod down firmly. It moaned. It shook its head. In vain. The knife ran across its beautiful long neck. A fountain of dark-red blood sprayed out. Theodora gasped in horror, turned, and ran off, choking on her tears.

Dorothea caught up with her. "I've changed my mind," she said cheerfully. "There are plenty of exciting things to write about in this country. Take what we've seen, for example. It was amazing."

Theodora was crying. "It's a wicked country. They slaughter gazelles," she said.

7

A desert that soothes the soul.

Endless sand and stone.

It's wise and has seen everything, so what could take it by surprise?

Many others like them had come that way before.

Theodora felt it seeping into her soul.

Nothing but silence. The sounds of the caravan and the songs sung by Issa the caravan leader sounded thin and pale against the majestic silence of the desert.

The Lord dwells in this wilderness.

8

The caravan traveled for days.

It's a long way from Suakin to Berber. They told them it would take twenty days.

They went past valleys and watercourses. Once they saw a herd of wild cows in the distance, running toward the horizon.

They lived on milk, meat, and bread. But Theodora refused to eat meat after the slaughter of the gazelle had left an unhealed wound in her heart.

They crossed grassy pastures in the wilderness. The unreal land they were traveling through was far from monotonous. It might be sandy desert for a time; then it would forget about being sandy and change into hard stony ground, and if it tired of that it would turn green and grassy like a meadow in spring. Rocky mountains loomed on the horizon and then suddenly disappeared as if they had grown weary of staying there and had moved on. Then other mountains would appear.

Issa the caravan leader never stopped singing. He only spoke the language of the desert or, if he spoke Arabic, he spoke it with an obscure, mysterious accent that Theodora didn't understand. He had a vast head but his limbs were so thin that he might have borrowed them from a child. His eyes were crazed and never stopped blinking. He had light down above his upper lip. Whenever Theodora looked at him, he was smoking an old pipe. If he saw her, he laughed, raised his pipe, and said proudly, "Pasha . . . pasha."

She didn't understand what he meant, but she guessed that some pasha had given him the pipe. He was a heavy smoker and sometimes he took a lump of tobacco and chewed it.

Father Johann, who had agreed to pay Issa five hundred piasters for the journey, told her that Issa was the finest camel driver in the east of the country. His camels were unmatched. He had an affectionate relationship with them. He spoke to them and sang to them. Some people claimed they understood him and replied to him. Theodora once saw him bend down, whisper in a camel's ear, and laugh. She swore to Dorothea that the camel smiled and mumbled something back with its thick lips.

Dorothea insisted she was mad and that Issa was mad too.

But Issa was useful when Father Pavlos had a fever on their fifth day. When the priests gathered around anxiously, praying to the Lord and looking in their baggage for medicine for fevers, Issa looked around on the ground and picked some herbs, which he crushed and then mixed with some boiled milk. Father Pavlos was shivering, and Issa insisted he drink the mixture. Pavlos sweated profusely, but in less than an hour he had thrown off the fever and was ravenously hungry.

Members of the mission asked Issa what the herbs were, but he just laughed and chewed his pipe tobacco without answering.

They stopped at a well but the guide said the water was undrinkable.

"The water's bitter and no good for drinking," the commander of the guard explained, with his son translating from his strange dialect. "It used to be sweet and the local people came here for water."

"What local people are there here in the desert?" Dorothea asked in surprise.

The man pointed to the hills in the distance, which looked like large pebbles.

"There. There's a tribe on each hill, and this is their land that we're crossing," he said.

"But this is desert," said Father Pavlos in puzzlement. "Isn't it government land?"

The man laughed his toothless laugh. "No government. The land, the mountains, and the sky belong to the people who live here," he said.

"Even the sky?"

"Our tribes own even the sky," the guide chipped in. "When a cloud escapes in the fall and it rains on another piece of land, we chase it to find out where it's rained and force the people there to pay compensation."

"Even the khedive of Egypt doesn't own the clouds," commented Father Pavlos.

The commander of the guards resumed his story about the well: "The tribes fought here with the invading Arab Bedouin. The Bedouin brought their animals to this land every summer seeking water, and they tried to take over the wells and the pasture, but the local people prevented them. One year there were many people killed and when the fighting was over all their blood had drained into the land and the wells had turned bitter."

Everything in this country was different from the things Theodora had known before.

In their tent at night, Hortensia told her about eastern Sudan, which they were leaving now for the central part of the country. Hortensia had visited Sudan a year earlier. Her uncle was a bishop in Khartoum. She knew many things and she liked this amazing black country; this monotonous land where nothing earthshaking had happened since it had been annexed by Mohamed Ali Pasha. Theodora listened with interest and wrote notes in her diary. She thought she might include some of these stories in her next letter to her mother. Dorothea listened with interest too and thought about the book that Theodora would have published when they went back to Egypt.

The country was a beautiful dream. A beautiful, languid dream. That's why Dorothea kept praying to the Lord to make interesting things happen to her.

9

On the way they met a group of people from the hill tribes. They were black people who owned the hills, the plain, and the sky with its clouds.

A little clan. The men were naked except for one piece of calico, and wore no trousers. Barefoot. On their heads they had a single clump of curly, greased hair. Their fingers were decked with silver rings of a kind that Theodora had never seen before. There were two women with them. Thin, the color of dirty copper. They weren't as black as the men. Their hair was carefully plaited. On their legs they had silver anklets.

The nuns tried to speak to them but they had no language in common. Hortensia asked to draw one of the women. Issa, the caravan leader, jabbered with them. He laughed and smiled. Then he told them that they refused to be drawn.

He didn't tell them much about the local people. The travelers exchanged ignorance for ignorance with the local people and then left them to their secrets.

10

Two days' journey from Berber the guard gave Theodora a sparrow. She loved the gift very much. The sparrow was so tiny that it didn't even fill her little hand when she held it. Its wings were the color of coffee and it had an elegant tail and a white breast. Its sweet chirping saddened Theodora and annoyed Hortensia in the tent. But it died a few hours before they reached Berber. While it was still alive Theodora had found a hole in its chest with a trail of ants coming out. The bird's breast was still trembling but the bird was unable to move.

She tried to seek help from the guard or one of the guides. But the friendly guard had left the encampment and gone off to check the rest of the route to Berber with two of the other guards. She then resorted to Issa the caravan leader, but he just smiled at her and repeated cheerfully, "It's a sparrow. Yes, it's a sparrow."

He couldn't understand why she was sad or why she was asking for help. And then the sweet bird died in her hand.

11

The caravan stopped in Berber for a day before heading south toward Khartoum.

What made Theodora happiest was that she was able to have a bath in a closed room. Washing in the desert had been most embarrassing, but in Berber the Lord had finally given her a mud-brick room where she could feel safe. She washed her hair, which had turned bronze from the desert dust, and asked Hortensia to help her dry it.

She didn't like Berber much. It was a poor, dingy town, surrounded by orchards of doum palms. Father Pavlos told her that prostitution was rife in the town. In Berber she ate some pomegranate. She liked it and asked where it came from. She discovered that traders brought it from Egypt to the markets in Berber and Shindi.

As they were leaving the town, her guard friend pointed to a house in the distance and said, "There's a man who's a hundred and sixty years old in that house. One day I'll invite you to visit him. He likes to have guests."

"A hundred and sixty years? How can that be?"

"That's what I'm telling you, and he's in good health. He's been married eight times and has thirty-seven children and a tribe of grandchildren and great-grandchildren. The Europeans come to visit him and he likes them. I'll invite you to his place someday."

Theodora smiled and said, "I'll take that as a promise."

He laughed and shrugged his shoulders.

The desert in those parts was harsher than the desert they had crossed on their way from the Red Sea. Although their route kept close to the Nile, Theodora wanted them to go even closer so that she could see if it was different from the Nile in Egypt, but the river was still some way off. She caught glimpses of the water sparkling, but not from close up. They had the option of going up the river by boat but one of the gray-haired Catholic women said she was afraid of the river.

What kind of idiot would be afraid of the river? Theodora thought.

But she didn't object because it wasn't her decision. The mission decided to continue on land and to pay Issa a hundred piasters extra.

Theodora saw swarms of locusts. Hortensia, who had started to travel alongside Theodora and Dorothea instead of with her fellow Catholic companions, said the Nubians who lived in northern Sudan ate them. Theodora remembered John the Baptist, who ate locusts in the Judean desert. She thought about the friendly guard and wondered whether he ate locusts too.

Half a day after leaving Berber she asked him about his accent. Unlike the other local people, he spoke in a way she could understand.

He laughed, as he did whenever she asked him about anything. "I try to speak in a way you'll understand," he told her. "I've met many Egyptian traders and Turkish civil servants and I know how to speak to them in a hybrid dialect that isn't too difficult for them."

She liked his intelligence.

"He has a social awareness you wouldn't expect from barbarians," she told Dorothea.

They covered the distance to Khartoum in seven days. On the last night before they entered the city, they had a feast. The guards brought another gazelle. Theodora begged her guard not to slaughter it, so he left the task to his brother. Dorothea insisted on watching them slaughter the animal and cut up the meat, while Theodora stayed in the tent, partly in anguish, but also secretly thanking her guard for refusing to take part in this crime.

They called her out of the tent when the food was cooked and all traces of the gazelle were gone. Issa the caravan leader laid claim to the gazelle's head and hid it in a piece of cloth. Father Pavlos said he was going to sell it in Khartoum. The guards sang for them while they were eating. One of them had a sweet voice. He sang, and the others answered him stridently in unison:

"*Yubani hiya yubanain*
Allayl bubi yal-mitqal."

And the refrain was:

"*Ana rasi indar.*"

The melody was light and jaunty, and everyone liked it. They clapped and smiled and nodded their heads. Theodora looked at the priests and saw that they were as happy as children. Even the Catholic nuns had loosened up and broken into beaming smiles.

Issa danced and pranced to the rhythm of their clapping. He was shaking his big head to and fro and waving his hand in the air in rhythm with the music.

When the party was over Theodora asked Hortensia what the lyrics meant, but she didn't know. Theodora stood by her tent and called her guard friend. He swaggered up, with eyes like a snare.

"The song says: 'O my love, the night is over and my head is heavy with drowsiness, so come and sleep with me,'" he said.

Theodora laughed and thought he was teasing. But he assured her he was telling the truth. As the women were about to go to sleep, she said to her companions, "Who would imagine that in this desolate country the people sing things like that?"

"I don't like that guard and the way he tries to ingratiate himself with you," Hortensia said grumpily in the darkness.

"Don't be such an old woman," Dorothea retorted defensively. "He's just a friendly guard."

"Believe me," said Theodora, "he would be a good friend if it wasn't for what he is."

"What do you mean?"

"He's just a black savage, Hortensia," Theodora said.

12

After a week in Khartoum, Theodora wrote to her mother Laskarina.

We reached Khartoum after a journey that lasted twenty-eight days. It's a beautiful city surrounded by gardens and shady palm trees. We were met by the members of the Catholic mission on the banks of the Nile, along with some of the consuls. Delighted that the exhausting journey was over, we walked to the buildings of the Catholic mission with them, past gardens full of flowers. In the main hall we found some of the Turks and Europeans who work here. Pleasant people who love life. One of them told me about his wars against the slave traders. There's a German doctor who smokes heavily and is a big talker. He doesn't seem to believe in the Lord. In the afternoon we went to our mission buildings and found a crowd of Greeks and Egyptians waiting for us there. They celebrated our arrival and cheered for us. They are really nice people. I live in a beautiful house with a garden. Outside my window there's an orange tree. Every house in the area has a garden, so the city has a pleasant smell, which covers up the strange smell of the people. It was sad to part with Hortensia. She promised she would visit but she hasn't done so yet. Their mission is traveling west to a town called Obada. Khartoum is beautiful, Mama. It has spacious buildings, mostly made of stone and brick, and a little mud brick. There are no less than three thousand houses. The Catholic mission is really vast, although most of the Europeans are Greek Orthodox. Yesterday Uncle Panagiotis and Auntie Maria visited me. They send their regards to all of you. I'm going to the Khartoum gardens with them the day after tomorrow, and we'll visit the Christian cemetery in the Salama Pasha district. I'm going to love life here. Pray for me, Mama, so that the Lord will look favorably on me.

Six

1

SADNESS FADES AND TENDS TO dwindle with time. But when
Theodora received bad news about her father she was devastated for months and almost wasted away. Dorothea looked
after her and comforted her as much as she could. Theodora
lost weight and turned into something like a ghost. At night
she cried for long periods.

"I didn't know that sorrow could be as poisonous as this
sadness of mine," her mother had said in her letter, but she
didn't give many details.

There had been some rioting, some madness in Alexandria.
Egyptian Muslims had killed people in the street. Dorothea
looked into it and discovered there had been a big massacre
in the city. Theodora's father, Andreas Eleftherios, had been
killed at the entrance to his house. He was no longer worried
about her chastity. He was dead.

When Father Pavlos tried to console her, Theodora said
in a daze, "They killed him on the front steps of the house.
Who's going to help my mother wash away all the blood?"

Fadl al-Aziz the servant went up to Father Pavlos and whispered, "The girl's going to lose her mind. Read the Rahman
chapter of the Quran to her."

Father Pavlos took no notice. But he was startled when Fadl
al-Aziz put her arms around Theodora and said sadly, "Ask
Allah for forgiveness, my dear, and say '*There is no god but Allah.*'"

He told the old servant off and threw her out of the room. She went off muttering Muslim invocations.

Theodora was in bed with fever for two weeks. Then she spilled her guts out for some days, with vomiting and diarrhea. The Armenian doctor visited her when the medicines that the church had didn't work. He said she had dysentery. And when Father Pavlos told her she was grieving, the doctor shrugged indifferently and said, "Grief and dysentery."

Khartoum didn't have a flood drainage system. That fall pools of water had gathered in every corner and there were many mosquitoes. Typhus, smallpox, cholera, and dysentery were widespread.

Dorothea stood by the window looking out at the wet, sweltering streets and watching the mosquitoes bouncing against the screen over the window.

"This isn't a city. This is a cesspit," she said.

That August, when the letter arrived from the widowed Laskarina, the mission had already been in Khartoum eighteen months.

As the days passed Dorothea had lost her admiration for the boring city, whereas Theodora had become more and more enamored of it.

Uncle Panagiotis and Auntie Maria were family to Theodora and they found in her a replacement for their own daughter, Sara, who had died four years earlier. They showered on her the pent-up parental feelings they had no other way to express.

Uncle Panagiotis saw himself as a native of the country.

"After nineteen years here I've turned completely savage," he joked with Theodora as she drank tea in their spacious sitting room. "Even my skin has almost turned black."

Two years later, when the Europeans decided to flee the city because the dervish uprising was approaching, he objected. "Where would I go?" he said. "This is my country. I've forgotten any language other than the Arabic that the people speak here. And my skin's so black I wouldn't feel at home anywhere else."

Auntie Maria tearfully accepted his decision to stay. "I won't abandon dear Sara's grave and run away," she said.

To visit Theodora Auntie Maria had to walk across the city to the Orthodox mission in the Mosque district. She helped her bathe and get dressed. Proudly she looked at Theodora, who shone like an icon in her white habit. When Theodora went out to visit the school or for the weekly sermon Maria walked with her to the garden gate and prayed for her safety with verses from the gospels and mothers' prayers. She competed with Fadl al-Aziz for the task of washing Theodora's clothes but the black servant imposed her will emphatically.

"I'm the servant in this house and that's my job. You're an honored guest who comes and goes. If I let you wash the girl's clothes, what would become of me?" she said.

Auntie Maria cried at being called a guest but Theodora consoled her and made her happy by starting to call her "my kind mother." But for the rest of her life Fadl al-Aziz never forgave Auntie Maria her attempt to intrude, and she always had a hostile, defensive attitude toward her. Dorothea often heard her talking to herself angrily in the kitchen.

"My God," the servant said once, "that foreign woman expects to wash the girl's clothes! You count for nothing, Fadl al-Aziz. That'll really be the day!"

Then she addressed the heavens, saying: "O Lord. Send the Mahdi soon because the world's gone mad."

2

How bitter death is, Father.
    Why do you die far away,
    Leave me, and disappear?
    Is crossing to the other shore so easy, so simple?
    You leave me here and ascend to the Lord.
    Why do loved ones have to die when we are far from them?

When we part from them, why don't they tell us this will be the last meeting, so that we can take strength from them?

They promise that we will meet again soon. We busy ourselves thinking about the coming meeting and with our daily lives. Then they betray us.

They die suddenly when they are still in our thoughts, and then we have to suffer.

I won't forgive you, Father, for imposing this sadness on me. I will never forgive you.

3

Why, you do know not what will happen on the morrow. For what is your life? It is just a mist, that appears for a little time and then vanishes away.

James 4:14

4

Ten days after they arrived Hortensia fulfilled her promise to visit.

She came to the Orthodox mission accompanied by a black eunuch who stood waiting for her at the gate and gave all the passersby wary looks.

The three girls sat with each other and reminisced about their recent journey. Theodora told them the story of the ostrich that her guard friend had told her.

"He said that when God created the birds every species said, 'I will fly if God wills,' except for the ostrich, which said, 'I have wings and I'll fly.' It didn't say, 'If God wills.' God punished it by depriving it of the power of flight, and it has remained earthbound ever since, while all other species of bird can fly."

The other two girls laughed.

"After a little while in this country," Hortensia said, "you'll discover that for every strange phenomenon they have an explanation that has something to do with the sky or heaven.

Their religion is strange, but Father Johann advised me not to interfere with the beliefs of the local people."

She didn't forget to make pointed remarks to Theodora about Younis the guard.

Fadl al-Aziz came into the room and they teased her by asking questions. They had fun listening to her answers and opinions.

Hortensia invited them to go out for a walk along the Nile and they agreed. Dorothea went to tell Father Pavlos but couldn't find him. She found out from the workers that he had gone to the governor's office. The three girls went out and the eunuch followed them to protect his precious charge. They crossed clean, wide streets. The government was regular about sweeping them and sprinkling them with water every morning to keep the dust down. They walked along the paths of packed red dirt in the shade of massive mimosa trees, looking at the strange mix of peoples. Several Europeans greeted them. Dorothea drew her friends' attention to a smart young man who greeted them with exaggerated friendliness in an attempt to strike up conversation.

Groups of Egyptians passed by. The fezzes on their heads made Theodora anxious, by reminding her of the gentlemen in Alexandria. But none of them pestered her with comments in the way she was used to. Guiltily, she wondered why she felt disappointed. She didn't like the remarks that passersby used to make. She used to ignore them and say a prayer. But now she missed the devil that she used to ignore.

The city was a pageant of people and fashions. Smart European clothes with fezzes. Old Turkish clothes such as baggy trousers and waistcoats. Egyptian and Indian turbans.

As they were going into the gardens, a Sudanese man passed by near the Austro-Hungarian consulate that overlooked the Nile. He was riding a donkey and when he was level with them he jumped nimbly off the donkey's back and walked on foot until he had gone past them. They looked at him and saw him getting back on his donkey. He went off without a word or a glance.

Hortensia asked the eunuch why. "Out of respect, madam," he answered curtly.

The gardens were wonderful little pieces of paradise. They walked under mango, orange, lime, and guava trees. They jumped over watermelons that were lying on the ground. Theodora liked the swollen trunks of the banana trees. The birds were of many species and every color.

"If there was a sea here, this would be the most beautiful city in the world," Theodora said.

Dorothea pointed to the clear Blue Nile nearby. "The Nile has its own magic," she said.

They watched the sun sink toward the west. It lit up everything bright red. They praised the Lord, then headed back.

This city is the pearl of the world, Theodora was thinking. I'll be sad the day I leave.

She could understand why Uncle Panagiotis and Auntie Maria loved it so much. Every time she walked back to the mission from their house in the district around the governor's office, close to the granary, she thought about how they belonged to the city. They were no longer Greeks or Egyptians. Khartoum was their real home.

She was curious to see the rest of the country and she envied Hortensia, who had traveled west to see other places and different towns inhabited by black savages, unlike European Khartoum.

Hortensia left in March, a month after they had arrived in Khartoum. She had left by boat, heading up the Nile. She had promised to write letters but hadn't kept her promise. When they met once again under sadder circumstances, Hortensia told her she hadn't forgotten the promise but it had been impossible to fulfill it.

Theodora fell in love with Khartoum and prayed to the Lord to let her belong to the amazing city. The Lord heard her prayer, and when she died on the west bank of the Nile, years later, they took her across the river to the east bank and buried her in the city she had loved.

5

The Orthodox mission was in the Mosque district—the district around the main mosque that Khurshid Pasha had built when the city was founded in 1830. It was the largest and noisiest district in the city. It had four main streets and several grand mansions, the most famous of which were the mansions of Georges Chiadi and Ali Khulousi, as well as several European consulates. It had the Catholic mission church, the Prussian Protestant mission, and the headquarters of the Orthodox mission.

The Orthodox mission was built of baked brick. It was divided into two wings, a northern and a southern, surrounded by a garden with an area larger than that of the buildings. In the garden there were so many trees that it looked like a little jungle. All kinds of birds spent their time there. A gravel path cut through the garden to the entrance, shaded on each side by four mimosa trees.

The main entrance to the building was from the front garden. It had decorative brickwork and at the top a cross in white stone. There was a side entrance into a narrow street that led to the street where the arsenal was. The side entrance was generally used by the sick and poor people who received financial support from the mission, and by traders selling cheese and milk. For some reason Fadl al-Aziz saw herself as the guardian of this entrance, and on her wrist she kept a copy of the key to the black iron gate.

Beyond the main entrance there was a long corridor that ended in a large hall. In the morning the sun shone into it through large stained-glass windows, and on the walls there were pictures of Jesus, the Virgin Mary, and many saints, as well as African spears brought from Bahr al-Ghazal in the south of the country. On the right side of the hall low steps went down to the kitchen, where Fadl al-Aziz permanently supervised four black servants, who later became three. On the left were the dining room and two rooms, one of them a large library with books in Latin, Greek, English, French, and Italian. On the eastern wall of the library was a large mural of the Holy Family. The other room belonged to Bishop Antonios, who was in charge of the mission, and the only people who went in were the bishop's assistant, Father Pavlos, and sometimes Fadl al-Aziz. On the left of the hall there was a narrow corridor that led to the north wing of the building, where the men's rooms were—Bishop Antonios, his assistant, Father Pavlos, and five others: four Greeks and the fifth half-Abyssinian.

At the end of the hall there was a staircase made of thorn wood that led to the upper floor where there were rooms for the nuns and the mission workers. Theodora's room was on the upper floor and looked out over the northern garden. In front of the window was an orange tree that hid some of the view, but it gave off a pleasant fragrance in the evening.

On the wall of the room there was a picture of Saint Mark sitting in a cave, a halo around his head, writing on a tablet with a quill pen, with a lion crouched beside him. In prominent letters underneath was written: "The Christ that I believe in delivers me from all adversity." Aunt Maria had given it to her and Theodora was delighted with it.

About four months after arriving in Khartoum, Theodora and Auntie Maria ran into Father Johann sitting waiting in the large hall. Theodora was pleased to see her old traveling companion. She asked him about Issa the caravan leader and the toothless commander of the guards and his friendly son. He said he had run into Issa once, and that the others were no doubt in the desert making a living as usual. Theodora introduced him to Auntie Maria. The joy that lit up Theodora's face made Auntie Maria feel that Theodora liked Father Johann, so she invited him to lunch in their house the next Saturday. Father Johann tried to decline the invitation, but Auntie Maria insisted.

On the Saturday, Theodora and Dorothea went early to Auntie Maria's house to help her prepare. Theodora had good memories of that day because before the visit was over Uncle Panagiotis and Father Johann had become close friends. Theodora later heard from Auntie Maria that they started spending hours together in the coffee shop that belonged to George Tensiari the Greek in Bahr Street, playing chess.

When Theodora prayed before going to bed, she thanked the Lord for the blessing of the friends He had given her in Khartoum: "Our Father Who art in heaven, may the blessings of friendship last forever."

In her notebook and letters to her mother she recorded all her moments of happiness in that black, European country.

6

Sunday, February 6, 1881

The governor lives in great luxury. He and his family live in a grand palace with a large retinue of servants and slaves, and he keeps wild animals in the palace garden.

In front of the palace on the Nile side there's an empty space shaded by a large sycamore tree, and the governor and his guests spend the evenings under the tree, talking and smoking and drinking coffee. The governor, Raouf Pasha, invited us there and we had a pleasant time.

Then we went to the reception that he held for us in a hall near the palace, which was decorated with colored lamps. The garrison troops danced military dances. They were all Negroes. The army band gave a concert that Father Johann liked very much. I learned from Father Pavlos that he had been a musician in his youth.

After that we went into the dining room. It was a large square room decorated with a life-sized portrait of Mohamed Ali Pasha. The cutlery and tableware were crystal and silver.

A British engineer sat next to me. I noticed that although he was polite he didn't say grace before eating.

Thursday, February 10, 1881
The people of Khartoum are a mixture. They divide the inhabitants into categories based on their color. Every race has its own color, starting with white and then gradating through various degrees of black until it reaches pitch-black.

They divide black into strange colors. They say "a blue man" for someone who's pitch-black, and "a green man" for someone who's dark brown. Their idea of white is funny. They consider brown-skinned Egyptians to be just as white as Europeans, but they say that the Turks are red.

Friday, February 11, 1881
The inhabitants of Sudan include people from different groups and many tribes.

The majority are blacks, the Negroes who are the indigenous inhabitants of Africa. They are the lowest breed of humanity. The only ones in Khartoum are slaves. They are in a state of nature, without any culture or civilization or even craftsmanship. In their own territory they farm the land as well as they can and go fishing.

Then there are the Arabs, who are more noble and intelligent and civilized. They have some savagery left but we can easily rid them of that. Most of the Arabs in Khartoum are merchants or work with the government. They smoke tobacco and wear Turkish dress.

7

Theodora went to the mission school along Meshraa al-Qadi Street. She taught on Friday and Tuesday, while Dorothea taught on Wednesday and Thursday.

The school was a modest mud-brick house that the mission rented from a Turkish merchant and used for teaching and nursing. Theodora loved the children. Most of them were Greek or Egyptian, some were Abyssinians, and a few were Sudanese Negroes.

The Negro children were mostly orphans that the mission was bringing up. They were from pagan or Muslim families but their parents had died and the mission was taking care of them. They lived in poor districts that Theodora never visited throughout the four years she lived in the city. But she had heard about them. Fadl al-Aziz told her about them and about the amazing things that happened there. There were the Tubjiya district, the Teras district, the Huboub Darbani district, the Nuba district, and the Kara district. Theodora didn't believe the stories. She thought they were figments of the old woman's disturbed imagination.

When Theodora went into the classroom, the children smiled at her and were as cheerful as colorful little birds. She loved their innocence.

She taught them the Book of Genesis and stories about the saints.

She discovered in herself a gift for telling stories when she saw the children's eyes widen in amazement as they listened to her. They fell silent and held their breath when she spoke. Sometimes they cried. But they always cheered happily when the story of a saint ended with the Lord helping him triumph.

The other days of the week she volunteered in the school's nursing department. She eased the pains of the sick. Most of them had fever or alcohol poisoning. The Greeks didn't catch the fevers often because they were used to the climate. But the Egyptians, Syrians, and Prussians were always getting fevers and typhus.

When she went back to the mission in the afternoon she wrote in her diary, which was full of her happy thoughts. She wrote down observations and made references to memories that came to her out of the blue. She was careful to record her memories because, after about a year in Khartoum, they had become elusive and indistinct, as if the events had never happened. They would show up suddenly and take her by surprise, and then she would try to remember the details and ask herself whether these things had really happened or were just stories she had heard from someone else.

She loved the parties the Catholic mission held in its large new church nearby. She went to them with the other mission staff. The priests wore caftans and gowns, while the nuns wore trailing white dresses and headdresses with long trains.

Theodora went to several houses on different occasions. The Europeans in the city had parties for various celebrations—for New Year's Eve, for example, or for the day the kings of their countries ascended to the throne. The biggest parties were the ones the consulates held on their national days.

When the Orthodox mission celebrated its first anniversary in Khartoum, Theodora realized that most of her clearest memories were about things that had happened in the past year. They were about all the new things she had seen in the city. She was putting down roots and the more she settled down the more remote and hazy her previous life seemed to be.

8

The mood in the city was as serene as the Nile in summer.

But it turned somber without warning. When Theodora saw the autumn storms for the first time, she was terrified.

The sky turned dark by day, with red clouds reminiscent of hell. It rained sand. The howling wind carried off clothes, clay vessels, and tree branches. From her window Theodora watched the orange tree bend so low it almost snapped.

When the stifling rain arrived the city turned into a vast swamp that stank of rotten fruit. Everyone was trapped where they were when the rain caught them. They might have to stay where they were until the sky relented. When the rain stopped, the city looked washed and fresh.

Theodora was appalled by what she saw, but Auntie Maria reassured her that she would get used to it.

9

When she was getting ready to go out one day, Theodora found that her little silver cross was missing. She looked for it among her things but couldn't find it. She asked Dorothea, who was surprised it was lost. They tried looking together but to no avail.

Dorothea asked her when she had last seen it. Theodora remembered wearing it the previous evening. She had taken it off after praying and combed her hair with the comb that was on the same table. But she didn't remember seeing the cross on the table.

"It's been stolen," Dorothea said with confidence. "Someone came into your room while you were asleep."

The idea startled her—that someone might come in when she was asleep, when she didn't know what was happening around her. When she was weak and defenseless. A stranger wandering around her room and meddling with her things. They told Father Pavlos and he said, "Before we make a scene, we have to think about who we should accuse."

They quickly ruled out Fadl al-Aziz, and their suspicions centered on the four young maids. Father Pavlos called in Fadl al-Aziz and asked her. He didn't tell her about the theft but he asked her about one of the maids who was known to leave her room at night after bedtime.

"Angela doesn't sleep," Fadl al-Aziz said simply. "She's always moving around the building. Several times I've caught her hovering in the hall or going upstairs to the sisters' rooms."

"Have you told anyone about that?"

"I'll never complain about my girls to anyone. I know how to punish them," she replied.

Father Pavlos told her about the disappearance of the silver cross. The old woman stood up straight. Her eyes flashed with resolve. She took them down to the kitchen and through to a small adjoining room—a room no more than four feet wide, where Fadl al-Aziz and the maids slept. Fadl al-Aziz searched Angela's few possessions. She found a prayer book that Bishop Antonios had lost a few months earlier, four valuable wooden combs, a cloth bag lost by a nun whose assignment had ended two years earlier, a brass mirror with a Gothic inscription, some Majidi riyals, an ornate pawn from a chess set, a pocket watch of unknown origin but apparently of some value, and seven silver chains. They didn't find the cross. Fadl al-Aziz searched the belongings of the other maids but didn't find anything. What they had found among Angela's things was enough to accuse her of theft. Father Pavlos took the things away and went up to Bishop Antonios's office.

Bishop Antonios told the governor's office and a few hours later the police came and arrested the terrified maid.

Angela was a thin black girl from the Shilluk tribe in the south of the country. She had fine features, like an ebony carving. When they arrested her, she screamed and frothed at the mouth. She resisted and swore that she wasn't a thief. She said she had found all these things inside the building on various occasions after the owners had left, or she had found them in the street. She swore that Bishop Antonios had given her the prayer book, but the bishop said he didn't remember doing so. They took her into the garden of the mission building and tied her to a large mimosa tree. The birds were chirping in the sky. They bared her back and gave her two hundred lashes of the whip until she almost expired.

The whip, with five tails and small iron balls on the ends, fell on the girl's back and shredded it. The iron balls dug into her flesh and the policeman had to pull hard to get the whip out of Angela's body. She screamed. She called for help. She begged for someone to show mercy on her. The whip came down again. When it hit her back she stopped breathing and held in her screams for a moment. The pain was brutal and she started to bang her forehead madly against the trunk of the tree, but the police held her head in case she died on them without confessing.

She fainted several times from the whipping and the screaming. And then the officer, a Turk decorated with ribbons and many feathers, ordered his men to stop the flogging until she came around. Angela didn't go back on her story. She didn't admit stealing. She implored Bishop Antonios to remember the day he gave her the prayer book. She said he had blessed it and she had kissed his hand in gratitude.

Her eyes were full of tears and her nose was running. Her forehead was dripping with sweat. Her black back was covered in blood and her white flesh showed through where the whip had broken the skin.

The members of the mission and some of the passersby who gathered watched her denial with incredulity. The Turkish commander asked Bishop Antonios if he wanted only to have her punished and then to let her continue working. But the bishop declared that there was no place in the mission for a thief.

"So we'll take her to the governor's office," the Turkish officer said. "We'll brand her and sell her as defective goods. Please drop in on the clerk tomorrow and he'll give you some compensation for her."

Theodora asked about the branding the officer had mentioned. He looked at her and said, "We'll burn a mark on her cheek."

The idea pained Theodora. She asked Father Pavlos whether it wouldn't be enough just to dismiss her. But Bishop Antonios said, "At the end of the day it's not us punishing her. These are the Turks' laws. We have nothing to do with them, my daughter. But I promise to pray to the Lord to save her soul and guide her."

Father Pavlos tried to placate her, saying, "It's a lenient sentence. Remember that the Muslims cut off people's hands in cases like this."

The policemen took Angela away and none of them ever saw her again. The governor's office apologized to the bishop for one of its citizens committing a crime against the mission. The bishop was magnanimous, because the police clearly couldn't prevent criminals from committing their crimes.

Theodora never found her silver cross. But she kept praying for Angela, asking the Lord to save her soul and guide her.

In her diary with the leather cover, she wrote how surprised she was:

"People are savage and ungrateful. The more the shepherd tries to guide the lost sheep of the Lord, the more they try to do him harm. Today a black maid stole my silver cross."

10

Theodora was getting over her sadness when a second letter arrived from her mother.

Like everything else, sadness fades. But when it first strikes it seems overwhelming, with no end in sight. It plays havoc with your mind and makes everything in life taste bitter. But it gradually abates until all that remains is a faint ache deep inside.

It was the middle of October 1882 and Theodora was about two months short of completing her two-year assignment at the mission. The letter arrived with the mission mail. Dorothea took it up to her friend's room, and Theodora asked her to read it. The news was disturbing. Her mother Laskarina, who was now a widow, told her the details of the massacre that had taken place in Alexandria and how the angry mob had killed her father and some of the Europeans they knew. The unfortunate events took place after the peasant unrest led by Orabi Pasha. The Egyptians hated the Europeans, who wished only the best for them. The Egyptians were ungrateful for the favors the Europeans had done them. She wrote lamenting that the city was no longer as it had been and that their lives were in danger. Her brothers had agreed to go back to Greece. The family would go back to the land where it had its roots. They expected Theodora to join them there when she finished her term in the Khartoum mission.

Theodora wept in silence as Dorothea read the letter. Her world was falling apart around her. Her father had been slaughtered far away in Alexandria and she suddenly felt like an orphan. She had only found out a month later—a month during which she had been laughing and having fun, going to the mission school and talking to the children about the Lord, love, and the teachings of St. Paul the Apostle without knowing they had killed her father at the entrance to their house. And now she would never be going back to her city. The sea at Alexandria would never enchant her again. She wouldn't hear its waves calling her name, in a whisper in case the seagulls overheard. She would go as a stranger to Greece, a country she had never seen before.

Why had the Lord condemned people to live in exile? she wondered.

Every day Fadl al-Aziz brought her the tamarind infusion that the Armenian doctor had prescribed. And at dawn Dorothea would wake her up to drink buttermilk on an empty stomach. She obeyed the doctor's orders and let Father Pavlos read verses of the Bible over her forehead to comfort her and restore her health. Every afternoon Auntie Maria visited her to cry with her. Alone, without the others, she thought about her future.

When she could walk alone without wobbling she asked Dorothea to come to Auntie Maria's house with her.

Her aunt was happy when she saw the two girls arriving that morning. She hugged Theodora and cried. She kissed her on the cheeks. When Theodora told her she was thinking of staying in Sudan she agreed with her without hesitation.

Khartoum was not a place for transients. Everyone who came fell in love with the city, even those who were annoyed by the changeable climate, the rains, and the dust storms. The priests who waged war on debauchery loved it despite the depravity of the local people, the brothels, the endless homosexual parties, and the shady Europeans who made a living by cheating. Theodora decided that she didn't have anywhere else to go. She wasn't going to throw herself into another foreign country. Once her family left, she would no longer have family in Alexandria. But here in this city, founded by Turks in the European style, she had memories, family, and friends. Where would she go if she left all this?

"I'd be a stranger anywhere else," she told Auntie Maria. "But here I'm happy with you. Why should I leave?"

"Don't leave. This is your country. Panagiotis and I realized that a long time ago."

"So I'll stay here with you, mother," Theodora said hesitantly, her eyes wandering.

Auntie Maria hugged her tight. Dorothea, who was impatient to leave, didn't know what to say. She loved the city like Theodora, and hated it at the same time. The political turmoil frightened her. Five months earlier the new governor of the country, who had been governor of Suakin when they landed there, had arrived to deal with an insurgency that had broken out. Whenever Father Pavlos came back from the governor's office, he was yet more anxious. There was a disaster in the making, but no one knew what it would be. The rains that year were like harbingers of death. Though she was usually as happy as a lark, Dorothea's heart shook in trepidation for the future. But she didn't know how to dissuade Theodora from her unintelligible decision.

"I'm going to stay, Dorothea," Theodora said.

There was nothing she could do. Dorothea departed alone in March, leaving her friend in a city that was prey to rumors. The unrest was escalating. There was news about uprisings sweeping distant towns. A Muslim fanatic was claiming he had been sent by God to fight the infidels. Hortensia was said to have fallen into captivity. Nothing was certain. But Theodora had made up her mind that this was the only country she had, so why would she abandon it and go?

Stoically she said farewell to her friend and to Bishop Antonios, who left the mission in the charge of Father Pavlos and two other priests.

After two years and a month Theodora began a new life in Khartoum. She was a citizen, not a transient.

She would live in Sudan, serve the Lord, and find happiness. That's all she wanted.

When she and Auntie Maria came back from saying goodbye to the travelers, she vowed to be the saint of the city.

Something inside her told her that in the waves of the Nile she would find something to make her forget the enticements of the sea in Alexandria, but she tried hard to fend off such wicked thoughts.

"Nothing but serving the Lord. That's how I will enter the Kingdom of God," she said.

11

But he that received the seed in stony places, the same is he that hears the word, and immediately with joy receives it.

Matthew 13:20

12

Fadl al-Aziz was a dimwitted old woman. The teeth of time had chewed her up and turned her into a wrinkled black lump. There wasn't a part of her body that was firm. It was just rolls of rippling fat. She had been working in the mission since the day it was set up, and before that she had worked in Turkish, European, and Egyptian houses. She claimed she had worked with a troupe of Egyptian dancers, but Theodora couldn't believe that this old woman had ever been shapely enough for that kind of work.

Most of what she did in the house she did wrong, and in fact the four maids that she supervised were always correcting her mistakes.

But from the first month she acted as if she were Theodora's teacher. One evening she looked at the girls sitting in the big hall and singled out Theodora to address.

"You, girl," she said. "You don't speak properly."

It was a surprise to Theodora and to all the nuns.

"Listen to the way you speak," Fadl al-Aziz continued. "I'll teach you how to speak. You're pretty but it's not right you should have such a defect." The servant imitated Theodora's accent, making fun of the hard *g* she used instead of *j*, and other features of the way Egyptians speak.

Theodora tried to explain to Fadl al-Aziz that she didn't want to change her accent and that she was perfectly capable of communicating with everyone as it was. But Fadl al-Aziz was as stubborn as a mule. She followed Theodora everywhere, and whenever she talked about her or even mentioned her in passing, she described her as "the girl who doesn't know how to speak."

On the advice of Father Pavlos and Bishop Antonios, who valued Fadl al-Aziz, Theodora had to defer to the old woman. She started to sit with her for an hour or so every day to have her pronunciation corrected and to learn words and sayings.

"*Kawkar* means to get someone in trouble. Come on, say it after me. Baking bread is called *uwwaasa*. Don't pronounce it that way, girl. Say *uwwaasa*."

Fadl al-Aziz pointed to her injured arm. "This is called *uwwaara*. An injury is an *uwwaara*," she said.

When she told her proverbs and explained what they meant, she added some advice: "Bless the Prophet with me. Blessing the Prophet will help you remember."

Theodora laughed and didn't know how to remind the old woman that she was a Christian.

"'His feet are in the river and his mouth is open for the raindrops.'" Fadl al-Aziz continued. "It means he's greedy. He dives into the river but he still wants more water. Do you understand? You won't understand if you don't bless the Prophet. The word for foot is *rijl*, so don't say *rigl*."

Theodora learned much. The old woman was useful despite being dimwitted. Dorothea was surprised. "Why did she choose you rather than any of us others?" she asked.

No one knew the answer. Fadl al-Aziz didn't say, but she vowed to herself that Theodora would perfect the local dialect. Theodora started speaking Sudanese Arabic fluently, but with a childish accent. The way she pronounced the letter *j* was engaging and the words tripped readily off her tongue.

Fadl al-Aziz told her about the legends and customs of the country and little-known aspects of the poor quarters. She told her about the Mahdi who would soon appear and said that people had found his name written on hens' eggs and on the leaves of trees.

"But there's nothing written on the leaves in our garden," Theodora said with a laugh.

"You're infidels, so your trees are unclean," Fadl al-Aziz said contemptuously. "The angels only write that on the trees of believers."

Theodora asked her if the Mahdi was the same person as the rebel who was giving the government trouble in faraway parts of the country.

"Only God knows these secrets. If he is the Mahdi he'll come into this city and slaughter the infidels and bring about justice."

"Does 'the infidels' mean us, Fadl al-Aziz?"

"Of course, my girl. He'll kill you, and on the Day of Judgment you'll all go to hell," she said.

"And you, Fadl al-Aziz, will you let him kill us? Don't you love us?"

The old woman frowned. "I love you all, and you especially, my girl," she said. "But who can say no to the man that God has guided? That's God's command and we have to accept it."

"She's a crazy old woman," Dorothea said.

When Dorothea said good-bye to Theodora, between tears at their parting, she said, "Be careful. The nonsense that Fadl al-Aziz talked about might be imminent. The Muslim rebels are advancing."

"All of that will end soon, Dorothea," Theodora replied. "The government's strong and it won't be defeated by some black savages."

Bishop Antonios gave her a rosary with black beads. He advised her to pray and to look after the mission school whatever happened.

"I have confidence in you," he said.

She kissed his hand and reassured him.

"Don't worry. Things will calm down," she said.

When they left, Theodora gave them some letters to send to her family in Greece. She thought of writing to Georgios, the son of the man who sold olives, to tell him that she still remembered his sin but she had forgiven him and prayed to the Lord to forgive him and cast light into his heart. But she couldn't find an excuse for doing that. She wasn't frightened by the thick clouds gathering on the horizon. Uncle Panagiotis and Auntie Maria shared her opinion. Nothing would happen.

But when 1884 began, about a year after Bishop Antonios and Dorothea had left, the nonsense Fadl al-Aziz talked about looked like it might become a frightening prophecy.

A new English governor arrived in Khartoum at the beginning of the year: the famous English hero Charles Gordon. The Europeans were delighted that he had come. This hero of the empire had never been defeated. He also had previous experience in Khartoum and the Sudanese liked him. He tried but failed to evacuate the Egyptian troops and the European community. The rebels held most of the country. Gordon sent his meager forces out to fight but wherever they went they came back defeated, or didn't come back at all.

One night Theodora heard a wailing that seemed to tear the city apart. She rushed downstairs in bare feet to find out what was happening. She found the mission workers standing there in fear, with looks of terror on their faces. Father Pavlos told her that a force of five thousand fighters had gone out to meet the rebels but they had all been killed. Not a single one had come back.

Fadl al-Aziz was delighted with the news.

"This is the army of the Mahdi," she said. "It can't be defeated. He'll kill the lot of you, God willing. Pray to God to help the Mahdi triumph over the infidels."

When the middle of April came the city was surrounded by thousands of rebel dervishes and completely isolated from the rest of the world.

Theodora stood in her room looking at the campfires of the besieging forces shining in the dark. It was a carpet of lights. In her anxiety it struck her that maybe Fadl al-Aziz was speaking with the voice of the Lord. The rebel army would enter the city and kill them all.

Seven

1

Bakhit expected someone to remember him and set him free. But when he appeared in court the judge sentenced him to indefinite imprisonment.

He harbored a false hope that his detention would not last long. A month or two months. The crime they were punishing him for wasn't even mentioned.

They had caught him drunk in the street, in a city where everyone was a drunkard by night and a jihad warrior by day. He was shouting out her name at the time. He had a sword in his hand but couldn't remember where it came from. He was staggering down the street screaming and asking the Mahdi, high in the Creator's Heavens, to put out the fire burning inside him. But the fire hadn't gone out and the nightmare tormented him endlessly.

The patrol beat him and dragged him along the ground to the judge's house. The judge woke up irritated and in a foul mood. He listened to the patrol. He examined Bakhit to see what state he was in, ordered that he be thrown in jail, and went back to sleep.

"I know I won't be here long," Bakhit told Father Johann.

"My son," said Father Johann kindly. "Don't let your hopes carry you away."

*

When the prison guards took him down from the post and shoved him into the chamber of wonders he was bleeding profusely. He didn't care that he was losing so much blood. Am I losing my love for her with my blood? he wondered anxiously.

In the chamber of wonders the few prisoners surrounded him. All of them were white, but soiled by the prison filth. Among them his blackness was like a crude laugh.

They bandaged his wounds with rags and he discovered that they had a cold barley drink. They gave him some. Rifaat Effendi al-Salamouni told him that Touma made it for them. For three riyals a week Touma supplied the cell with everything they needed. She brought okra, bread, barley, milk, coffee, and some meat if it was available. In the cell there were three Egyptians, an Austrian, and a crazy Moroccan. They were all wearing patched Mahdi-style jelabas. It was Father Johann who had seen Bakhit chained to the post and asked after him. He felt sorry for him and wanted to do him a good turn. He bribed the guards and they took him down to join them in the cell. In the morning Jawhar came into the cell in a worried state but he found Bakhit being well looked after.

Father Johann reassured Jawhar. "My son, we are all children of the Lord," he said. "We'll take care of your friend, so don't worry."

Father Johann took Bakhit under his wing. He felt sorry for the tormented soul that he saw in Bakhit's limpid eyes. When Touma brought food, he set aside a large portion for Bakhit and watched him affectionately as he ate. The Moroccan ate alone at the far end of the room. Jawhar was frightened of the Moroccan and avoided him when he visited them.

"He doesn't speak much," Jawhar told Bakhit. "But when he does speak he claims he's Jesus the prophet of God. The judge is going to sentence him to death at any moment, so don't go near him. They might think you believe in him, and then you'll find yourself hanging from the gallows in the market with him."

He tried to stick to Jawhar's advice, but found it hard to tame his curiosity.

One night he went up to the Moroccan, watched by his smiling cellmates. He sat next to him and asked him his name.

The Moroccan didn't answer. Bakhit tried to lure him out of his shell by mentioning some of the Moroccans he had known in Khartoum in the old days. Friends of his Turkish master. But the Moroccan seemed to be somewhere else. At a loss, Bakhit looked to Father Johann. "Don't try," said the priest. "He doesn't speak unless he wants to. And if he does, you'll hear some weird things."

Bakhit crawled away from him.

"I knew your master, Abdüllatif Effendi Mazhar," Rifaat Effendi al-Salamouni told him. "He was a good man, may God have mercy on him."

Bakhit Mandil wouldn't have ventured to describe his old master as good. The scars on his back didn't allow him to do so. But he didn't object.

"The last time I saw him was when he invited us to a party," Salamouni continued. "He had brought a troupe of dancing girls and they performed some theatrical pieces and comic sketches."

Mustafa Shaker, who had been the manager of the public baths, also remembered the party.

"The acting was beautiful. I still remember some of the scenes. The late General Gordon was also there. He was laughing cheerfully despite the threats the city faced," he said.

"I wonder where the dancing girls have gone," said Salamouni.

"As far as I know, they left Khartoum before it fell," replied Mustafa Shaker.

Another of the prisoners, a man by the name of Mahmoud al-Jirjawi, was silent. He had never been to Khartoum or seen it. He had come to Sudan a little over two years ago, and they had caught him in Berber and jailed him on a spying charge.

"Those Egyptians," Father Johann whispered to Bakhit, "they never stop moaning and lamenting the past."

Bakhit noticed that he hadn't heard Father Johann talking about his past. He asked Jawhar, since there are no secrets in prison.

"Father Johann was a missionary in Khartoum," Jawhar said. "The Mahdi's followers captured them and brought them here to Omdurman. Some of his colleagues died and others escaped, and God showed some of them the way to Islam. But he's remained an infidel, though he has a good heart."

So Father Johann was a reminder of past friendship.

It's no surprise that he felt sorry for me.

Was it you who sent him, Theodora?

Or maybe he saw how upset you were for my sake and he sympathized with me.

"How strange these Christians are. Nice people, but they'll end up in hell," Bakhit said in amazement.

"And their whiteness is so horrible! God didn't give them a beautiful skin color so he made them kindhearted instead."

Bakhit Mandil no longer found fault with the whiteness. Before Theodora came into his life, he had wondered why God had disfigured these people. Their bodies looked as if they had been skinned and then painted red. They had eyes like vicious cats and they smelled of rusty copper. That day when Buthayna, the Turkish daughter of his rough old master, burst in on him, he had almost vomited. She had a strong, putrid smell. Her eyes followed him for ages with looks that he couldn't explain. When he was standing in the courtyard of the house wearing only a short pair of trousers, she was all smiles at the sight of his chest. He felt uncomfortable. The day the fourteen-year-old girl decided to attack he was moving the furniture from the east room in his master's mansion into another room. She came in and closed the door behind her. He braced himself for trouble. She came up to him and stroked his bare chest. "So handsome," she said, breathing heavily.

He stepped back in fear, but she came after him, her eyes flashing with desire.

"You're ugly. So ugly you're beautiful. My God!" she said.

"What are your orders, my lady?" he said.

She slipped her fingers down inside his trousers.

"You're not human. You're a wild beast. Take me," she said.

She pulled him toward her and he felt as if she were digging into him. Her body was brazenly white. She smelled of rust. He hated the color and smell of white people.

She reached down to find the shaft of his penis. She took hold of it and gasped.

"I bet your sperm has worms in it. I want them," she said.

He felt his stomach turn. When she dropped her dress, he shuddered at the sight of her nipples. They were red like pimples.

"Not all whiteness is horrible," he told Jawhar, remembering what he had learned from his master's daughter.

Jawhar looked at him in surprise. "That Christianity has messed up your head," he said. "How can you see anything pleasing in their color?"

"Jawhar, we are all the children of the Lord," Bakhit answered thoughtfully.

Jawhar was shocked. "By the Mahdi!" he cried. "You're talking like the Christians."

Bakhit turned to his apprehensive friend. "There's nothing to be surprised about, my friend. She's in my blood, but I fear I may have lost some of her when I bled," he said.

2

Out of gratitude for their kindness Bakhit took a vow to act as messenger between his cellmates and Touma.

If they wanted anything he jumped up and looked for her to fetch it for them. He went from one cell to another. He said hello to the prisoners, joked with some of them, and avoided others. He was afraid of revenge by Younis Wad Jaber's comrades in the Jihadiya. He was wary of them even though Younis had left prison a week after Bakhit had been taken down from the post.

"I've known Younis for years," Father Johann said. "He's a good lad."

But Bakhit wasn't interested in the Austrian's testimonial. What does that foreigner know about the bastard? he said to himself.

What upset him was that, by knowing Younis, Father Johann reminded Bakhit that Theodora had also known Younis.

Why am I obsessed with Younis? Bakhit wondered. I'll be damned if I don't bring a bloody end to this obsession, he thought.

Touma had golden-brown skin and a massive frame. Her body was as soft as if it were stuffed with fat. Her backside wobbled jauntily. Bakhit went into her enclosure and conveyed his cellmates' orders. She smiled at him and was friendly. Whenever he came to see her, she asked him flirtatiously, "Won't you visit me one day for something other than to tell me what the Christians are ordering?"

Bakhit frowned and didn't answer, but she never tired of asking.

He asked Hawa, his angel, for forgiveness. He complained to her about the way he was treated and she comforted him sadly when she visited him at night in his cell, enveloped in a mist.

"I don't want any woman other than you, Hawa," he said.

"Don't be sad, Bakhit. For my sake, don't be sad."

He pushed his fingers through the cracks in the door and whispered, "I want to touch your hair."

She frowned. He could hear her breath and sense it as something almost tangible beyond the door. "Please," he begged.

Her chestnut locks dangled onto his fingertips. He stroked them lovingly. When he pulled his fingers back they smelled of musk and he was worried the smell might wake up his cellmates.

"I saw Younis here," he told the specter of Theodora.

"I know."

"Forgive me, but I'm going to kill him."

In the old days he used to tell her the same thing in anger. Shaking from jealousy, he'd shout that he would kill Younis. She recoiled from him and said testily, "Why? You've no right to do that. What do you want from me?"

Bakhit was taken aback. "You know," he said nervously.

"I don't know. All I know is you annoy me," she replied. "Why are you harassing me? What do you have against Younis? What have you got to do with me?"

He tried to apologize but she wouldn't accept his apology.

"Go away. I don't want to see you," she said. "Don't meddle in my affairs again."

She pushed him out of the courtyard and closed the door on him. Sometimes he didn't go away. He just sat waiting outside the door until he woke up at dawn. Then he would have to leave to avoid a scandal. She kept away from him for days. She might meet him in front of Idris al-Nubawi's stand in the vegetable market but she wouldn't speak to him. Her face would be seething with anger. But a few days later, when he passed nearby, she would whisper to him, "Is there no end to this torment?"

He shuddered and almost made a scene. He pulled himself together with difficulty and asked, "What torment?"

"The way we live," she sighed. "Isn't that Khalifa of yours going to die? Or maybe the Lord will raze the city to the ground and we can all breathe a sigh of relief."

His heart rejoiced to be forgiven. He made a promise to himself that he wouldn't make her angry again. But whenever he made a promise he broke it, and she never tired of losing her temper and then forgiving him.

One day he dared to ask Father Johann about his mission.

"I was with the Catholic mission in the Mosque district," Johann said curtly.

Bakhit's heart skipped a beat, and suddenly the priest smelled of musk. He had lived near her in the Mosque district. If only Bakhit could kiss his hand.

But he, the wretch, knew Younis Wad Jaber, just as she did.

No matter, because he was going to kill Younis.

She wouldn't be angry with him this time.

3

Anxiety consumed Khartoum and then blew the city out as smoke. Unease descended on every household. The Europeans unlucky enough to have stayed did not know what was in store for them, but they were certain it was bound to be bad.

Father Johann kept busy in the mission inspecting the meager supplies that remained. He checked the sacks of grain and biscuit stored in the cellar. The siege of the city went on and on. Hunger stalked the streets; thefts and assaults followed in its wake. Sudanese savages emerged from their lairs in the remote districts of the city to invade the area around the governor's office and the Mosque district. They attacked houses looking for food. The mission kept its gates firmly locked for fear of looting. But reports of robberies in the houses nearby frightened the residents. The savages looted Ali Khulousi's mansion. They even took the furniture. The consulates called in troops for protection. The British consul advised Father Johann to do likewise to protect the mission. Father Pavlos followed the example of the consulates and had the Orthodox mission protected, but Father Johann preferred to save what little money remained and just lock the large iron gates.

Every day he went out to visit the governor's office and meet General Gordon. He found the consuls, the important Europeans, and the prominent local people there. They came out with promises that the storm clouds would soon clear. The relief expedition was on its way from Cairo. Father Johann left with Father Pavlos.

"Do you believe them?" asked Father Johann.

"It might be true."

Father Johann snorted angrily. "I think it's a fantasy, Pavlos. There doesn't seem to be any hope in prospect. The siege is strangling Khartoum," he said.

"Don't worry. The Lord won't abandon us."

In the afternoon Father Johann met Uncle Panagiotis in George Tensiari's coffee shop. They sat on cane chairs, despondent. Everyone was thinking about death. When people met they looked at each other like dead people. Uncle Panagiotis ordered a coffee without sugar. Father Johann asked him why. His stomach was upset, he said. They shared their anxieties. Uncle Panagiotis was as anxious as Father Johann but he was clinging in hope to a reed that would prove to be broken.

"This is my country, Father. It won't do me any harm," he said.

"It is your country, Panagiotis, but these dervishes are dangerous," said the priest.

"No, Father, a bunch of savages won't scare me. I refuse to run away like others have done. I won't abandon my country to that black rabble."

"We no longer have the option to run away, Panagiotis," Father Johann said bitterly. "We're all staying even if, unlike in your case, this isn't our country."

Father Johann gave the mission workers orders not to open the gates after sunset whatever happened. Only death stalked the streets of the city at night. The classes stopped at the school and the weekly sermons were postponed until salvation dawned. But the night dragged on and grew darker and darker.

Uncle Panagiotis came to visit Father Johann in a state of anger and agitation.

"Have you heard the news?" he said. "Those bloody Egyptians!"

Father Johann didn't know anything. He was depressed by the news that the town of El Obeid had fallen and the people there had been captured. He was busy praying to the Lord to save the lives of the members of the mission there.

"The governor's office has uncovered a secret organization that's helping the dervishes. A group of Egyptians. It's called the National Association. It includes some idiots who were followers of that bloody Orabi," Panagiotis said.

"Followers of Orabi here? In Khartoum? After all these years?"

Panagiotis swore. "Imagine!" he said angrily. "They've been spying on the city's defenses and sending messages to the dervishes."

Father Johann scurried in alarm to the governor's office in search of more information. In the outer hallway he met Mr. Power, the correspondent of the *London Times*. Power was in as much of a panic as he was, if not more so. Power told him that some of the Egyptians who had been exiled to Khartoum on charges of supporting the Orabi rebellion had set up a secret organization to support the Sudanese rebels. He told him that the secret organization had tried to contact a group of prominent Sudanese, but one of them had given them away.

"Gordon Pasha should honor him. He wasn't an informer. He was a hero," Power added.

Johann asked who he was and was told that his name was Sheikh Ibrahim Wad al-Shawwak.

Johann went out looking for the man. He was told he had a shop in the European market. He walked around asking until he found him. He was an elderly man in his late fifties. Short, with a fine cotton cloak and eyes as sharp as a flashing blade. Johann introduced himself.

"I know you, Father," said Sheikh Ibrahim. "No need to introduce yourself."

He went into his shop. It was a large shop selling animal feed. There were sacks in lines along the sides, two wooden benches, and a chair.

"I've come to you as a European citizen to thank you for the valuable service you have done for the country. I haven't come to you as a priest," Father Johann said.

Sheikh Ibrahim smiled. "I haven't done anything. It's just talk."

"You're a modest man. I heard from the governor's office that it was you who reported the traitors."

Sheikh Ibrahim glowered for a moment, and then he broke into a smile again.

"Father, don't believe everything people say," he said. "In these bad times many things are said and all kinds of deeds, good and bad, are attributed to people who never did them."

Father Johann was puzzled, but Sheikh Ibrahim didn't give him time to ask more questions.

"Whatever its purpose, your visit deserves to be honored, Father," he said, and called over one of his workers.

"Go and look for my son Abdel-Gayoum. Tell him to get home before me to prepare lunch. Father Johann will be our guest today."

Father Johann muttered words of thanks and tried to decline the invitation. But Sheikh Ibrahim said with a smile, "There's no escape, Father. Besides, I want you to tell me about things you're bound to know better than me. A well-informed man like you will help to reassure ordinary people like me."

Father Johann was delighted and, over lunch at the sheikh's house, he didn't hold back any of the information that he had. His information wasn't reassuring but Sheikh Ibrahim Wad al-Shawwak welcomed it.

The city was dying. The English governor was mad. Cairo had promised to send a relief expedition that never came. Supplies were running low and a famine was preparing to overwhelm them. The city's defenses were worryingly inadequate and the gates in the wall would not hold out long. The Sudanese savages were grumbling and talking about the European infidels and describing the dervishes and their Mahdi as the Ansar of God, as if the Mahdi were like the Prophet.

On his way back Father Johann felt pleased with himself. Although Sheikh Ibrahim had denied he was a hero, the priest was confident he had had the honor of meeting a righteous man who had done the city a favor by telling the governor's office about the organization of traitors.

4

The city had lost its peace of mind. At night it was on guard.

Everyone heard the music. The bugles and trumpets were playing from the governor's office. The tunes were sad, like warnings of danger.

When he heard the music through his window, Father Johann hurried to open it. The sound came into the room. He bowed his head in submission. It was the wail of bagpipes. A sense of gloom came over him and wrenched his heart. Tears welled in his eyes. He knew they were playing in mourning for the city.

The music rustled the leaves at the tops of the trees and seeped into the houses where the windows were open to receive it. It twisted and turned with the river. It pierced people's hearts. Why had Gordon chosen this music that night?

The city was trembling with fear, cloaked in a sad despair.

When the trumpets fell silent, a deep silence prevailed. A painful silence.

The whole universe was struck dumb.

Then the rockets fired by the attackers exploded in the sky over the city.

5

Bakhit told his Egyptian cellmates about his time as a prisoner in the Egyptian countryside. He recited the poems about Qays and Leila that he had learned from his master. They laughed at the simpleton that he was. They made light of the humiliation he had been subjected to in Egypt. He asked them about Youssef Effendi Said, but no one knew who he was. He told them how impressed he was by the city of Cairo.

"It's enormous and it's clean. The people there wear strange clothes and speak even more strangely," he said.

They told him the history of the landmarks he had mentioned. They praised the khedive. They remembered Egypt with unrestrained nostalgia.

"I knew a girl from the church," Bakhit told Father Johann.

Father Johann looked up at him.

"Did you meet her in Egypt?" he asked.

"No, I met her here in Omdurman. She was working in the Orthodox mission before the conquest of Khartoum," Bakhit replied.

Father Johann was interested. "I knew all the women who worked in the Orthodox mission before Khartoum fell," he said. "Do you remember her name?"

Of course that was the last name Bakhit would ever forget. His heart was awash with love for her, purified by his longing for her. Or else he wouldn't have spoken her name.

Father Johann fell silent and looked somber. "May the Lord have mercy on her soul," he said finally. "I knew her. She was like a daughter to me."

May the Lord have mercy on her soul. What if the priest knew what she meant to Bakhit?

There was a sparkle of love in Bakhit's eyes. Father Johann could read his sadness and was intrigued. Was it possible? The Lord worked in mysterious ways and He might favor a black slave. He remembered the words of Solomon: "But Your providence, O Father, governs it: for You have made a way in the sea, and a safe path in the waves, showing that You can save from all danger." Maybe Bakhit had been her path, her helper in what she faced. Maybe he was a fresh breeze that eased the pain of her torment. He looked at Bakhit's blackness and remembered how dazzlingly white she was, like the brilliance of a holy day.

"We are all children of the Lord," he said to himself.

Father Johann's eyes filled with tears. But Bakhit did not weaken. His sadness gathered inside him in the form of determination. Revenge.

As he looked guiltily at Father Johann, his determination gained strength. The names came together in his head. He wouldn't let any of them get away, whether their guilt had been big or small.

Mahmoud al-Jirjawi crawled close to him. He told him how he had been captured. He claimed to be a merchant. He showed him where two of his fingers had been cut off as a punishment.

"They caught me in Berber," he said. "They confiscated all my goods and they didn't let me send letters to my family. They say I'm a spy."

"The best thing they did to you was to stop you sending the letters," said Father Johann. "The letters we send are being read and we are questioned about every word in them."

"I have a wife and she doesn't know if I'm alive or dead. All I'm asking is that they take pity on her."

Bakhit was about to tell him the story of Youssef Effendi Said's wife, who fell in love with a neighbor. But he changed his mind. That story would be no consolation to the poor man.

Mahmoud al-Jirjawi slapped his head and his cheeks and wept. They tried to comfort him, but he curled up in a fetal position in the corner and sobbed.

"That's how he is," Father Johann told Bakhit. "Whenever he talks about his wife and children he cries. One day he'll die of grief."

"Is he really innocent?" Bakhit asked.

"I don't know, my boy. No sane man would enter the country and go all the way to Berber just to do business. He's either greedy, stupid, or a spy."

Mustafa Shaker reminded Bakhit that it was time for prayers. He went out with him to the prison yard. The prisoners who hadn't gone out to work gathered for prayers at the eastern wall. Bakhit got into line next to Mustafa Shaker. He was looking for Jawhar but couldn't see him. Prayer helped him forget his worries. He asked God when he would get out. His fourth month was almost over.

They finished praying. Bakhit turned and saw the guards standing at a distance, watching them warily. Mustafa Shaker took him by the hand and walked him toward Touma's enclosure. Mustafa was chatting casually with him, asking about Egypt and the coffee shops there. Whenever Bakhit said anything Mustafa laughed and clapped.

"You're incredible, Bakhit!" he shouted. "Goddamn you, man!"

There was nothing funny about what Bakhit had been saying. Bakhit thought the Egyptian was just happy to be reminded of his country. Nostalgia plays with the minds of the homesick. It turns them into children.

"I haven't seen Egypt for fourteen years," Mustafa said. "But I never tire of dreaming about seeing it again."

They reached Touma's enclosure and she welcomed them. Mustafa Shaker left Bakhit, went up to Touma, and started whispering. She clicked her tongue in protest and said, "My husband has the day off today."

"Get yourself ready," said Mustafa.

He put four Majidi riyals into her hand. She stopped and thought for a moment.

"Can you do us a favor?" she asked Bakhit.

"What do you want?"

She came up to him.

"I'll give you five piasters if you stand at the door to the enclosure to make sure the coast is clear," she said.

Mustafa Sahker was startled. "You mean here?" he said.

"Any shady place is good."

Bakhit politely refused. But she held on to his arm before he could leave.

"Don't be a coward. All you have to do is clear your throat if anyone comes close. I'll give you five piasters for this simple task."

Bakhit looked at Mustafa Shaker and could see he was hesitant.

"Five piasters and a mug of beer," Touma said.

It sounded like a good offer. Bakhit thought for a moment. Then she winked at him and said, "Five piasters, a mug of beer, and whatever you want."

"Five piasters and a mug of beer," he said.

She laughed and Mustafa Shaker laughed nervously with her.

Bakhit stood a few feet from the enclosure with his back to it. He watched the path that ended in the large prison yard. Behind him he could hear Touma grunting, his friend panting, and the shackles clanking. He sneaked a peek and saw them locked together.

He turned the five piasters in the palm of his hand and waited.

6

Bakhit crept warily into the servants' quarters.

He went past the bedrooms. If anyone caught him he would say he was looking for his friend Sabah al-Kheir. But he didn't meet anyone on the way. He didn't hope for anything more than a look at her.

His desire got the better of him. He couldn't control himself and he grew reckless. When it was time for the sunset prayers he had waited for the streets to clear and then slipped in. He had gone into the servants' quarters through the back door and then through into the yard. He didn't hope to speak to her. She was angry as usual. He only wanted to have a look from a distance in the hope that this would satisfy his craving and cheer him up. When he saw her face, his desire didn't diminish, but his world was set to rights and he felt strength course though his veins. If she was absent, he felt life draining out of his body. She had some psychic power.

He approached her room and stood at the window. Craning his neck, he looked in. The room was empty. He suddenly had a frightening notion that she was behind him. He started and turned. There was no one there. But maybe she would take him by surprise. He decided to withdraw disappointed.

Then he heard the sound of water. He was in great danger. But seeing her was worth the risk. If they caught him, he was dead. He would make the excuse that he was looking for his friend. But they wouldn't believe him. He didn't care. He followed the sound of the water. There was a matting screen in the corner of the yard. He went toward it on tiptoe and looked through the gaps in the matting.

The smell of musk overwhelmed him.

Oh Mahdi, have mercy on the wretched.

His spirit soared.

The water was running over her body. She was as naked as a wild rose. As white as the milk of bulbuls. Her wet chestnut hair stuck to her neck and cheeks. Her neck was as long as a gazelle's. Her breasts were like two baobab fruits.

His head spinning, he stepped back. He stumbled and fell to the ground, making a noise. He heard her catch her breath behind the screen.

He didn't stop to think, but dashed off at a run.

7

"You're very pretty."

"You're my black brother."

8

He went out with Jawhar in a chain gang. His friend seemed anxious but he didn't explain why.

Bakhit pressed him. Jawhar gave him a brief smile.

"Where's your usual good cheer and chattiness?" Bakhit asked.

"Look at my shadow. It's pale," Jawhar said after a struggle.

Bakhit looked at his friend's long shadow on the ground.

"Your shadow's just a normal shadow. What's wrong with you?"

"It's not. My shadow's faded."

"It's your brain that's fading."

His second year in prison was about to end. He told Jawhar openly that he was thinking about taking revenge as soon as possible.

"I'm going to rot here before I have a chance to kill them, Jawhar," he said.

Jawhar looked at him blankly. "You wouldn't have time to kill them all if you escaped now. They'd catch you and kill you," he said.

"I'm worried I won't have time to kill any of them. I've waited so long. I'll grow old in prison."

Jawhar leaned back against the wall. When he moved his feet the chains on his legs clanked. He didn't answer.

"But I know that killing one of them wouldn't be enough," Bakhit continued. "Tell me: If I can only kill one of them, which one should I choose?"

Without thinking Jawhar said, "Younis."

Bakhit thought for a moment, then asked, "Why him?"

"It would make you happy, wouldn't it?"

"But I did find him and God saved him. God might save him from me again. Maybe God doesn't want me to kill him."

"Aren't you going to kill him with the other five?" asked Jawhar.

"With the other five! I will, but I won't take the risk of making him my first choice."

Jawhar thought about the six names. Sheikh Ibrahim Wad al-Shawwak, Abdel-Gayoum the son of Sheikh Ibrahim, al-Naim the son of al-Hajj Taha, Younis Wad Jaber, Taher Jibril, and Mousa al-Kalas. They were all the same to him. He shook his head in indecision.

A guard shouted when he saw them whispering. He rushed over, raised his arm, and brought his whip down on them.

Before they could shield themselves the whip struck Jawhar's cheek and drew blood. Bakhit protected his face with his forearm. Jawhar sat on the ground and shouted, "God, O God, by the honor of the Mahdi!"

The guard cursed at them and ordered them to shut up. No one had come forward to employ them that day. They had remained on offer all day long, but to no avail. Bakhit remembered the day he was put on display in Khartoum Market. He was still an adolescent at the time. He had stood there for two days. Several people inspected him. They lifted up his arm and felt his young muscles. A large European came up to him, a man with a red face as if he'd been boiled. The hair on his chest was visible through the gaps in his shirt and it was soaked in sweat. He was bad-tempered. He opened Bakhit's mouth and examined his teeth. He took down his trousers and inspected his penis. He laid it on the palm of his hand. "Does he have syphilis?" he asked the trader.

"He's as clean as a new whistle, Mister."

He ran his hand over Bakhit's coarse hair. Thoughtfully.

"He's a good lad," the trader said. "He doesn't wet his bed or snore, and he's a good price."

Next to him there was another boy like him and a man. And some Abyssinian and black girls whose skin glistened with animal fat. They all had their feet tied with ropes. Bakhit had almost reached manhood and had the surprised look of someone still discovering the world.

The European looked at Bakhit's flat nose.

"He's an ugly monkey, just as I want. How much is he?" he asked.

"Only three hundred and fifty piasters, and on the standard terms: one-fifth of the price up front and you can try him out for three days."

"That's too much."

The trader raised his hand as if taking an oath and said he wouldn't make much profit at that price. "He's cost me two hundred piasters in food since I bought him, Mister," he added.

The man twiddled Bakhit's nose. Bakhit's trousers were still on the ground and his body was exposed.

"Where's he from?" the man asked.

"They brought him from a stockade in the west. I guarantee his quality, by my honor."

The European man sighed. He had innocent-looking eyes despite his brutish body. He agreed to the price. He paid seventy piasters and asked for Bakhit to be delivered to his house.

"Don't let me down at the man's house," the trader said as he led Bakhit away. "He clearly doesn't want you to do housework. He wants you to serve him. Be a man."

Bakhit didn't understand Arabic well at that stage. He still struggled with it and spoke the language of the faraway western mountains. But the way the European man touched him spoke to him in a language he understood. When his master summoned him at night he found him lying naked, facedown on his bed.

"Come here, my ugly love," the man said.

On the third day, before the man returned him to the slave trader, Bakhit's resistance collapsed. He couldn't take the flogging and he had lost strength from hunger. The European man had locked him in a small dark room. The man came into the room growling and tried to kiss Bakhit, who recoiled. The man flew into a rage and got out his whip. Bakhit's eyes filled with tears. On the last night Bakhit couldn't wait. He promised himself that he had only to hold out a few hours and he would be back in the market. But the torture broke him.

"I'll do it, sir," he said. "I'll do it."

The man's face lit up.

"Good boy, good boy," he said.

The man didn't wait. He rubbed Bakhit's penis to arouse him and helped him penetrate him. He screamed. He spoke a lot in a language Bakhit didn't understand. When he'd had his fill, the European lay down panting and left Bakhit to his sadness.

"What a stud of a monkey you are," the man said ecstatically. "You're the lord of the stud monkeys!"

After five years satisfying his master, Bakhit was given away to Abdüllatif Effendi Mazhar, a senior official in the police department. His old master kissed him as he said good-bye.

"I'll miss you, lord of the stud monkeys," he said.

Bakhit was overjoyed at becoming a house slave. He happily took on the task of serving in the household of his new Turkish master. He spat on the memory of the enormous European and lived for the moment.

When he and Jawhar went back to prison after failing to find work, Bakhit went to see Father Johann. He tried cautiously to get him to talk about her. Father Johann had told him everything about her several times over during the previous two years, but Bakhit never tired of trying to slip her into the conversation. Father Johann knew his tricks, but he didn't begrudge Bakhit his efforts. He told him about their journey from Suakin to Khartoum and Bakhit reveled in the memories. He knew the stories by heart, so much so that they had become part of his own history. He remembered sailing on the steamer from Suez to Suakin. He could smell the coffee in the guesthouse kitchen. He could see the tomb of Sheikh Barghout, which the sailors hailed when they passed.

An hour before it was time to lock up the cells, Jawhar interrupted the reminiscences Father Johann was sharing with Bakhit. He stood at the door and called him. His voice was sad.

"Bakhit, I need to speak to you," he said.

Bakhit wasn't in the right frame of mind to listen. "Tomorrow, Jawhar," he said.

Jawhar didn't reply. Bakhit looked up at him, expecting him to leave. Jawhar nodded and turned away, saying, "I'll see you tomorrow, brother."

But no one saw him again.

Eight

1

THIRTEEN DAYS AFTER JAWHAR DISAPPEARED, Bakhit saw Merisila for the first time.

He was sitting apart, plagued by uncertainty and loneliness, when a guard called him. He stood up lazily.

"There's a woman asking after you," the guard said.

The guard took him to the western gate. They went past
Touma's enclosure and then past the guards' houses and the
kitchen. At the end of the western courtyard he found a tall,
spare woman. Her lower lip was pierced and there was a
silver pendant hanging from it. Her eyes were crazed. Beside
her stood a girl of fifteen, short and plump, with a round
nose. Her thick hair was carefully braided. Bakhit stood
there puzzled.

"We're looking for news of Jawhar," the woman said.

"Who are you?"

"I'm Niamat al-Sater, and this girl is his sister's daughter."

Bakhit looked at the girl. There was something pretty and
mature about her face.

"You're Jawhar's niece?" he asked.

The girl didn't answer, but looked at Niamat al-Sater, who
answered for her.

"Her name is Merisila," she said. "Her mother died years
ago, in the sixth year of the Mahdi, and I've been looking
after her. I was keeping her for her uncle when he came out,

but then we heard he's disappeared. We came to ask and were told that you'd be the one who knows."

Bakhit mulled over his woes. He thought about the fact he, the person asked, knew less than the person who was asking. He told them what he knew—nothing to throw light on the darkness of uncertainty.

It was a day like any other. The sky didn't look sad. The sun had given no warning of what would happen. In the afternoon a sandstorm blew up, blazing hot because it was summertime. When the cells were closed the prisoners shouted out that Jawhar wasn't there. At the same moment all the cells suddenly complained that he was missing. Every cell was under the impression that he had stayed only in that cell. Bakhit didn't know why the whole prison suddenly missed him.

"So what should I do with the girl?" Niamat al-Sater asked on her next visit.

Bakhit looked at her.

"Keep her with you as a daughter. Nothing has changed," he said.

The woman snorted and cursed. "Everything has changed. I can't keep her at my place forever. Her uncle was going to come out of prison one day. I was looking after her with that hope in mind. Her crazy mother can't force me to keep her for the rest of my life."

Now the girl spoke up. "Don't insult my mother," she said pugnaciously.

The woman punched her on the shoulder. "Your mother was a whore," she said in anger.

Like an angry cat, the girl leapt at the woman's chest, screaming and scratching the woman's cheeks with her nails.

"Don't insult my mother, you damned woman! I'll kill you!" she said.

Bakhit held on to the girl and pulled her back. He grabbed her around the waist and wrenched her away from Niamat.

"Little bitch! Your bitch of a mother produced a girl as crazy as herself!" the woman shouted.

Naimat's cheek was bleeding. Bakhit held on to Merisila, who was in a rage. Her chest was heaving as she panted. If he had let her go, she would have killed Niamat. He begged them to calm down.

"The girl belongs to me," Bakhit told the woman. "I'll be her uncle if Jawhar doesn't show up."

Niamat weighed him up, wiping the blood off her face with her hand. "Jawhar used to pay me one riyal a month," she said doubtfully.

"I'll pay Jawhar's riyal."

"And you'll take her if you get out?"

"I'll take her if I get out."

Merisila looked up and gave him a fierce look. He was worried she might attack him. But when she looked into his clear eyes, she calmed down.

"And when are you coming out of prison?" Niamat al-Sater asked him.

That was the question that kept him awake at night. Whenever he had the chance he begged the prison governor to bring him news. But the governor just laughed at him and said, "Don't trouble yourself. You're my property forever."

"Many people get out. I'm here indefinitely and yet I've repented. Put in a good word for me, for the Mahdi's sake," said Bakhit.

"It costs a hundred riyals to have a good word put in," the governor said dismissively. "And I can't guarantee it would work."

The governor left him to his despair and sadness. "My boy, don't tire yourself out with hoping," Father Johann advised him again.

So Bakhit lied to the woman. "I'll be out soon," he said.

2

Merisila had been ten years old when her mother ate her younger brother.

The sixth year of the Mahdiya was a year of madness. The land produced no crops and the Nile was so low that kids played in the riverbed. Swarms of locusts filled the skies, blocking out the sunlight for days on end. The army commanders sent letters complaining to the khalifa.

"Living conditions have continued to deteriorate for everyone—old and young, fighters and their families. They have even started to eat carrion and pick seeds of grain from the wayside and garbage dumps. If my lord could see the condition they are in now, he would feel sorry for them."

Fastidious people locked themselves up at home and died of starvation inside. The hungry broke down the doors of their houses, went in, and ate them.

A few months earlier Ata Minnu had had a baby boy by a Jihadiya soldier who she couldn't remember. She tried to persuade each of her visitors to claim paternity of the child and to support her and the baby and Merisila, but her customers weren't foolish enough to agree.

In the second week of starvation, her eyes bulging, she said to Merisila, "Fetch me the ointment."

The girl brought the clove-and-sandalwood paste and let her mother rub it into her skin. Her body glistened with the oil and she smelled good. She went out to the street with her. Ata Minnu dragged her along, with the baby strapped against her chest. Her breasts were just wrinkled folds of skin that produced only bile. When someone passed, she stopped them and offered Merisila to them. The emaciated passersby didn't want to buy the girl. Ata Minnu offered her for sale for a pound of grain. Then, when she was getting desperate, she offered to give her away for nothing. A man who looked like he was dying of hunger agreed to take her. He took hold of the girl impatiently. Ata Minnu wanted to tell him what a good girl she was but he wasn't interested. "I'll take her, I'll take her!" he blurted out.

He pulled the girl to go, but Ata Minnu's heart sent her a warning. She ran after the girl and shouted, "What are you going to do with my daughter?"

The man pushed her away.

"Go away, woman," he said. "My children haven't eaten for days."

Ata Minnu screamed and hit the man with her free hand.

"Help! He's going to eat my daughter!" she said.

People gathered around and freed Merisila from the man. He was furious. Weeping, he shouted, "Leave me alone. My children are hungry, you bastards."

Ata Minnu pulled Merisila and went back home sadly. She shut herself up in the only room and left Merisila in the court-yard. Merisila could hear crying at night. Her sobs mingled with the wailing of the baby. Ata Minnu tore the night sky with her cries. In the morning she opened the door and went out in a daze to her daughter. She woke her up. She rubbed her face and wiped the sleep out of her eyes. She gave her a hug and smelled her coarse hair. She kissed her, then took her to the gate, pushed her out, and said, "Don't come back."

"I'm frightened, Mama," Merisila whispered.

"Your father won't abandon you," Ata Minnu said reassuringly. "He'll come for you."

Merisila didn't know where to go. She sat leaning against the wall of the house. She watched the passersby in fear. They looked at her greedily. Her stomach rumbled from hunger and her eyes glazed over. When afternoon came she overcame her fear and disobeyed her mother. She stood up and pushed aside the gate to go in.

In the only room she found her mother on the ground, weeping and stained with blood. The remains of the baby boy were in a copper pot.

3

One day soon after Bakhit first went to prison, Jawhar had invited him to Touma's enclosure and said that the food would be on him. Touma smiled at Bakhit and said, "A new wretch. Welcome. You bring baraka to the Sayir prison."

Jawhar asked her to make them asida, a kind of sorghum gruel. As she got up to start work, she said to Bakhit, "For Jawhar's sake I fed you when you were tied to the post. If Jawhar wasn't dear to me, I wouldn't have agreed."

"It wasn't just for my sake. I promised you one week's earnings," Jawhar objected.

Touma laughed. "And would your earnings have made it worth my while if the guards had caught me and my husband had found out?" she said.

Bakhit remembered her during his ordeal at the post, like a bird stuffing food into the beak of its young. He thanked her and asked, "Do you have any children?"

She splayed her fingers. "Five," she said. "My husband, Kakoum, is energetic."

"He's energetic and you're insatiable," Jawhar added.

She laughed her laugh and left them to start her work. Jawhar told him about himself, how he had escaped after the destruction of Khartoum, how he asked a military commander for help and the commander freed him from his Egyptian master. Like Bakhit, he had started working for wages in people's houses and in the markets.

Touma heard him talking and said, "Have you told him about your brother-in-law?"

Jawhar pulled a face and scolded her.

The woman laughed and said, "Poor us. People envy us women because we have the prisoners and the Egyptians, but there are other women who take their pleasure with the djinn."

Bakhit gave him a quizzical look. Jawhar's face glowered like the sky in autumn. "My sister had a child with a djinni," he said tersely.

Bakhit laughed in surprise, thinking it was a joke.

"I'd give all the men in the world in exchange for someone who could give me a night with a djinni," said Touma. "All the men except you, new boy," she added, looking at Bakhit.

Ata Minnu had spent one night in the ruins of Khartoum. She had fled Omdurman when the patrols were looking for her on a charge of making sorghum beer. She panicked and swam across the Nile to the dead city. She took shelter in the ruins till the morning. When she went back to Omdurman she was exhausted. She told inquisitive women about her night. She was trying to forget her worries and go to sleep when the djinni possessed her. He was tall and white. His penis was a rod of flame.

She didn't scream and she wasn't frightened. When he was finished with her he turned into a whirlwind and disappeared. The women didn't believe what she said. They said she had run off with some infidel foreigner. They said with disgust that the rod of flame was his uncircumcised penis. But three months later Ata Minnu gave birth to a girl who was as beautiful as a summer's night. The women of the city were stunned, but they said it was only uncircumcised infidels who could produce children in three months.

And when Ata Minnu ate her baby ten years later, the women who believed her story said that the djinni's penis had unbalanced her mind.

"What mother would eat her child?" they whispered. "The djinn were angry with her because she had a child with someone else, so they took their revenge."

She cried and cried and Merisila joined her in mourning. The evening cloud passed by, weighed down by the tears of their sadness. Ata Minnu was screaming and slapping her face.

When midnight came she fell silent and caught her breath. Her chest was tight. She found it hard to breathe. Her face was flushed. Before dawn the whole of Omdurman could hear her cry: "O my child!"

She died when the muezzin called the dawn prayers.

4

Jawhar never reached his cell. He lost his way somewhere between the chamber of wonders and his cell. No one knew what happened to him, and no one could understand how he could disappear.

He didn't die, because the dead leave their bodies behind them. He didn't escape, because the guards didn't keep it a secret when they helped people escape.

It was said that the djinn had abducted him, or that he had never existed and was just a devilish figment of people's imaginations.

The last people to see Jawhar were Bakhit Mandil and his cellmates.

He had promised Bakhit sadly that he would see him the next day, but he didn't fulfill his promise.

He vanished like a day that is past and all that remained of him was a sad memory in the heart of Bakhit Mandil.

Nine

1

"Why are you so patient with him?" Hortensia asked. She was mystified.

Theodora's gaze wandered. She remembered his deep sadness and nobly tragic face.

"I don't know. I feel guilty when I hurt him," she said.

"He's not your responsibility. He's just a savage."

Bakhit's eyes were as wide with wonder as a child's. As clear as a stream. The pain he felt haunted her.

"He's not like the others," Theodora said. "Believe me, he's not like the others."

He showered her with affection. He was attentive in a way she wasn't accustomed to. He beguiled her more than the Mediterranean had ever done. He courted her with his eyes in a whisper that was more tender than the words of the shopkeepers, the carters, the itinerant fruit sellers, the gentlemen, the fishermen, and the breeze from the sea. His soul was as pure as the light of the saints. She felt sorry for his soul, trapped in a black body with thick lips. As ugly as the city of Omdurman. But his soul was as radiant as Alexandria.

She came out of her master's house every afternoon to go to the vegetable market. He was punctual about keeping the appointment they had never made, every day at Idris al-Nubawi's stall.

"What are you doing here?" she asked.

"Nothing. Just a coincidence," said Bakhit.

But she knew he was waiting for her, whereas she had come by chance. She hadn't gone out to see him. She had no reason to go out for him. She just went to the vegetable market every day and went past Idris al-Nubawi's stall and found him there. She spoke to him for a few minutes. Or she might speak to him for hours. Then she left. There was nothing to it. They were just chatting. He told her things she had never known. About worlds she had never imagined existed. Sufferings she had only heard about. She read to him from her secret diary, things she hadn't read to Hortensia.

When he said, "You're very dear to me," she heard words of love in languages she had never imagined he knew. Her spirits rose.

"And you're very dear to me, like a brother," she replied. "We are all children of the Lord, born of suffering, Bakhit."

2

On a Friday, eleven days after the fall of Khartoum, Theodora and Hortensia were separated again.

The Mahdi visited the city to inspect what his followers had done. More than twenty thousand people had been killed. The city had been plundered and the women taken captive. The Mahdi stood near the corral where the women had been gathered together. He gave orders that the women should be sorted out before sunset. Those who had husbands should go back to their husbands, and those who didn't should be married off. As for the infidels, such as Theodora and Hortensia, the military commanders and the wealthy men could take possession of them.

Like a prophet, the rebel dervish was surrounded by admirers. He spoke softly. His eyes were restless. His beard gave a determined impression. His words were like the Ten Commandments, immediately obeyed.

Hortensia went off with her new master, Malik Aribi, and Theodora was taken by Sheikh Ibrahim Wad al-Shawwak.

Hortensia and Theodora had met in the corral two days after the fall of Khartoum, before they were separated by the Mahdi's command.

It was Hortensia who caught sight of Theodora and called her. Theodora rushed to her and hugged her tight. They both burst out crying and each looked to see what state the other was in. Hortensia had lost weight, looked darker, and had lice. Her skin had turned hard and rough. Her blue eyes looked terrified. In the last two years, she had seen untold suffering.

She told Theodora how she had fallen into captivity in the west of the country. Two of the other nuns had died. The priests were crawling around in chains somewhere. They had brought all the women to one place and locked them up. She didn't believe it when she saw Theodora. Finally she had found a vestige of the happy days that were gone. Since leaving Khartoum she had seen only hardship in all its forms.

El Obeid had fallen to the rebels. The siege and hunger had worn the town down. The fighters were like specters that stumbled as they walked. The people of the town had eaten carrion, dogs, and the gum of trees. The sky turned black with noisy vultures circling. When death seemed inevitable the city opened its arms in surrender. The dervishes came in beating their drums and blowing their onbeia trumpets.

They took the priests to their encampment and tied them up in the open air. They kept asking them to convert to Islam.

"A Coptic man called Iskandar used to come to see us," Hortensia said. "He had abandoned Christianity and followed the Mahdi. He had changed his name to Abdel-Tawwab. He sat with us and tried to tempt us to convert."

He told them about the delights of the afterlife that the Mahdi's followers would enjoy. He tried to frighten them by saying that those who rejected the Mahdi would come to a bad end and have a painful death. Fear and the bad air made most of them ill. When they heard that an order had been issued to share the nuns out among the military commanders as slaves some of them died of shock.

"But they didn't do that," Hortensia said. "And they didn't kill us, although Iskandar had warned us several times that we'd be killed. They used to walk past us in the place we were held, in the open, and curse and insult us. When one of us died they wouldn't bury the body. They said the Christian dogs didn't deserve to be buried. They let the bodies swell up in the open. We saw them rot in front of our eyes. We couldn't sleep at night for the horrible smell of our dead colleagues."

She asked Theodora about Dorothea.

"She went back to Egypt years ago. We wrote each other a few letters but that stopped once the city came under siege."

Theodora was in torment. Her voice was hoarse from screaming.

The dervishes had swept into Khartoum at dawn. The dam had burst and they rushed in. They spread like locusts.

Father Pavlos stepped back from the gate and knelt to pray. The nuns clung together and wept. There was the sound of death in the streets and the metallic smell of blood was stifling. They could hear screaming from behind closed doors. The hiss of fires grew into a roar. The beautiful city of Khartoum was dying.

"Pray to the Lord to have mercy on us," said Father Pavlos.

Theodora felt powerless. Fear had immobilized her. She tried to think of biblical verses that she knew by heart but she couldn't recall any. Her face was covered in tears. I don't want to die, she thought.

Before the middle of the day the dervishes arrived. They broke down the gate, walked over its remains, and came toward them. They slaughtered Father Pavlos. Four of them grabbed him and one of them slit his throat, shouting "Allahu akbar!" Father Pavlos's blood covered his white clothes.

Fadl al-Aziz came trilling from the kitchen. She was overjoyed. But one of them impaled her with a spear in the chest. A big shiny spear. It buried itself in her body. She choked on her trills as she fell. The dervishes shouted and Fadl al-Aziz passed out.

Theodora screamed. They dragged her out of the building. She didn't see any of the other nuns again after that. The last thing she saw was their bodies being dragged behind her. She knew nothing of what happened later. Her headscarf was torn. Her hair was all over the place. Her body was battered and bruised when they dragged her along the ground.

Black men were all around her. Their voices were horrible. She didn't understand what they were shouting. The smell of them was disgusting and made her retch. They were covered in dust and full of zeal.

The only thing in her mind at the time was that they would kill her. They would cut her throat. "I don't want to die!" she begged.

3

Bakhit read with difficulty from her diary:

> Don't let the days of your life make you sad as they pass. It is
> a pain that is over and deliverance is nigh.

4

Theodora's new mistress, Nuwwar Bint al-Hajj Qasim, whose father was of North African origin, received her with a smile.

She was friendly and tried to cheer Theodora up. She was a slim woman, with fine bronze skin and a pretty dimple in her chin. It was her nature to smile. She took Theodora into the bathroom and brought her some cheap soap, apologizing that nothing else was available. Gently she told her to wash and then to dress up.

"Your life with us won't be bad, my dear," she said.

Theodora was frightened. She didn't know what was expected of her. She was anxious about her future. Sad about the people from whom she was parted. She hadn't forgotten the sight of blood spurting from Father Pavlos's neck. She locked herself in the bathroom and cried. She bathed as well as she could, washing the dust of her detention off her body. She rubbed her skin to purge it of the smell of her captors.

But the soap wasn't strong enough. When she poured water on her body to rinse off the soapsuds she found that the smell was too strong. She sobbed and collapsed on the floor. She felt sorry for herself. She remembered them dragging her along the streets and shouting. Her head was bumping in the dust, and the smell of them was killing her.

She came out of the bathroom sad and soaked in water. Nuwwar sat her on the ground and dried her hair, then combed it tenderly. She tried to plait it into little braids but it wouldn't stay in place when she tried. So she brought it together and plaited it into a braid. She gave Theodora a bright calico dress to wear.

"What are you going to do with me?" Theodora asked.

"All's well, my dear. You're one of us now," Nuwwar said. "We'll look after you in a way that pleases God."

Theodora looked around her. The room was opulent and suggestive of wealth. It had fancy mirrors.

"Are you going to kill me?" she asked.

Nuwwar laughed. "Why would we do that?"

"I don't know. You kill Christians."

"No, my dear. We're followers of the Mahdi. We only want the best for people."

Theodora thought about the suffering she had seen and the death of people she loved.

"But you're Khartoum people," she said.

"We've believed in secret, my husband and I, for some time. My husband was helping the Mahdi from inside the city."

"Will be I be a maid in your house?"

She could see a fleeting sadness in Nuwwar's face.

"You're not a maid, my dear. Sheikh Ibrahim has taken you for himself," she said.

Theodora didn't know what that meant.

"Perhaps that's best for you, my dear," her mistress continued. "I don't mind."

5

Trouble and anguish have come upon me, but your commands are my delight.

Psalm 119:143

6

Saturday, February 12, 1881

The city is full of slaves. The slaves are half or more of the inhabitants. We're in a big slave encampment. Everyone in Khartoum has at least one slave, and there isn't a single house that doesn't have a black slave girl sitting on the threshold grinding grain. I'm told that the slaves here are of various races. Some of them are Abyssinians; others are from all parts of Sudan and from central Africa.

Yesterday I saw a slave from the equatorial swamps. They say they're cannibals. He smelled horrible.

Tuesday, March 8, 1881

Uncle Panagiotis told me the first people to bring slaves to Khartoum to sell them were the government of Mohamed Ali Pasha about fifty years ago when Sudan was annexed to Egypt. The Arabs in Sudan love to have slave girls. The slave girls don't usually become free unless they produce children. The Arabs like black women, but most of the Turks, Egyptians, and Europeans like Abyssinian women. I must admit they are good looking. They are the color of fine coffee and are good natured.

Wednesday, March 9, 1881

What I've noticed is that masters usually treat their slaves with compassion. So the slaves like their masters more than they like the places where they grew up. The Turks and Egyptians rarely mistreat their slaves. But unfortunately cruelty is widespread among the Europeans. I don't know how European men can allow themselves to do this. Perhaps it's the influence of this barbarous country. The government has had to pass a law to prevent foreigners from beating their slaves. This is an insult to civilization and the civilized world.

Wednesday, June 15, 1881

The Egyptian traders here are agents for the trading houses in Cairo. They live in luxury in large houses with harems of black slaves. They eat, drink, and smoke in great opulence but, like all Egyptians, they look forward to going back to Egypt.

Sunday, July 3, 1881

I've realized that the poor Egyptian workers live in the same quarters as the Sudanese. Some of them are married to Sudanese women and live as established families. These workers came to Sudan after the Egyptian conquest because there aren't any local people who are good at technical things or at the jobs common in the civilized world. Why have they ended up living with blacks in this way? Is it because they are poor like them? But how can they have forgotten that they are part of a great nation while these blacks are merely their subjects?

Friday, August 5, 1881

I've discovered that the British engineer is not an engineer and is not even British. He's a Belgian adventurer who used to work in the slave trade on the White Nile. Ever since the French slave trader Vissier and later the Sardinian trader Bruno Rolesu grew rich in this way and transported thousands of Sudanese slaves to Cairo, other Europeans have been trying to imitate them.

The Belgian adventurer tricked the Egyptian traders. He sold the slaves himself and then fled to Khartoum. He claimed he was a British engineer as a cover until he could find someone who could help him go abroad. I found out he had left a month before I discovered who he really was.

I was surprised when Dorothea admitted she had met him several times.

7

Her mistress Nuwwar interceded on Theodora's behalf after months of maltreatment.

Sheikh Ibrahim succumbed to his wife's entreaties and gave Theodora to her as a servant. After that she could go out when she wanted and Nuwwar didn't object to Hortensia coming to visit her.

The new city of Omdurman wasn't at all like Khartoum. She felt lost when she went out in the streets.

"It's not like Suakin or Khartoum," she told Hortensia.

"It's not like El Obeid. It's an amazing city. It looks like everyone's about to suddenly set off on a journey," said Hortensia.

The houses were all of unbaked brick. There were scruffy tents set up here and there. Goats, sheep, and donkeys wandered among them.

"Are you still in pain?" Hortensia asked her.

Theodora moved her thighs carefully and remembered the pain and the horror she had been through.

"No, there's no pain now," she said.

"What monsters they are!"

They had both been ordered to convert to Islam. Hortensia had soon obeyed her master. She didn't have anyone around her to help her resist, unlike in El Obeid. Malik Areeby was delighted with her. His eyes full of tears, he said, "If God loves a slave, He uses him or her to show the way to someone who has gone astray."

He changed her name to Maymouna, saying it was the name of one of the Prophet's wives.

"He offered to marry me."

"Are you going to accept?"

"Maybe. That would give me some security while I think about my situation," she said.

Theodora was more stubborn in the beginning. Then she relented and converted to Islam. Nuwwar chose the name Hawa for her. She taught her how to pray and promised to help her memorize parts of the Quran. But Hawa didn't make progress on that. "It's confusing at first," Nuwwar said to console her. "That will pass. Don't worry."

She didn't know whether she was in a daze because of what had happened to her or whether she didn't really want to memorize the verses. But she pretended to believe what her mistress had told her.

When Bakhit Mandil proposed marriage to her, it brought back memories of those pains.

"I want to have children that are the same color as me and have eyes as beautiful as yours," Bakhit told her.

She started in horror, as if her flesh was being cut under a blade. "Don't say that!" she shouted.

"What's wrong?"

She jumped to her feet. "Don't say that. I don't want to hear you say that again," she said.

"But I love you," he mumbled in confusion. "I want to marry you."

She put her hands over her ears and shouted, "Shut up! Shut up!"

Her shouting startled Idris al-Nubawi. "You're going to attract people's attention," he told them firmly.

Hawa didn't wait. She picked up her things and left, leaving Bakhit standing bewildered at the vegetable stall. When she was gone, Idris asked Bakhit, "What's up with her?"

Bakhit wrung his hands. "I don't know, Idris," he told his friend. "She's mad."

"All white people are mad," Idris said with a laugh.

Bakhit looked toward the crowd that had swallowed her up. "But I love her, mad as she is," he said.

Ten

1

BAKHIT HAD HAD A GRIM WEEK.

He hadn't seen her in the market. He went to Idris
al-Nubawi's stand every afternoon and sat underneath waiting till the evening call to prayer. When Idris started packing
up his wares, Bakhit stood up lazily.

"Don't be so sad," Idris said.

"Without her I'm nothing, Idris," said Bakhit.

Idris scowled. "Be a man," he said. "You're acting like a
mother who's lost her child."

Bakhit left him and went off toward Sheikh Ibrahim Wad
al-Shawwak's house. He wandered the streets aimlessly. He
passed by the dome of the Mahdi's tomb and stopped awhile
to say a prayer to his Lord. When he reached his destination
he walked along the mud wall. He stopped at the servants'
gate. He pushed the door open gingerly and called Sabah
al-Kheir. His friend hurried over with a smile on his face. He
could see how sad Bakhit was and he knew what was wrong
with him. He led him away by the arm. They stopped in an
open space to the north of the house.

"Are you looking for Hawa?" he asked.

"Is she well?"

"Very well, you idiot. What's up with you?"

He was delighted she was well, but at the same time deeply
anxious that she was well but hadn't come to see him.

"Why hasn't she been coming to market then?"

"I don't know," said Sabah al-Kheir. "She asked the mistress to excuse her from running errands to market. Do you have anything to do with that?"

Bakhit didn't answer the question. Instead, he asked his own: "Is she well? Is she sad?"

"No, she's her usual self. Yesterday she was singing Egyptian songs to the mistress to make her happy. The mistress was laughing with pleasure. And your friend has a pretty voice."

"She was singing?"

"Are you sad that she was singing?"

He didn't know if he was sad that she was singing. He left Sabah al-Kheir standing there and went on his way.

"Where are you going?" Sabah al-Kheir called. "I want to take you somewhere fun tonight."

Bakhit didn't answer. Sabah al-Kheir called after him again: "Shall we meet in Idris's house?"

Bakhit only wanted to leave. The beer he would drink at Idris's place wouldn't help him. He let his sadness carry him along and wandered around the streets. He went from place to place thinking of her. She wasn't sad. She was singing. She had a sweet voice. But she didn't come to see him. Maybe it was because he had annoyed her and made her sad. Why else would she abandon him to despair and disappear?

The world looked bleak. His heart ached. He couldn't go out to work for a week. His body could only just carry him to Idris's stall, where he would wait in vain. The fear of losing her hurt him deep inside. Waiting to see if she would come made him physically ill. But she didn't come and now he had found out that she was well, and that she had been singing.

Was he sad that she was singing?

He didn't tire of going to Idris's stall. He sat pensively under the stall. Whenever Idris asked him about her, he said, "She's singing."

Then she came.

Her shadow fell on him before he saw her. He smelled the scent of musk. He looked up and found her standing over him. He didn't know what to say. He just looked at her looming over him.

"Bakhit!" she said.

"Yes."

"Take me to the river. I want to see the sunset."

2

They sat down to the west of the jetty. In front of her was Tuti Island in the middle of the river. The ruins of Khartoum were visible far behind it. The sun went down behind them and their shadows stretched across the ripples on the surface of the water. The birds screeched at each other to leave before darkness fell. The hubbub of Omdurman seemed as distant as a dream. The surface of the river was calm, as was her mood.

"It's no use, Bakhit," she said.

He didn't know what to say. Anything he said might be the wrong thing—something that would make her angry.

"I can't deny that I care for you," she said. "You're not someone I was on my guard against. You're not someone I expected to meet. But all this is pointless."

"Are you asking me to give up loving you?" he asked cautiously.

"You have to, Bakhit."

"Why? What is there to stop us getting married?"

"It's no use."

"Why not? I'll ask your master for you. We can live together in my house. You needn't be a maid ever again. I'll work and get you everything you want. We'll have our own yard. I'll buy a sheep for milk, and you can keep pigeons. We'll have children, three of them. Four, with one girl as pretty as her mother."

"Bakhit! Bakhit!"

He stopped. His silence walked with her into the void. Darkness closed in on them.

"I can't. You're not part of the life I imagined. My whole life hasn't been the life I imagined. I wouldn't be able to, Bakhit."

She didn't tell him about her pains. She kept her thighs firmly together. She remembered Alexandria and the Mediterranean. Georgios, the son of the man who sold olives. The darkness in the damp church when he kissed her lips. Her master Sheikh Ibrahim's room. Crying at night. The years of torment in captivity before Bakhit came into her life. Bakhit's smell, which was like a familiar sore.

"You came to me too late, Bakhit," she said.

"Tell me when I should have come," he said, stubborn as a child. "I'll turn time back to then. I'll tell the sun to go backward and come to you before it's too late."

"It's no use. There's no point, Bakhit. Please."

Her master, Sheikh Ibrahim, had bought her for his bed. He had been looking forward to her virgin body. The Christian girl who was as white as milk.

Nuwwar had passed her to a servant girl, who took her by the hand down a long corridor spread with camelhair rugs. The girl took her into a large room with an Egyptian-style brass bedstead. She stood there trembling. No one told her what would happen but she could smell trouble in the air. She heard the door behind her. Sheikh Ibrahim came in. His head was uncovered and he was wearing a fine short shirt and leather sandals on his feet. He smiled at her.

"Praise be to the Lord, who has granted the faithful victory over the infidels," he said.

She didn't understand what he meant. "Thank you, sir, for saving me from the stockade," she said timidly. "I'll be grateful to you for the rest of my life."

He sat on the bed and beckoned to her to come closer.

"You don't owe me any gratitude. It's the grace of God that has made you mine. You're from Greece, aren't you?"

"I'm from Egypt, sir. My parents are from Greece."

He looked into the distance and said, "I saw you before in the market, in the company of a woman from Greece, the wife of Mr. Panagiotis. I thought you were her daughter, but I asked around and learned that her daughter died a long time ago. They said you were a teacher in the Orthodox mission."

She mustered all the politeness she could to override her fear. "It's by God's grace that you recognized me and saved me, sir," she said.

"Come and sit down," he said. "Why do you insist on saying I saved you? In fact I chose you for myself before anyone else did. I wasn't going to leave your beauty to some idiot dervish follower of the Mahdi."

What he said heightened her fears. She went up to him but didn't sit down. He reached out and took hold of her hand. Her body was cold.

"Frightened?" he asked.

She didn't speak. She couldn't speak. What did he want?

He tugged her hand, pulling her into his arms. She shuddered, cried out, and shied away, then collapsed on the floor.

"No," she said.

He slowly stood up.

"Don't be frightened. I won't hurt you," he said.

"No," she said again. "Stay away from me."

He reached out to touch her hair, but she screamed. He bent over her and she kicked him in the stomach. He fell in pain.

"You bitch!" he said.

She jumped up to escape, but he grabbed her foot and she fell on her face. He crawled on top of her. His smell was stifling. His body was repulsive. His face was up against her face, and he was groping with his hand, looking for the hem of her dress. He wanted to strip her naked. She kept screaming. She closed her legs tightly. She spat in his face and he slapped her. He backed away for just enough time for her to push him off. She tried to crawl away. But he clung to her hair. Her braid came unraveled. He pulled and it hurt.

"I'm not going to let you go, you uncircumcised Christian!" he said.

She wriggled to escape his grip but when she heard Nuwwar's voice she was embarrassed. Her dress had been torn off her.

"That's enough, Sheikh Ibrahim," said Nuwwar.

"What's it to do with you? Get back to your room!" he shouted.

"That's enough, Sheikh. Have pity on the girl. She's frightened."

He stood up in a rage and straightened his shirt. From where she lay she could see he had nothing on underneath. With his foot he looked for his sandals but couldn't find them. She could see them far under the bed. He was walking around the room barefoot and swearing.

"I had to grovel to ten dirty dervishes and I paid her weight in bribes to get hold of her. And then she spits in my face?"

Nuwwar helped her sit up and smoothed her disheveled hair.

"You have to be gentle, Sheikh. She's a frightened girl. Have pity on her."

But he didn't know what pity was. Every night he tried to take her, and her fear helped her triumph. He wasn't able to take her virginity despite his attempts. Once he stripped her naked, touched her with his erect penis, and tried to press it deep inside her, but she darted out of reach like a curtain in the wind.

She bit his cheek and he flew into a rage.

"I'll teach you a lesson, you Christian bitch!" he shouted.

He left her weeping on the floor. "Never mind, my girl," said Nuwwar. "We've all been through this process. It's just that you're a little older. But the pain will pass. Don't be frightened."

3

"I know a trader who smuggles goods from Egypt," Bakhit told her. "I'll bring you some Egyptian candy. Would you like that? And we can name the girl after you. I'd like to have two Hawas. If you'd like to run away to Egypt I'd go with you and leave Omdurman. Or we could run off alone into the wilderness. I'd change my name. You'd be Eve and I'd be Adam, and we'd be the first human beings in the world. We'd create a new world far away."

"You don't understand," Hawa sighed. "You're blind."

4

When Bakhit came back from Egypt he threw himself back into the life of the city. He had acquired experience and had seen a world he wouldn't have dreamed of.

But he hadn't lost his childlike innocence, which was surprised by life. He told everyone he had dealings with about the wonders he had seen in Egypt. His Egyptian master, Youssef Effendi Said, was a marvel, he thought. He didn't understand what his master had said about love until he met Hawa but he remembered it by heart and recited it to people with admiration.

He worked at every trade that required hard work—a porter at Omdurman port, a peddler in the market, a guard at the ammunition depot, a worker in the tailors' market, a clerk in the gunpowder factory, a carpenter in the carpenters' market, a building navvy, a well digger, and a gravedigger. It was in the last trade that he met Sabah al-Kheir.

He was sitting in the firewood market one day with some other gravediggers, as they were wont to do. A black slave with a limp came up to them and said, "I need a gravedigger, folks."

A group of men jumped up and offered him their services. He examined them at length, then picked Bakhit from among them. Bakhit knew it was fate that had chosen him over his colleagues on that day. Carrying his tools, he walked with Sabah al-Kheir to the grave site.

"The wife of my master, Sheikh Ibrahim Wad al-Shawwak, died this morning. He's a kind man. If you do the job well, he'll reward you handsomely," he said.

"It's God who rewards," said Bakhit.

He walked with Sabah al-Kheir to the house where his fate awaited him. He stepped into his destiny, unaware that it was the start of a new life. He found the usual commotion. Crowds of men and women. A suppressed, tense grief. The Mahdi had banned public displays of mourning for the dead years before, and the Khalifa had upheld that policy. Abdel-Gayoum, Sheikh Ibrahim's son, met him. He was standing among a group of Mulazmin officers and sons of rich men. Abdel-Gayoum took a long look at him and said, "Are you going to do a good job?"

Those were the only words Abdel-Gayoum spoke to Bakhit Mandil until Bakhit killed him eight years and five months later. He didn't say anything else. But he deserved to die by Bakhit's sword.

Bakhit went out to the cemetery in the northern part of the city, between the Dongolan quarter to the north and the Muslimaniya quarter to the south, which was home to the Copts who had been forced to convert to Islam. He chose a spot at random between the graves and started to dig. He slowly planted his mattock in the ground, then filled his basket and emptied it some distance away. He had finished digging the main trench before Sabah al-Kheir arrived.

"Haven't you finished yet?" Sabah al-Kheir asked.

"All that's left to do is the niche in the side wall."

"Goddamn! The funeral procession's on its way. Hurry up."

Bakhit wasn't rattled. The hard part was over. The ground in Omdurman was stony and rough. But he had finished digging the grave to knee depth. There was only the niche left and that wouldn't tire him out. He estimated he would finish by the time the body arrived. And so it was. He got out of the grave and stood aside to watch the impressive funeral procession arrive at the grave he had prepared. He saw a venerable old man, short of stature, surrounded by important people, including Commander Yaaqoub, the brother of the Khalifa; Ali Wad al-Hilw, one of the men the Mahdi had chosen to succeed him; Commander Othman Azrag; and other dignitaries of the Mahdist state. Sabah al-Kheir invited Bakhit to come back to the house with him.

"You're a skilled worker and you look like a nice guy. What's your name?" he said.

"I'm Bakhit Mandil."

"And I'm Sabah al-Kheir."

He embraced him as a mark of brotherhood. They walked along, chatting. Sabah al-Kheir told him about his master, Sheikh Ibrahim. He wasn't very different from Bakhit's Turkish master, Abdüllatif Effendi Mazhar, but he wasn't as good at insulting people in the Ottoman language. Sabah al-Kheir spoke about his master with hatred.

"I'll tell you something stranger than that," Bakhit told him cheerfully. "I fought in Wad al-Nujoumi's campaign in Egypt and saw some amazing things."

He went through the gate into the servants' yard with Sabah al-Kheir and sat on the ground in a remote corner. He watched the many servants bustling around like busy bees. They were carrying food and answering calls. Sabah al-Kheir brought him the remains of some stew.

"This is some of what's left over from the lunch that the gentlemen had before the funeral," he said.

Bakhit dug into the food. Sabah al-Kheir disappeared for a while, then came back with three riyals. He threw them at Bakhit, who took them gladly. He wanted to leave but destiny insisted that he stay. Sabah al-Kheir asked him to keep him company for a while. He stretched out his leg for Bakhit to see and said, "I have a limp, as you can see. I'm no use on occasions such as this. They need stronger servants. Let's chat a little."

The moon was bright. He was happy to have a full stomach and he had three Majidi riyals. Why not stay?

He happily agreed. Sabah al-Kheir asked him to tell him about the wonderful and amusing things he had seen in his life. He gave his new friend some of what he sought. Sabah al-Kheir laughed and clapped his hands in amazement. Then Bakhit smelled the scent of musk.

The smell filled the whole universe. He looked up to see what it was. His most beautiful dream. She was walking in the yard, with an intriguing hint of sadness on her face. She looked at him without seeing him. But his heart felt hot as if he had a fever. She passed by like a vision.

"Who's that white woman, Sabah al-Kheir?" he asked.

"That's Hawa. The late lady's favorite servant. She's been with us for five years."

"A Christian?"

"She converted. She had some complicated Christian name. She's from Egypt."

Bakhit watched her go. "No. She's not from Egypt. I've been to Egypt and she's not from there," he said.

When he met her in the market by chance five days later, he stopped her. She looked at him in surprise at his boldness.

"I have one question," he asked her.

She looked at him with her sad eyes. From then on he loved sadness.

"From which country inhabited by angels do you come?" he asked.

5

"I'll do the impossible for you to be happy," Bakhit told her. "Tell me what you want. Wish for the impossible and I'll die trying to make it possible for your sake."

She was about to take hold of his black hand. The skin on his fingers was wrinkled like a camel's knee. Having second thoughts, she pulled back.

"Bakhit, let me give you some advice," she said.

He opened his clear eyes wide. As innocent as newborn day.

"Don't trouble yourself doing the impossible," she said dolefully. "Nothing can make me happy. And the little I could do couldn't repay you for doing the impossible."

He shrugged his shoulders dismissively. "I don't care," he said.

6

So her kind mistress, Nuwwar Bint al-Hajj Qasim, had left her and died.

She had lived five years in her shadow, protected and shielded by her. She had taken shelter under her wing from the midday heat of enslavement. Nuwwar had interceded on her behalf when Sheikh Ibrahim was cruel to her. She had guarded her from Abdel-Gayoum's temper. She had commiserated with her when life was tough. She had been closer to her than Hortensia, dearer to her heart than the memory of her mother far away.

When Nuwwar heard by chance news of Theodora's Uncle Panagiotis and Auntie Maria, she came joyfully to Theodora. Theodora had told her so much about them that Nuwwar had almost fallen in love with them. Theodora found out they were living in the Muslimaniya quarter. They had been forced to convert to Islam, and in order to prove it Uncle Panagiotis had married one of his servants. Nuwwar gave her permission to visit them.

At noon one Wednesday she went off in high spirits to see them. Nuwwar promised her she would soon visit them too with her. "Go by yourself first," she said. "Restore contact with them and reassure yourself that they're well. After that I'll visit them with you. Your family is my family too, my dear."

But she came back in tears and poured out her sadness to Nuwwar.

"My auntie Maria is crippled. She's lost her mind and doesn't know what's going on. And Uncle Panagiotis is under the control of the maid he married. He's sad all the time."

Nuwwar hugged her to comfort her.

"The maid threw me out of the house. She said, 'We don't know you and we don't want you.' Uncle Panagiotis was standing behind her watching her as she pushed me out of the house. He didn't open his mouth to say a word."

Theodora wept bitterly. She put her arms around Nuwwar and buried her face in her bosom.

"I no longer have any family in this world. They've all abandoned me," she said.

"I'm your family, my dear," said Nuwwar.

But now Nuwwar had abandoned her, like everyone she had loved.

Nuwwar had been proud like the rich women of the dead city of Khartoum. She had the faith of a pious woman who feared the Lord in her dealings with people. When Sheikh Ibrahim punished her by inflicting genital mutilation on her it was Nuwwar who nursed her. She looked after her wound until it healed. She comforted her and eased the physical and mental damage.

When Theodora heard the voice of Sheikh Ibrahim looking for her, she took shelter in the servants' yard out of fear. She curled up in a ball and trembled. She saw him standing at the door to the yard. He beckoned her but she couldn't get up and go to him. She knew that something serious was meant to happen to her. The threat he had made some days earlier was not a joke. Now she knew the time had come for him to carry out his threat.

The servants grabbed her. They pinned her body to the ground. She resisted and her dress got torn. Her white thighs seemed to glow in the dark abyss around her. She refused to submit but they outnumbered her.

"You claim to be Muslim. Now we're going to complete the process," Sheikh Ibrahim said.

"Leave me alone!" she screamed, bursting into tears.

"A Muslim woman can't be uncut. That would be haram."

She cried for help at the top of her voice. But her cries disappeared into the void. Umm al-Shoul leaned over her and looked between her thighs. She was a black circumciser. As massive as a stone wall. She pushed her fingers inside her. Theodora screamed. The pain overwhelmed her, like an explosion that sent brutal jolts through her body. Umm al-Shoul rubbed warm oil into her skin. Her legs shuddered. Then she pressed the blade into her flesh.

"Help me, Jesus!"

"I knew she was an infidel!" shouted Sheikh Ibrahim angrily. "I knew it!"

"Shut up, infidel," said Umm al-Shoul. "God curse you."

The servants were still holding her body down, and the pain was giving her convulsions. The blade cut into her and she could feel the blood running down her thighs. Her urine ran cold. Umm al-Shoul took the blade out and looked up. She picked up a rag and pressed it against the wound. Theodora's blood stained the rag. The smell of urine, blood, sweat, and fear was everywhere. A mixture of smells like rotting fish. Umm al-Shoul leaned over again and plunged the blade in. She took her time cutting Theodora. Whenever the blood bothered her she wiped it with a rag and cursed the uncircumcised Christian.

She sewed the wound around a straw to leave a small opening and sealed it tight by pulling the threads. As Theodora's body shook, small pieces of cut flesh fell off. Umm al-Shoul rubbed the wound with a cloth rag soaked in natron solution.

The liquid was caustic. Theodora's head throbbed with the pain, which drilled into her head. The air came out of her nose in the form of a scream. Her tears drowned the world. Her cries made the river bleed and ran aground on the riverbank.

In pain. Weeping. Defenseless.

They tied her legs to keep them apart. "We need to do this," Umm al-Shoul told Sheikh Ibrahim, "so that the wound doesn't go septic from the tightness and the rubbing."

Sheikh Ibrahim looked at her thighs, covered in blood and urine.

"Let it go septic and let her die. It doesn't matter any longer," he said.

He had promised himself that he would enjoy her uncircumcised, but now she was just a woman like any other. He wasn't going to leave her unpunished. Not after she'd spat in his face and bitten him. He knew he had ruined her life and it didn't matter to him if she was dead and buried.

She lay there naked to every gaze. Servants male and female passed through her room. They looked at her white body with curiosity and disgust. Flies landed on her and buzzed around the wound. The wound dripped blood. She lamented her pains and Nuwwar caressed her in an attempt to mend her wounded pride.

"Take it easy, my dear," said Nuwwar. "We've all gone through this procedure. The pain will soon pass."

Theodora cried but said nothing.

"All the pain will pass, Hawa," said Nuwwar. "We're all like you, and uncircumcised women won't go to heaven. It's what's best for you, my dear, so you have to persevere."

The pains of the body pass, but the psychological scars remain. Nuwwar nursed her as well as she could. She told her of her memories of life with her husband. She explained her faith in the Mahdi and how she was worried her husband might make a slip of the tongue and curse the Mahdi, as he did sometimes. She treated her as a daughter.

"How can I repay you for your kindness? If it wasn't for you, I would have died of fear," Theodora said.

But it was Nuwwar who died.

Sheikh Ibrahim heard Nuwwar whispering to him in the dark. "Oh the pain, Sheikh Ibrahim," she said.

He jumped up and fumbled to light the lantern. He saw her dripping with sweat. Her eyes were protruding and she was trembling violently.

"What's wrong with you?" he asked.

"It's fever. I'm on fire."

With the vomiting and diarrhea, Nuwwar lost touch with the real world. She rolled around deliriously for days on end. She tottered on the brink of the precipice. At her side Theodora fought on her behalf. She wiped her mouth and chest. She removed rags covered with excrement from under her mistress. She cooled her brow with water. She gave her subia to drink or herbal tea made with senna. Every morning she helped her swallow coarse bread that had been ground into powder. But Nuwwar was rapidly declining.

Theodora stood by the edge of the bed, clinging to the hem of Nuwwar's soul, tugging it to make it stay. But Nuwwar slipped away like the afternoon sun. She suddenly succumbed. She slipped through Theodora's fingers and fell into the void. Her eyes clouded over as she said, "I'm going."

Theodora embraced her head and wept.

"Don't go, my lady. Don't go, mother," she said.

"I'm going."

Darkness covered her eyes. "*There is no god but God*," she mumbled.

Then she plunged into the unknown, leaving Theodora alone.

7

Lord, how are they increased that trouble me! Many are they that rise up against me.

Psalm 3:1

8

Five days after Nuwwar's death Sheikh Ibrahim announced that he wanted a new wife.

He called Theodora and said, "You were like a daughter to my late wife. You were closer to her than any of the other servants. So I'm going to put you in charge of them and the house."

She went out sadly to the market. When Bakhit appeared she scowled. But before she could go, he said, "Do you want to buy some vegetables? I'll show you the best person to buy them from."

She followed him to Idris al-Nubawi's stall. Bakhit wouldn't stop chatting. She and Idris agreed that he would provide the vegetables needed for the wedding. She bought some things and was beginning to check her bill when Bakhit cried out, "Fourteen piasters!"

She looked at him inquisitively.

"Your bill is fourteen piasters," he said. Then he added proudly: "I know my arithmetic, and I can read as well."

He picked up her purchases and walked along with her. He didn't ask her anything about herself. He spoke to her with respect, as if she were the Theodora she once had been.

"Through his eyes I see myself as someone else," she told Hortensia.

"Do you love him?" Hortensia asked.

"Oh no."

"But he means something to you. Don't deny it."

Theodora stopped and thought.

"I don't know," she said.

"You've been meeting him for more than a month. Why would you do that if he wasn't a close friend?"

"I don't know. Maybe I need him."

He beguiled her, like the sea in Alexandria, and she frightened him, like the river. By day her silence hurt him and by night his longing for her pained him. He switched like the face of the sky when the sun sets.

"You're becoming obsessed with that white woman," said Idris.

"I don't care," Bakhit said stubbornly.

9

Hassaniya Faraj came to Sheikh Ibrahim's house in a festive bridal procession. She was a middle-aged widow who had clearly been pretty and retained some of her prettiness. She wrapped her head in a black scarf with two strands of hair hanging out. She put kohl on her eyes. Her father was an Egyptian officer and her mother was from the Shaygiya tribe. Her husband had been killed by the Mahdi's followers.

Theodora couldn't like her at first. She was completely different from her late mistress. Theodora was wary of Hassaniya, and Hassaniya was wary in return. But Theodora grew used to her within a few days. The new bride was confident that the white maid did not have designs on Sheikh Ibrahim. Theodora hid her aversion to Hassaniya in her heart.

"She's nothing like my old mistress Nuwwar," she said to Bakhit.

"So why did he marry her?"

"I don't know."

But she knew he'd been dreaming of having an uncut woman in his bed. Hassaniya was a distorted version of Theodora. When Theodora went into the bathroom after Hassaniya to clean it and saw signs of what the couple had been doing in bed, a chill ran down her spine. Theodora thought that Sheikh Ibrahim was trying to sleep with her through Hassaniya.

"Why did the man marry a woman he doesn't love?" asked Bakhit.

Theodora looked at him inquisitively. "I wouldn't have expected you to ask that," she said with a smile.

"Of course," he said proudly. "Love's all we have. He who seeks God finds Him in love. He who seeks happiness finds it in love. He who seeks wealth finds it in love." Then he added grudgingly: "And he who seeks misery finds it in love." These were the words of his Egyptian master, Youssef Effendi Said, and Bakhit had only now understood them.

Theodora sighed and looked into his eyes, which were now the color of sadness.

"Bakhit, it hurts me to cause you pain," she said.

"I'm happy, Hawa," he replied.

"Oh no, you're not happy. I'm hurting you. I know that. Let's agree on something—I'm mad. I know what I'm like."

"We can agree on anything you like," Bakhit said excitedly.

"Don't go back to talking about love and marriage. That way we can be the best of friends. That would be wonderful, better for you and for me, Bakhit."

She saw his face cloud over. The pain showed through, but he faked a broad smile.

"Anything to please you, Hawa."

They sank into silence. She could hear his love busy inside him from his eyes. The clamor of his heart was too loud to ignore. "We've agreed and he's given me a promise," she said to herself.

When their time was up she got up to go. He walked with her to the house. They avoided the main streets. They slipped through the back lanes. He stopped at a distance from Sheikh Ibrahim's house. She smiled at him and took her things from him. Before she left, he said, "Tell me that happiness is possible, Hawa." A frightened child seeking reassurance.

"I can't give you any good news," she said dolefully. "You'll have to put up with sadness for the rest of your life. You'll have to put up with sadness as long as you love me. I know myself better than you do, and the worst may be yet to come."

Then she left.

Eleven

1

THE FIRST TIME THEODORA SAW Bakhit, she didn't know what to think.

No one had ever accosted her in the street in Sudan. Memories of Alexandria came flooding back. On her daily walk there she had been approached by all sorts, even the sea breeze. In this black country, on the other hand, nothing. She looked at him: a black slave with peppercorn hair. Thin and slim, without a single hair on his face. He had a horrible nose and his fingers were swollen. His knuckles were wrinkly and he had dirt under his fingernails. His smell was pungent and unpleasant. But when he spoke he distracted her from all of that.

Day after day he seeped into her, like a fleeting shadow. Something inside her trusted the warmth in his eyes. He gave up asking to marry her. He never spoke again about his dreams of having children, including a girl called Hawa who looked like her. But she could sense the love that rampaged inside him like a wild horse.

He sang the songs of the city to her:

O Lord, preserve her,
By God, I would treasure her like a mirror,
Or like a piece of sugar in my mouth.
O my tongue, sing her praises,
And may the saints follow her to protect her.

She laughed, but didn't really understand the strange language of the song. He explained the words to her. Between the lines of the song she read his hopes for her.

"Would you do anything to please me?" she asked.

"I'd die to please you," he exclaimed with candor.

"You'd die and abandon me?" she teased. "Who else do I have in this country?"

"I'll protect you whether I'm dead or alive."

Hortensia had escaped four months after Theodora met Bakhit. Now she didn't have anyone else. He was the only person who made her feel she was alive. She lapped up his expressions of affection. She wanted him badly, and she pushed him away violently.

When she and Hortensia were saying good-bye, Hortensia said, "I'm not worried about you. Bakhit will keep you alive."

"What can he offer me? He's like me—weak, maybe weaker."

"I know he's weak, Theodora. I know he's not real. He's an illusion. But through him you'll find what it takes to stay alive. Whenever this country wears you down and you need some solace, you know where to find it."

Tearfully she kissed Theodora on the cheek. Parting was cruel. Parting was horrible.

Hortensia tricked her master, Malik Areeby. He came to trust her, unaware she was hatching a plot with a group of captive foreigners. He thought the years they had been married had made her his. But she had been waiting. Waiting patiently. When she saw an opening she quickly slipped through it.

Her escape plan had been carefully crafted. There were six Europeans—a consul, three merchants, and two young women. They gathered the money they needed, recruited a guide, and hired an escort. The number of people slipping out of the city had increased in recent times. When someone found a gap in the siege and fled, the siege was tightened on those who remained. But they didn't stop leaving.

Hortensia had confided in her that she would be escaping the next day.

"You and your boy?" Theodora asked.

Hortensia scowled. "By myself. I'm not taking him with me," she said.

Theodora didn't understand. Two years earlier Hortensia had given birth to a baby boy who was as pretty as a little statue made of mud.

"He's black like his father. He doesn't belong with me. I don't want anything that reminds me of my days here," she said.

"Perhaps staying here will be safer for him," said Theodora.

Hortensia asked about Theodora's diary. "Should I take it with me? I could get your writings published in Cairo or in London," she said.

"No, what I write isn't for publication. It doesn't concern anyone but me. I'll miss you."

"I miss the civilized world. I've had enough of blackness and blood."

The next day Theodora tried to write something about Hortensia's escape. She couldn't do it. Everything she wrote was just the same short phrase: "I'm thinking about Bakhit Mandil."

2

Theodora rarely spoke about herself.

She always spoke about him. She wanted him to talk. She flirted. She laughed. But when he steered the conversation to talk about her she withdrew into silence.

He tried to draw her out. But she looked at him, puzzled. When she did speak, she said, "You don't know anything about what I've suffered."

"I want to know."

But she wouldn't say. He tried to bribe her with stories about himself. She reacted. She enjoyed them. He could see her face light up in happiness. But she wouldn't tell her own story.

He tried again to persuade her, but she always gave the same reply: "You don't know anything about what I've suffered."

3

Theodora went out on her usual errand after an absence of two days. Bakhit welcomed her with the impatience of a man who has been fasting. His eyes feasted on her face and he basked in her presence. He didn't reproach her. She could see the effect her absence had had on him, but she pretended to ignore it. He walked behind her in the bread market. He helped her carry the things she had bought. She moved on to the part of the market where the barbers were and told a barber that Sheikh Ibrahim was waiting for him. She went back to the vegetable market, greeted Idris al-Nubawi, and sat hunched up on the ground under his stall. Bakhit put his bags down and crawled in beside her.

"Why are men pigs?" Theodora asked.

He didn't know what to say. He didn't know if this was an insult aimed at him or if she was just making conversation.

"Abdel-Gayoum, Sheikh Ibrahim's son, never stops looking at me whenever he's at home. His father has already given him not one wife, but three. But he's still as he was. Whenever he comes into the house I feel his eyes undressing me."

Bakhit jumped and banged his head against the underside of the stall. Idris bent down to see what was happening.

"I'll kill him!" Bakhit shouted in a rage. "How dare he? I'll slaughter him."

She reached out toward him but pulled her hand back before touching him.

"Calm down, Bakhit," she said. "Don't be crazy. Nothing has happened. I'm just complaining to you that he annoys me. Don't turn it into a big drama."

Bakhit got out from under the stall, primed for action. He was fuming.

"Get back inside," Idris scolded him. "You want to kill the son of Sheikh Ibrahim Wad al-Shawwak because he looked at a maid in his own house? Are you mad?"

"I *will* kill him," Bakhit said defiantly.

Idris came out from behind his stall and sat on the ground facing Theodora.

"Don't listen to this braggart. He won't do anything. He doesn't have the guts to kill him. If you'd seen him dropping his weapon as soon as the infidels surrounded us in Aswan, you'd understand."

"You were with him in Aswan?" Theodora asked Idris.

"We went to attack the Turks. I got back, but he was taken prisoner and didn't come back for a year."

Theodora called Bakhit and he turned toward her.

"Come on, tell me about that," she said. "You didn't say that Idris was with you."

"Most of the people you see here in the market were with us," Idris said. "Bashir Wad Rahmatallah the butcher, Bahar Dara the watchman in the firewood market, and Ismail Abdel Zaher who sells vegetables. Do you know Saleh Jarr?"

"The one who sells bread? Yes."

"He was with us too."

She called Bakhit, who was angry again. "Come and tell me about those people," she said nicely. "Put your anger aside. Do you want them to kill you, leaving me alone?"

Bakhit sat down next to Idris. "I'm not frightened of dying," he said uncertainly. "I'm frightened I won't see you again."

"So stop this madness and you'll see me all the time."

She gave him a sweet smile and he felt dizzy. He calmed down. Idris looked at him in amazement, then jumped up and clapped his hands. "*There is no power or strength save in God.* The man is hopeless," Idris said.

As for Bakhit, he took Theodora on a tour through the labyrinths of his stories. He took pleasure in the fact that the two of them were alone with the stories; that he was sharing his history with her.

He bared his soul to her with great pleasure, because with her, and with her alone, he felt alive.

4

Bakhit came to see her on the sly. He waited on the wasteland north of the house and she came out to see him. They went for a walk, sharing the intimacy of silence.

They sat down near the river.

"I've brought you a present," he said. He handed her an amulet made of leather.

She smiled. "No one's given me anything for ages," she said. "What's the occasion?"

"I found a job in the soap factory."

She smiled again. "Congratulations! And what's the amulet for?"

"Open it up."

She opened the leather cover and found it was empty. She looked at him in surprise.

"It's full of my wishes. That's what will protect you. That's what I hope will always be with you," he said.

Her face lit up with delight. She hung the amulet around her neck.

"I don't know what to give you in return for this beautiful present," she said.

"Just keep well," he said warmly. "That would be the most beautiful present."

5

"I've brought you something valuable," Theodora told Bakhit.

He looked up to see. She took out her notebook. She had read parts of it to him several times. She held it and read out what she had written. He listened intently, but didn't understand what she was saying. She was reading what she had written in English. She didn't translate any of it for him. He tried to read the sense of it in her face. When she had finished he asked her, "What was all that about?"

"About things that make me sad."

His face looked pained.

"Things that happened to me when I was in Khartoum. Memories," she said.

He beamed with joy and told her his own memories of Khartoum. If he told her about his time with his European master he would get embarrassed and his black face would blush. But he didn't tell her about Buthayna, the daughter of Abdüllatif Effendi Mazhar, his Egyptian master.

She opened her notebook and took some sheets of paper out of it. She waved the sheets and said, "Do you know what these are?"

He looked and saw some pages in Arabic and some others in a foreign language he didn't know.

"These are statements from your Mahdi," she said, "and decrees from the old government that it used to circulate in Khartoum."

"The printing press prints the Mahdi's statements," he said, unsure what she meant.

"I know, I know. But these are old statements. They were circulated in Khartoum, written by hand, before the city fell. I found them at Sheikh Ibrahim's. But the government's statements are very rare. Did you know that these letters are valuable?"

He smiled. "I have some papers like that from the Wad al-Nujoumi campaign," he said. "I saw that Youssef Effendi Said was interested in them so I took some. Are they valuable too?"

"Not here. But in the civilized world they're worth a lot."

"You mean the infidel world?"

"Bakhit, my dear, you're a naïve child."

She unfolded one piece of paper and read it out: "From the slave that seeks God, the Mahdi, son of Abdallah, to his friends

191

in God who believe in God and His book. It is no secret that times have changed and old practices have been abandoned, and those who have faith and discernment do not approve."

She looked in the margins of the letter and said, "This is the summons letter, the first that your Mahdi sent out to people. It's written here that it was circulated in the year 1298."

She was trying to do the arithmetic on her fingers and convert the Islamic year into the European year, when Bakhit said, "The year 1881. I'm good at arithmetic."

"This letter is now ten years old, and every day that passes makes it more valuable," said Theodora.

She went on reading from the letter: "And the Lord of Creation, may God bless him and pray for him, has informed me that I am the long-awaited Mahdi. He has invited me to sit on His throne several times, in the company of the four caliphs, the Sufi masters, and the prophet al-Khidr, peace be upon him. He has supported me with his favorite angels, with saints living and dead from the time of Adam to our present days, and with djinn who are believers. In the Hour of War the Lord of Creation, may God bless him and pray for him, also attends with his gracious presence, along with the four caliphs, the Sufi masters and al-Khidr, peace be upon him. And He has given me the sword of victory from his presence, may God bless him and pray for him, and I have been told that through him no one will be granted victory over me, neither humans nor djinn."

She looked up at him and smiled. "Do you believe all that, Bakhit?" she asked.

"Whatever the Mahdi said, peace be upon him, is true."

Theodora pursed her lips in surprise. She chose another page and looked at it, then said, "This is a letter from him to Gordon Pasha, may he rest in peace."

She skimmed the letter and smiled. "Listen to this," she said, and read out loud: "'I'd like you to know that if you come to us as a Muslim we will instruct you and show you light at which your heart will take comfort and at which your desires for the world and for worldly things will fade away. After that, if we think you bring blessings and righteousness for Muslims, then we will make you ruler.'

"Imagine! He's inviting Gordon Pasha to convert to Islam. Gordon Pasha, a man who had the Lord in his heart. He always had the Bible to hand. And he promises to put him in charge. Isn't that ridiculous?"

"Why's that ridiculous?" asked Bakhit, unimpressed.

"Don't you know who Gordon Pasha was?"

"An infidel who was killed by the Ansar."

Theodora laughed. "An infidel like me?" she said.

"You're Muslim, Hawa. Stop joking like that. It's frightening."

"Very well, don't get angry. Gordon Pasha, my black brother, took part in the Crimean War, fought in China, and was governor in Khartoum twice. He was an important statesman."

She saw a vacant expression on his face. She leaned over his shoulder and said playfully, "You don't know about the Crimean War and you've never heard of China, have you?"

"I don't care," he said, shrugging his shoulders.

She laughed blithely. Her sadness was just a silly thing that people talked about. It was no longer for real. Or rather it had escaped her and lodged in Bakhit.

"What do you care about, then?" she asked.

He looked at her with his clear eyes, and in them she could see what she had done to him. She bowed her head. "Bakhit," she said.

He didn't speak. She looked up and said, "Every time I see you I'll bring some of these papers for us to read. I'll tell you about the civilized world, and maybe I'll teach you English. What do you say?"

When it was time for her to go he stood up with her. He said good-bye to Idris al-Nubawi and promised to visit him in the evening. He had a beer-drinking session with Idris every evening. As they were passing through the crowded market, she stopped and looked around. She thought she had seen a face from the past.

"What is it?" asked Bakhit.

"Just a moment! I thought I saw someone."

The man emerged from the crowd again. "It's him!" Theodora exclaimed with delight.

She slipped away from Bakhit and rushed off. "Younis!" she shouted.

Twelve

1

HASSAN AL-JERIFAWI AND THE OTHER men put Bakhit on one of the two horses and took him off toward al-Musallamiya. Despite all their desire for revenge, Hassan still had enough authority over them to stop them killing Bakhit. But Hassan did at least let them give Bakhit a good beating.

Hassan watched Bakhit bleed. Bakhit stared into space as though he were looking at ghosts. Blows rained down on his body but he didn't cry or groan. He didn't make a sound till they grew tired of hitting him.

"He's crazy," one of them said.

They searched his belongings and found a notebook that they didn't understand. Hassan picked up a tattered piece of cloth, examined it, and put it back where he'd found it. They took out some papers. One of the men looked at them, and then passed them to Hassan, who smiled in surprise.

"Someone who believed in the Mahdi," he said.

"Those are some of the treasures I've collected in my life," Bakhit replied weakly.

Hassan had a quick look through the letters. He couldn't see what might be valuable about them.

"They're just ordinary letters," he said.

"These letters have never been seen in Egypt. These letters are important to them. The English and the Turks would pay a good price for them."

"That's strange."

He pulled out a letter dated the twenty-eighth of Dhul Qaada, 1306, and read the preamble out loud:

> In the name of God the Merciful, the Compassionate, praise be to God, the Patron, the Bountiful, and blessings and peace on our Lord Mohamed and his family. From the worshipper of his Lord and the prisoner of his acknowledged guilt at his own shortcomings, Abdel-Rahman al-Nujoumi, to his master, his pillar of strength, his firm bond, and his means of contact with his master, the Khalifa of the Mahdi, peace be upon him, the Khalifa Abdallah bin Mohamed Khalifa al-Siddig. God has graced us with his guidance and has restored to us His blessings. Amen.

He pulled out another letter and read out a similar preamble. He went back to the first letter, skimmed it quickly, and read aloud again:

> My lord and my pillar of strength, after conveying honorable greetings and kissing your honorable fingertips and the soles of your feet, I bring to your honorable attention the fact that we have received your gracious letter and your august order of the third day of the month of Dhul Qaada, and the instructions it contained to be decisive, vigilant, and alert and not to overlook the people who are with the Turks, such as Bashir Abu Jibran and others, because they are not reliable even if they pretend to be compliant and obedient.

Then he skipped forward and resumed:

> I report to your honor that we began to enter enemy territory and the countryside on Tuesday, the third day of Dhul Qaada, and the field of battle was at Argeen on the river. In the twenty-three days since then we have been in

their territory, moving from encampment to encampment, from one district to another, and none of them have come to join us, or come seeking religion or for worldly objectives or for trade or anything else. On the contrary, they have all taken the side of the infidels and have asked for their help. They have helped the infidels by denying provisions to our men, refusing to deal with them, and helping the infidels by bearing arms, fighting against the Ansar, and being hostile toward them. We haven't written to any of them and neither Bashir al-Mathkour or any of the other common people in the countryside have written to us or communicated with us. What we have seen of them and the way they are living suggests they have no sense of security, no faith, and no interest in religion, and are not receptive to the Mahdist movement.

He looked up at Bakhit. "Were you on the al-Nujoumi campaign to Egypt?"

"Yes."

"The local people helped the infidel Turks against you."

"There weren't any Turks there. It was the local Egyptians and our troops."

Hassan put the letters back in the notebook.

"I didn't join the al-Nujoumi campaign. I was fighting in the east," he said.

"You didn't miss much. We went there to die. And I'd thought I was going to escape death," said Bakhit.

For some reason, whenever he had a chance, Hassan al-Jerifawi leaned over his prisoner to speak to him. Maybe it was the guilt running rampage inside him.

His companions were surprised at how friendly he was toward the murderer they had taken prisoner. But Hassan saw him as a colleague.

"Are you going to kill me?" asked Bakhit.

Avoiding the question, he asked instead, "Why did you do what you did?"

Bakhit spat out a thick gob of spit. "It was on orders from God," he said.

"God made you a murderer?"

Bakhit looked deep into Hassan's eyes and smiled. "God makes us what we are. What did God make you, my Arab friend?"

Hassan was shocked. God hadn't made him a killer. God had called him.

"Sit down, my Arab friend, and listen to my story, because I think that you, like me, are the victim of what you carry within you."

Hassan sat down hesitantly, but his heart was somewhere else.

2

God has called me, Fatma.

Can't you see the disaster that has befallen Islam?

The times have changed. The land is filled with injustice. The Turks, the infidels, have replaced God's religion and humiliated Muslims.

Should I not answer the call of the man who calls people to God and His Prophet and who calls me to act in a way that will give me new life?

We will fight in the path of God. In God's cause.

We will invade Khartoum, conquer Mecca, and rule Egypt.

We will spread God's light across the darkened world.

God's promise is our Lord the Mahdi, peace be upon him. And God wouldn't renege on his promise to send his Mahdi, Fatma.

We have a duty to leave our old homes. We have a duty to help God.

I hurried to you, my Lord, in the hope of pleasing you. I hurried to you, my Lord, in the hope of pleasing you.

I hurried to you, and left Fatma behind me.

3

"Fatma and I have made a pact," Hassan told his sheikh, Salman Wad Hamad al-Duwaihi.

The sheikh bowed his head and said, "It's all in God's hands, my son."

"I couldn't bear to divorce her."

"My son, no good comes about when someone leaves home in God's cause while his heart is still attached to the things of the world. If you go you won't come back. Divorce her and you'll cut your ties to the world and devote yourself wholeheartedly to God."

He went into the room where Fatma was. She was prettier than he had ever seen her. Lush as the riverbank near the islands, steeped with longing. Her body glistened with his memories of her. He stood at the door, lost for words. But she helped him.

"Have you made up your mind?" she asked.

"I've waited too long to answer the call, Fatma," he said, torn by pain.

Seventeen months had passed since he had heard that the Mahdi of God had appeared on earth. The letters and reports hadn't stopped coming. The country was on fire around them. People were leaving home in their hundreds to join the Mahdi. The country's finest were pouring in from all directions. The only men still at home were the skeptics to whose hearts God had not shown the light, or men like Hassan who were hesitant and worried that it might be false hope.

The summons from the Mahdi pained him when it reached them. Sheikh Salman gave it to him and told him to read it. The words were inspired by God the Merciful. His heart raced as he read what the Mahdi said:

"The Lord of Creation, may God bless him and pray for him, has informed me that anyone who doubts my status as the Mahdi does not believe in God and His Prophet. He, may God bless him and pray for him, repeated this three times."

He worried he would fail in what he did; that he might lose the faith he had gained when his heart was filled with the love of God. But he couldn't decide. He asked the sheikh for help but the sheikh wasn't much help. "Ask your heart," the sheikh said.

His heart knew the answer but his fears still held him back. He yearned for light from the Prophet Mohamed, but his fears tied him to the ground.

"My mind is now at ease, Fatma," he said.

She rose from the bed. Her dress rippled on her body and swished as she walked, and his head spun. She went to a pile of clothes in the corner of the room. She rummaged in the pile, then came back to him, held her hand out toward him, and said, "Look at this."

He took an egg from her, lifted it up, and read: "There is no god but God. Mohamed Ahmad is the Mahdi of Allah." It was written in proper Arabic, engraved in the eggshell.

"The hens at the school have been laying eggs like this for some days," she said.

"You agree with me then?" he asked.

She took the egg from him and put it back in its hiding place. "I wouldn't stand between you and God's command, master."

"So what's to be done?"

She lowered her eyelashes and said firmly, "We've been together for some time and you've been a good provider. You've never been unreasonable with me. You've lived with me with affection and you've treated me kindly. I'm not going to pay you back by sending you to hell. There's a pact between us that you're not at liberty to break."

He relied on his faith, and held fast to his certainty. He felt a burning sensation in his chest. "I divorce you, Fatma," he said.

"It's in God's hand, master."

He could no longer see her for his tears.

4

Hassan threw himself into the wide world, leaving the school and his memories behind him.

He embraced the loneliness of exile, the pain of leaving one's home, the pangs of nostalgia. The last the town saw of him was the sight of his back receding into the distance on the sheikh's donkey, as seen by Fatma's tearful eyes. Nostalgia is misleading as well as futile for those who leave home. They just end up torn to shreds as the chains of the past pull them back and the winds of the future push them on. The farther he traveled on the donkey, which was Sheikh Salman's rather than his own, the weaker the bonds that tied him to home. In exile he would grow new sinews and cover them with new skin.

The donkey's tail swished as it chased its shadow toward the west.

Eleven years later, five days out of al-Musallamiya, when he remembered that moment of departure, he crept through the darkness, unseen by his companions, to Bakhit in his chains near the river. He shook him to wake him up and said, "I'll tell you my story, Bakhit."

Bakhit listened in silence as Hassan explained his doubts and his sufferings. He finished off by saying, "Whatever experiences one might have, parting with loved ones is always the most painful. God created us to rely on the group. That's how God made me."

"The group is bad," said Bakhit. "People are a nuisance. It's only those we love who matter. The world is just the people we love. If we have to part with those people, we part with the world."

"But the only thing that we gain from love is this misery we feel," said Hassan.

Hassan traveled for days, and the days stretched into weeks. He picked up scraps of news about the Mahdi. The Mahdi, peace be upon him, had moved west with his followers to Mount Masa in Darfur. Hassan followed the light to him. Everything he came across on his way strengthened his resolve. God's religion had been suppressed and the Turks, the infidels, had built their state on injustice.

"The world was very horrible, Bakhit."

"The world never stopped being horrible, even after the Mahdi appeared," Bakhit replied.

5

I have never forgotten you, Fatma.

The ground picks me up and puts me down somewhere else, but you are always on my mind. God has tested my heart through my love for you, but I have little control over my life.

How weak man is! The more the mysterious grace of God raises him to the heights, the more something inside him calls him back to the world, and to the vanities of the world.

6

Night fell.

They asked whether today would be the day.

Thousands of the faithful. Besieging the Turkish city of Khartoum, the capital of the country and the bastion of corruption.

Beyond the river there were houses and mansions built in defiance of God. It was a city where the very ground was depraved and the walls of the houses iniquitous.

God's command has come. God's command has come, Khartoum.

The dervishes were seething with fervor. The trumpets were sounded. The Ansar of God had come in groups from every quarter.

The towns had fallen one after another, and only the river now stood between them and victory.

Hassan al-Jerifawi sat among his comrades, shaking with the tension. He was wearing the patched cloak that the Ansar wore. What he had seen on his travels had set his heart at rest. It doesn't befit a believer to lose hope. The end times had come and the Mahdi was bound to emerge. He had been shocked by what he had seen in one of the towns along the way, so he had made up his mind to avoid going into towns as far as possible.

Maintaining his resolve, he had finally reached the Mahdi's entourage. On his travels he had gone into the town of Rahad and it had horrified him and made him renounce city life. He saw finery, and his curiosity had been piqued by an elaborate party. He asked what it was and they told him it was a wedding.

Then the wedding procession came past. A group of young men were dancing, their dark eyes flirting with the spectators. One of them winked at him and blew him a kiss. He stank of perfume and had henna stains on his hands and feet. The husband was a slim Turk wearing a red fez with a long tassel and an embroidered jelaba. On his feet he wore sandals of costly leather. In his hand he held a whip that he waved at the dancers, who made trilling noises in celebration.

That was his last encounter with a town until he swore allegiance to the Mahdi.

People had less than a day left until the time came. It would be the Mahdi's day.

The besieged city sent its poor and hungry to the Mahdi to feed them. From them the Ansar learned that hunger was eating away at the heart of Khartoum. Spies and shortages of supplies were taking their toll.

When those fleeing the city reached the Ansar encampment the commander called Hassan. He told him to keep an eye on one of the fugitives, a terrified servant. The commander left them and hurried off. Hassan looked at his charge—an emaciated black man, wearing only long trousers. His chest was wrapped in thin strips of leather. His left foot had an obvious deformity. The man looked around at everything that moved. Hassan tried to reassure him, but he wouldn't listen. The commander came back and said, "You're going to go with this slave to a place he'll show you. You'll meet a man who'll give you some letters. Take them and give him this." He handed him a piece of paper with the seal of the Mahdi on it.

He walked through the encampment behind his companion and then they went on into some waste ground. They walked through a small wood and reached the river. Hassan could see the man he'd been sent to meet, sitting on the alert in a wooden boat. He grabbed his sword. The slave ran off, thanking the Lord that he had survived.

"Peace be upon you," said Hassan.

The stranger got out of the boat. He was a young man about Hassan's age, thinly built. His front teeth stuck out. He smiled at Hassan. "And peace to you, and the mercy of God," he said.

"They ordered me to take some letters from you."

The stranger looked him up and down. "Who are you?" he asked.

Hassan told him his name. The stranger nodded.

"I'm Abdel-Gayoum Wad al-Shawwak," he said.

He passed him some folded papers. Hassan took them, then handed his own piece of paper to the man. The stranger looked at it, still smiling.

"I have something else to say that hasn't been written in the letters," the man said.

Hassan didn't comment; he listened without saying a word.

"Tell the Mahdi that an expedition from Cairo has reached Metemma. It will soon reach Khartoum to relieve the siege."

Hassan tensed at what he heard. The stranger reached out to shake hands. "May God grant you victory. We are helping from inside. Victory comes from God," he said.

Hassan shook the man's hand and turned to go. But then he stopped and looked back. The stranger and the slave were pushing the boat off to leave.

"Are there many like you in Khartoum?" Hassan called after them.

"There are believers everywhere," Abdel-Gayoum replied.

He waved the piece of paper that Hassan had brought him. "This guarantees my safety when you come into the city," he said.

"God be with us, Hassan," he shouted as the waves carried the boat away. "If God grants victory to His soldiers, then ask after me."

Hassan didn't know what was in the letters, but he knew they were very important. After he handed them over to the commander and told him what else Abdel-Gayoum had said, there was a flurry of activity in the camp. That night people said it might be their last night. Tomorrow might be the day, because God had revealed the secrets of Khartoum to the Mahdi.

Hassan kept to himself, not far from his comrades. He remembered Fatma. He remembered his travels and the jihad he had fought with the Mahdi. He remembered the corruption they had destroyed. The heresy they had fought against. The bodies of the infidels that had been burned after death. In his mind's eye he could see the bodies of the Christians and Turks on fire.

He looked forward to martyrdom. When he met the Lord, he would say to him: "O Lord! I was in the army of your Mahdi and I died fighting for your cause."

For such a death could there be any reward other than Paradise?

7

From the other bank they could hear the music. Brass instruments were being played somewhere.

A murmur ran through the camp. They were reciting the Quran. Hassan al-Jerifawi found himself reciting: "*And hasten to forgiveness from your Lord and to a paradise as broad as the heavens and the earth, prepared for the devout.*"

The peace of God reigned in the encampment. The angels walked among them with the glad tidings.

And when the sounds from Khartoum fell silent the Mahdi's herald was sent out to address the troops. "Swear allegiance to me, to fight to the death!" the herald cried.

Then their rockets exploded in the sky and they crossed the river.

Thirteen

1

MERISILA OFTEN WONDERED WHETHER HER mother ate her brother alive or killed him first.

Whenever she visited Bakhit in prison she shared her doubts with him. Bakhit didn't approve of what she told him. He tried to find out from her what was happening in the city—those small details that it was hard for him to learn when he went out with a work gang. But Merisila preferred to dabble in murky worlds. The day she learned how to make love potions, she came to the prison full of excitement. She hugged him, to the annoyance of the guards, and exclaimed: "I've mastered love!"

Bakhit laughed and said, "You're too young to have done that. You're just a child, my little one."

She frowned disappointedly. She put her hands over breasts the size of lemons and said, "I'm not a child. Women suckle babies with smaller breasts than these."

Bakhit laughed at her naïve enthusiasm as she told him about her love potions.

"If the man who's in love puts one under his armpit and soaks it in his sweat then the women he wants, whoever she is, will fall in love with him, even if she's the sultan's daughter," she said.

Why hadn't he had something like that when he was writhing, wounded and bleeding, in the snares of love? He put his hand on Merisila's head and said with a smile, "I hope that's true, my little one."

She yielded to his touch and looked up at him with eyes as innocent as a sparrow in the rain.

When Theodora's specter came to see him, he asked her, "Would a love charm have worked?"

She moved around the cell carefully so as not to wake up the prisoners who were sleeping. She looked at Father Johann tenderly. Then she sat next to Bakhit and whispered, "Your questions are getting more painful, Bakhit."

"I don't feel any pain. Are you in pain, Hawa?"

She moved her head close to his. The smell of musk excited him.

"Look at me," she said.

Her eyes were full of conflicting hopes.

"Oh Bakhit!" she said. "Those are the eyes of a man who's suffering."

He growled stubbornly. "Don't speak to me of my pain. I didn't want your sympathy, Hawa. I wanted you."

"If I answered you it would only add to your pain, so don't ask, Bakhit."

He grew used to Merisila and to the fact that her strength was in her weakness. Reluctantly, he told her details of his ordeal. Whenever he told people about his love, they tended to leave. There was something of a curse on his love, or else his love was a curse. Maybe that's why Idris al-Nubawi had disappeared: to save himself. Jawhar had been abducted, lost in the void. He had seen Idris as a patron and in Jawhar he had found sympathy. But Merisila listened to him and said, "To hell with that infidel woman, that daughter of a whore."

When he rushed to Theodora's defense, Merisila said dismissively, "Women don't like the men who love them. If you had put your thing between her legs to satisfy her uncircumcised lust, you would have won her."

He shuddered at the thought. He had never touched her. That's why he felt such anguish when she rushed to greet Younis. She put her arms around Younis in the middle of the market. He smiled at her and laughed. She took hold of his arm and shouted joyfully, "I'm happy to see you!"

Bakhit stood there holding her shopping, unsure what to do. Should he follow her or wait? He gave up trying to decide and kept waiting, without choosing.

When she came back to him, her eyes looked as happy as leaves in the rain. "Who was that?" he asked in a choked voice.

"That was Younis Wad Jaber," she said cheerfully.

He would remember the name well, and years later, when he sought him out to kill him, he would track him down, weighed down by the pain he had long borne.

"He's the first person I met in this country. He was one of the guards for our caravan from Suakin to Khartoum," she said. She stopped walking, turned to Bakhit, and said gaily, "He gave me a lovely sparrow. I love sparrows very much."

From then on Bakhit started catching sparrows to give to her, but he knew, unfortunately, that he couldn't match the happiness the first sparrow had given her.

2

His experiences with Buthayna, the daughter of Abdüllatif Effendi Mazhar, had left scars that were worse than those from his time with his European master, which he had forgotten. Buthayna followed him wherever she could. Into the storeroom or into the room where they kept charcoal. Her color when naked was disturbing. When her face was flushed it turned so red he was worried the blood was going to burst out of it. But as he was recreating himself in Omdurman, he discovered the beauty of being black. He tried the bodies of black and Abyssinian women, who hadn't washed for months. And in them he found a pleasure he hadn't known before. Luck was on his side and he wasn't arrested, although the Khalifa's spies harassed prostitutes and women who made alcoholic drinks. When famine struck in the sixth year of Mahdist rule, it was hard for him to visit the women he knew.

They put their prices up, to match other price rises, and some of them starved to death.

When he looked around him and saw death on all sides, he decided to sign up for the military campaign to invade Egypt. An Abyssinian woman he knew died that morning. At noon he heard that one of people he had worked for had eaten his fingers to alleviate his hunger. He was shocked, and decided that night to escape death. There was a report circulating in the city that an expeditionary force of Jaalin tribesmen was going to join al-Nujoumi's army. Bakhit slipped into a house where the vultures were screeching. The birds flapped their wings aggressively around him. He went in and saw the bodies laid out on their beds as if asleep. He ignored them and looked around until he found a sword and two spears. He didn't find a rifle. He looked for money but didn't find any. He made do with the weapons and left. With them he applied to the Jaalin expeditionary force. But they took his weapons from him and gave him a position in the supplies department. They assigned him to carry water and other things that the fighters needed. Idris al-Nubawi and Sabt Jawd al-Karim were with him. Like him, they went to war to avoid starving to death.

Their detachment left Omdurman on a Monday afternoon and headed north, determined to earn the honor of fighting jihad. They were told that the Egyptian countryfolk were waiting to be conquered by the Ansar of the Mahdi. Cairo would be one stop on their way to conquering the world.

"Maybe from there we could join the army and invade the lands of the Turks across the sea," said Sabt Jawd al-Karim.

Bakhit had never been to sea before. He had heard that in eastern Sudan there was a sea that separated Sudan from the Hejaz and Mecca, but he didn't believe there could be a stretch of water wider than the Nile that separated Omdurman, the Mahdi's city, from the ruins of Khartoum, the city of the Turks. The desert stretched as far as the eye could see from the Nile to Metemma. They stayed there two days. The Jaalin there were delighted to see the detachment of local boys. As they left to meet their martyrdom, the local people celebrated and commended them to death. Bakhit saw a mother kiss the head of her son, a soldier. "Don't come back," she said as they parted. "I want the joy of receiving your shirt stained with blood after you've died a brave death."

The small town of Metemma was teeming with soldiers. "In God's cause! In God's cause!" people shouted from their houses.

When Theodora was amazed at these stories, Bakhit Mandil told her, "Only when we give up the false celebration of life do we understand the value of death."

"But Bakhit," Theodora replied, "life is a gift from God."

"To die bravely is nobler than any life," said Bakhit. "There's no immortality like the immortality of having women sing of your valor after you die."

Theodora laughed in amazement at what he had said, and Bakhit began to sing:

"When the time to die comes, those lying in bed will die,
While those who die in the thick of battle will be spared."

A few days north of Metemma, deep in the desert before they caught up with al-Nujoumi's army in Sawarda, Bakhit and Sabt Jawd al-Karim were sent out to hunt, and while they were searching in vain for something to eat other than snakes and scrawny vultures, they came across an isolated house among the sand dunes.

Sabt thought it was a house for Turkish spies, off the caravan route. But when they knocked on the door they found a woman alone there. She was an Arab woman, good-looking by their standards. A stocky woman with plenty of hair. Bakhit said hello and asked, "Where are the men?"

The woman didn't move.

"Maybe she's one of the djinn," Sabt said to Bakhit fearfully.

"There's no one with me," the woman said after a long silence. "If you want to eat, go into the kitchen there and take what you want. But if you have evil intentions, then God will protect me."

"We're from the Mahdi's army, madam," said Sabt.

The woman didn't seem interested.

"Why are you alone?" asked Bakhit.

"My husband went to Dongola and told me to wait here till he comes back," she said.

"And when's he going to come back?"

"God alone knows. I'm waiting, as he told me to."

They went into the kitchen apprehensively and found large pots full of cooked food. Bakhit went out again and asked if they could take some of the pots, but she didn't answer. They took what they could and left. Bakhit went up to her to say good-bye.

"Thank you for your generosity. If your husband comes back tell him that the Mahdi's soldiers passed by," he said.

Before he left, he heard her say, "He went to see you to find out what you were doing."

Bakhit went back to find out what she meant.

"We heard about a righteous man who was said to be God's Mahdi," she told him, "so my husband went to Dongola to find out about him, and he told me to wait for him here."

Bakhit was amazed to hear what she said. "My God!" he said. "The Mahdi died four years ago."

The woman shook her head in protest. "Oh no," she said. "We heard that on Aba Island he was summoning people to fight jihad and that his fellow holy men in Dongola were going to join him."

"O Mahdi of Allah!" he exclaimed. "That was eight years ago. People rallied to the Mahdi and conquered the Turks in Khartoum. And the Mahdi died after that and the Khalifa is now in charge."

"I don't what you're talking about, stranger," the woman said irritably. "Now go away. I'm waiting for my husband as he told me to, and I'll have nothing to do with your stories."

From behind Bakhit, Sabt asked her warily how long she had been waiting.

"I don't know," she said.

"You're waiting for a husband who left years ago on a journey that would have taken just a few days? For sure you're a widow," said Sabt.

"He told me to wait here, and I would never disobey him."

They left the obedient woman where they found her. She hadn't stood up or even changed the way she was sitting, and they never found out where she had gotten the food she had cooked or how she had lived alone for so long in this wilderness.

"How can someone live for years waiting for a fantasy?" asked Bakhit.

"It's faith, my friend," said Sabt.

3

One Thursday Bakhit, along with Mahmoud al-Jirjawi and Rifaat Effendi al-Salamouni and a long line of other prisoners, went out to the nearby riverbank to fetch water. They left Father Johann behind in deference to his age and status, as well as Tajeddin the Moroccan, who insisted that in his capacity as Jesus the son of Mary he couldn't possibly carry water with commoners. The three prisoners filled as many containers as they could and staggered back to their cell with them. It was hard to walk with chains on their legs and with water sloshing around in the containers.

The days pecked lazily at the shell they were in like a trembling chick hatching out of an egg.

"My wife must be sad," Mahmoud al-Jirjawi lamented. "I wish some kindhearted person would tell her what's happened to me."

In one corner Father Johann prayed to God for relief that never came. Mustafa Shaker meanwhile wasted his riyals on Touma's plump body.

Each day was as bleak as the one before and promised the next day would be shamelessly bleak too. On Bakhit's feet the wounds from the shackles were festering. The days bled his spirit drop by drop. In the prison there was no hope.

Merisila visited him and revived him for a while. Theodora came to him from time to time and lit up his life. After that, he slumped in his chains. His spirits rotted away day after day.

But he never tired of dreaming of the day when his sword would shed the blood of his enemies in revenge.

4

Bakhit Mandil escaped death by starvation in Omdurman, but hunger caught up with him on al-Nujoumi's campaign. The grain ran short and the stores were empty. People ate inedible things and developed a taste for things they wouldn't have looked twice at were it not for the pangs of hunger. But they didn't retreat.

The infidels sent them intimidating messages, tempting them to surrender. They tried to cause a rift between them and the Khalifa who had sent them to their deaths. The local Egyptians didn't like them. The Egyptians ambushed them and made it hard for them to stay in any of the villages. But they didn't retreat.

Defeat seemed imminent. The army commander, al-Nujoumi, addressed them:

"Those who wish to go back may go back and I won't stop them. Whereas I have sworn allegiance to the Mahdi, peace be upon him, to fight to the death for God's cause. And I will die a martyr, as there is no hope of victory."

"Can an army of believers be defeated?" Sabt Jawd al-Karim asked in surprise.

Hunger was sapping their strength, while their faith drove them on. Control over Egypt was close at hand if they were patient. The country had bread and corn and things that were good in the eyes of God.

God had promised the Mahdi that he would conquer Egypt, Mecca, and Syria. God was testing them through hunger, but in the end victory was inevitable.

They marched with rumbling stomachs. They could see God's covenant shining at the end of the road. Then the infidels met them, with their army and their weapons and the arrogance of their heresy.

When the fighting was fierce Idris al-Nubawi threw down the firewood he was carrying and turned to his fellow servants. "Let's not die as cooks. Come on—to Paradise!"

They picked up swords and advanced. Sabt Jawd al-Karim went to Paradise, while Idris al-Nubawi fled to Omdurman.

Bakhit Mandil never suffered from hunger again, but he didn't get to Egypt as a conqueror. He arrived there as a prisoner.

5

"We were soon defeated. We hardly fought," Bakhit told Theodora. "Some people were killed and others fled."

"War is a scourge, Bakhit."

"Incompetence is a scourge, Hawa. We went off clinging to our faith and nothing else. We believed that Egypt was waiting to be conquered by us. We were told the Egyptians were dying to join the true religion. We went there flying the Mahdi's banners and they killed us. We were brave and they were brave. We were fighting for true religion and I don't know what they were fighting for. We didn't flag and neither did they. But our fighting was all in vain. A pointless endeavor. We hardly raised a sword or fired a gun. We were believers, but we were hungry. They won and the ground was covered with bodies."

Theodora looked at him in commiseration. "And you?" she said.

He was trying to forget that she had come up to him with Younis Wad Jaber. She was laughing with him and smiling when he spoke. Her eyes sparkled with happiness. Younis's face had darkened with desire. And she laughed.

Bakhit suppressed his troubling thoughts and said, "The man who captured me was an Egyptian with a good heart and rotten luck. His name was Youssef Effendi Said."

Bakhit knew he didn't qualify for martyrdom. The smell of gunpowder surrounded him and smoke covered everything. He could hear cries of "Allahu akbar!" that ended in screams of death.

He was terrified. The hand that held the sword was shaking. Sabt Jawd al-Karim shouted, "Death to the infidels!"

Sabt ran toward the enemy in the expectation of Paradise, but Bakhit threw down his weapon and lay on the ground. The Egyptian man pulled him out from under the other bodies and Bakhit followed him meekly.

He told her how his Egyptian master had taken him to his house. He threw him down at the door and went in to spread the good news. Two women came out to look at him. They were white, and wore black. One of them was old and grumpy. The other woman, her daughter, was the wife of Youssef Effendi. She was a good-looking young woman with a rebellious streak in her eyes. His master gave him a drink and the old woman complained.

"The other soldiers came back with booty and you come back with a skinny black man?" she said.

Bakhit slept tied to a peg in front of the door. He didn't think about anything. He shivered, as if the shock had given him a fever and made him jumpy. Once again he was a slave.

When Khartoum had fallen and he had fled, four years ago, he had been nineteen years old. He thought he had said farewell to slavery forever. He lived in Omdurman, learning how to be free. But now he was facing a new period of servitude.

He was so dazed that his mind was a blank. He looked around at the ghostly white houses that shone in the darkness among the palm trees. He could hear the local people noisily and excitedly celebrating their victory.

In the morning he followed his master to the place where the bodies of al-Nujoumi's soldiers had been abandoned. When they got to the first of the bodies they were surprised to find groups of people scavenging in the area. One of them called to Bakhit's master. "Youssef," he said, "some of the dervishes are alive."

They turned over some of the bodies that weren't moving and could see life in several faces. But the ones who were alive were almost dead from exhaustion. Some of the local people brought food and tried to force it into their parched mouths. It was no use. Then someone said that some bread soaked in water might work. Bakhit's master took him back home, and later left him and went out. He could hear him shouting at the old woman.

"They're human beings who need food," he said.

The other woman insulted him and sent him off with curses. He came out carrying a basket, which he pushed into Bakhit's hands.

"Off you go, my Sudanese friend."

Bakhit followed him in silence. His master was short, with bronze skin. He was wearing baggy trousers and a black shirt.

They gave first aid to some of the wounded and stole things from some of the corpses. Bakhit heard that the local people had taken alive so many prisoners like him that there was no longer room in people's houses for any more. They had decided to leave the other survivors on the battlefield for the government to find them.

He walked back behind his master, with the basket full of things they had looted: revolvers, spears, clothes with shot holes, tins of loose powder, Martini and infantry rifles that were no use, riyals, pounds and fragments of silver coins, beads, unfinished letters, notebooks whose importance no one could discern, and many other things.

Tajeddin the Moroccan didn't speak with Bakhit until after the mysterious disappearance of Jawhar.

At the time Bakhit had scarcely completed his second year in the Sayir prison. Merisila came into his life slowly. He was lonely despite having people around him. He thought about death and knew it was still a long way off. He longed for it and feared it. He wouldn't die till he had taken revenge. That's what he wanted. But he was tired. Life had worn him down. Whenever he thought he was free, he acquired new bonds. He had rejoiced to have escaped submission to his European master's whims, only to fall under the oppressive yoke of his Turkish master and the whims of his daughter. He had crossed the river to Omdurman in the belief that his troubles had come to an end when the walls of the city of Khartoum came down. Then hunger had held him captive. He had escaped to the land of Egypt and found himself enslaved once more. After a year he went back to Omdurman to be captivated by Hawa. He was drunk on being her slave and dreamed of a new life with her. Now that she was dead, he faced the burden of avenging her murder. Could death alone free him from his bonds? He would be embarrassed to be in her presence if he died without taking revenge on her behalf.

He was sitting pulling strips of dead flesh off his leg when Tajeddin spoke.

In the small room his voice sounded as deep as if it were coming from an ancient trunk. In the past he had never addressed Bakhit, who might as well not have existed. If necessary, he spoke in a whisper, but only with Father Johann. He might look at Mahmoud al-Jirjawi, Mustafa Shaker, or Rifaat Effendi al-Salamouni. But he looked right through Bakhit as if he were a phantom.

That day, after fetching water with Mahmoud al-Jirjawi and Rifaat Effendi al-Salamouni, Bakhit sat in the corner of the cell nursing the wounds that the shackles had caused on his leg. He heard Tajedddin speak. "The Word of God has spoken truly. He who has not brought about his own enslavement is not free," he said.

Bakhit didn't look up, thinking that Tajeddin was speaking to Father Johann. But then Tajeddin said, "Bakhit, don't trouble yourself seeking freedom that you will never obtain, you poor thing."

Mustafa Shaker laughed. "Praise be to God. God is pleased with you, Bakhit. Jesus the prophet of God is speaking to you," he said.

Father Johann stopped weaving the wicker basket he was making. Everyone looked at Bakhit.

"Are you speaking to me, Hajji?" Bakhit asked.

"God has spoken to all mankind, so why wouldn't His prophet speak to you? God has spoken to all mankind but they don't listen. You, you wretch, God has sent you prophets. But like all mankind, you thought that God was addressing the rest of the world and had forgotten you. You idiot! In fact God speaks to people individually."

Bakhit was confused by the abuse, and his cellmates laughed.

"By the Prophet, go easy on the man. He doesn't know what you're like," said Rifaat Effendi al-Salamouni.

Tajeddin had left his home in Marrakesh to go on pilgrimage to Mecca. He passed through Sudan during the years of turmoil. News of the Mahdi reached him and he decided to wait and find out the truth of the matter and to postpone his pilgrimage till the following year. He stayed in Khartoum, watching vigilantly and observing events. He was inclined to believe in the Mahdi but he preferred to bide his time. He did believe when he saw how the city fell miraculously into the hands of the Ansar. He swore allegiance to the Mahdist movement and expected God to triumph. But the Mahdi passed away five months after the conquest of Khartoum. He didn't invade Mecca or Syria and he didn't govern Egypt.

Tajeddin had some knowledge of numerology and bibliomancy. He consulted the Ibn Arabi manuscripts that he had in his possession to see what they had to say, and decided that God's divine decree had changed. He concluded that time was up for the Mahdi and the world could now expect the second coming of Jesus the prophet of God, who would break the Cross and kill the Pig.

"Hajji, I only want to rest," said Bakhit.

"You are the worst of beasts; you are at rest."

"I'm the prisoner of my shackles, Hajji."

Tajeddin looked at the men in the cell, who were following with interest. "Who's going to tell the idiot that a slave never finds rest until he brings about his own enslavement?" he asked impatiently.

Mustafa Shaker laughed. "O prophet of God," he said, "if we could understand what you say, we'd explain it to him."

"Stupid apostles never did the prophets any harm," said Tajeddin.

Bakhit told Merisila what Tajeddin had said and she laughed. She had a laugh as loud as a horse neighing.

"He's a madman saying things that only the mad would understand," she said.

But Bakhit, who didn't really understand what Tajeddin had said, felt there was a grain of truth in it.

When Youssef Effendi Said had spoken to him about love, Bakhit had thought it was nonsense, but he came to believe it when he met Hawa. And now he felt that Tajeddin's nonsense came from the same source. Wisdom is simply what we understand belatedly from the meaningless remarks of the mad.

He crawled through the dark cell, having given up hope that Hawa might come today. He sat cross-legged next to Tajeddin. He whispered his name until he heard him mumbling. "Hajji," Bakhit said, "tell me about the peace of mind that a submissive Muslim feels."

7

Saturday, August 27, 1881

The Europeans don't set a good example for how Christians or civilized people should be. How can we spread the word of the Lord when these people set such a bad example? There's a Frenchman who owns forty slave girls and has had children by some of them. He's imitating the Muslims.

Most of the Europeans who don't work with the government are adventurers looking for opportunities to make money. They are libertines who have no respect for anything and are far from virtuous. Corruption, deceit, and violence are deeply entrenched in them.

Wednesday, February 8, 1882

I saw the celebrations of the birthday of the Prophet Mohamed. The celebrations lasted eight full days and ended yesterday. I visited the scene of the celebrations to the east of the vegetable market. There were large tents decorated with flags and lanterns. There were fireworks, army music, and men drinking coffee. I asked Father Pavlos whether they had hymns.

8

The way Younis Wad Jaber looked at Theodora was unmistakable.

His desire had a smell and a presence. Bakhit could feel it stifling him. Whenever Bakhit ran into him in the street, Younis seemed to be laughing at him, with trickery in his eyes.

Bakhit asked Theodora about him.

"He's a friend," she said.

Bakhit was in torment but he held his tongue.

9

A month before Omdurman fell, he told Merisila that he would like to taste some of her homemade gruel.

"Food is scarce and prices have risen, but nothing is too dear if you ask for it, Bakhit," she said.

"Don't put any of your magic in it," he joked.

She came to see him the next day. He sat with her in the corner and ate with her. The gruel was soft and delicious and he smiled gratefully at Merisila.

"Do you still want to avenge the death of that infidel woman?" she asked.

"That's what I live for," he said.

She said nothing and looked into the distance. He could feel Merisila's affection for him, which had grown in her over the previous five years. He could smell what she was hiding, but he had left his heart on the other side of the river.

"The infidels are advancing," she said, breaking the bonds of silence. "They'll die on the walls of Omdurman and then the Ansar will head out to invade Egypt, and from there they'll invade the world. Rejoice, because this might mean the end of your imprisonment."

He looked at her quizzically.

"There are said to be many invaders. They might need prisoners who believe, as fighters," she said.

"This is no longer my battle," he replied.

"Bakhit, don't delude yourself."

He shook his head stubbornly. Everyone was saying the same thing. Even Hawa was against him taking revenge on her behalf. But he didn't care. He would carry out the mission he had lived for.

The debt that love imposes is heavy. The debt that love imposes is like a chain. But he had learned that freedom lies in being faithful to one's chains.

"Let the infidels come or let them go, it doesn't matter to me today," he said. "I'll keep waiting to take revenge until the right moment comes."

Merisila bowed her head. "What a mule you are, you filthy slave," she murmured.

Fourteen

1

THE BITS AND PIECES PICKED up from the battlefield were piled on the floor of the room. Nafisa Fouda, the wife of Youssef Effendi, and her mother sat on the floor sifting through them.

The old woman didn't like what she saw. Nafisa wasn't interested. Youssef Effendi stood by the door waiting for a kind word from them, but it didn't come. Disappointed and angry, he went out to where Bakhit was sitting and crouched beside him.

"You, Sudanese guy! I'm too poor to look after you, so you'll have to work for your keep until we work out what to do with you," he said.

He was in a bad mood and he looked miserable and feckless.

"Tell me, you Sudanese man. Do you know of any magic that will win a woman's heart?"

"I know how to write," Bakhit said. "And I'm good at several trades. Put me to work and you can have my wages, but I don't know magic."

"There's no work for you in the town but I'll find something for you to do," said Youssef Effendi. "If you knew magic like the other blacks, you could have done me some good, and yourself too. But it's my rotten luck that from the whole of Sudan all I get is a slave who knows how to write."

He patted Bakhit on the shoulder and stood up hesitantly. He walked away, leaving Bakhit alone.

Once again he was a slave. Whenever freedom came his way, he soon found himself a slave again. He submitted to his fate. He was adept at submitting to his fate. He was adept at being a slave.

Bakhit leaned over and lay down. He put his cheek on the ground. He breathed the unfamiliar air of Egypt. It was heavy with loneliness. He tried to think about anything. Any idea or memory to occupy his mind. But he couldn't find anything to think about. He made do with the void inside him. He smiled for nothing. He could hear the old woman complaining. He shut his eyes and tried to sleep, but the flies bothered him.

2

The loneliness of exile in a country that showed no mercy.

A friendless loneliness. Life in Egypt wasn't the life he knew.

He missed the cruelty of being in the Mahdi's army, the narrow streets of Omdurman, the inflated bodies of dead donkeys on the banks of the Nile, the wary arguments of drunks when they were full of beer.

A loneliness without a close companion. Faces of which he had no memories. On top of the hostility of exile there was the hostility of the enemy soldiers.

The houses around him were made of whitewashed mud brick. They seemed to glow at night. They were hidden away, dispersed here and there among the palm trees. Odd, squat palm trees with brightly colored fronds.

The very air was hostile.

Alone and helpless. Helpless and alone.

A slave in a country that showed no mercy.

3

At night, as Bakhit was trying to sleep with his head on a stone, Youssef Effendi threw him an onion and some millet bread.

Bakhit jumped hungrily at the food. He grabbed the onion and bit into it ravenously. Youssef Effendi sat down close to him and looked at him.

He watched him eating the bread—picking up the pieces and pushing them into his mouth.

"It's strange, my Sudanese friend," he said.

Bakhit looked at him inquisitively.

"You people!" he went on. "I can't understand you people. Why did you come to attack us? How could you think of invading Egypt? Why do you hate us? Haven't we treated you well? Is this because of the khedive? We all hate him. I was one of the people who supported Orabi Pasha. That's why they sent me here. But you hate all of Egypt."

His mouth full of onion, Bakhit said, "We're the soldiers of the Mahdi, peace be upon him."

"That dervish was a fraud. Egypt has treated you well. We ruled you honestly and properly. We respected your leaders and your tribal sheikhs. But you didn't return the favor." He paused awhile to think. "My friend Ismail Said was a loyal follower of Orabi Pasha. He was a sincere nationalist. They dismissed him from the army after the defeat. Then they reappointed him when the trouble broke out in Sudan. He went there with Hicks Pasha to set the country straight and put an end to the dervish who pretended to be the Mahdi and who ruined everything and sanctioned so much bloodshed. My friend was an honest, patriotic man. But you people killed him. What did his children do to deserve having their father killed just because you're mad?"

"The Mahdi told us to fight the infidels to bring about the reign of God."

"You're just ungrateful. Sudan was doing well under Egyptian rule, but you're religious fanatics," said Youssef Effendi.

Bakhit's eyes flashed with anger. His body tensed. He thought of pouncing on Youssef Effendi to wring his neck and then run off into the darkness. But his hopelessness held him back. Where could he run to in an unfamiliar country? He wasn't up to shedding blood, and then escaping in Egypt would be difficult.

He looked down despondently. He didn't reply to his master. Youssef Effendi mumbled something angrily. He stood up to go, leaving Bakhit to curse his impotence and feel guilty that he had failed to defend his faith in the Mahdi.

4

At the end of the week Bakhit was coming down one of the palm trees near Youssef Effendi's house when he saw a convoy of soldiers.

He was bare-chested, with a dirty wrap pulled tight over his lower half, partially covering his private parts but leaving some bits exposed. He was picking dates and throwing them to the ground under the tree. With his face hidden in the fronds, he heard the noise the soldiers were making. He leaned out to look but couldn't see anything. When he started coming down the tree trunk he saw their drab uniforms advancing toward the house.

He jumped to the ground and hastily bent down to pick up the dates in a piece of cloth. Then he ran barefoot toward the house.

He arrived as the soldiers stopped outside. They were a group of Sudanese soldiers commanded by a self-important Egyptian. The officer examined Bakhit carefully and asked, "Are you a barbarian?"

Bakhit's heart jumped. "Yes," he answered.

"What's your name?"

"Bakhit Mandil."

The Egyptian took off his fez. He wiped the sweat off his forehead. He told Bakhit to call his master.

"He's not at home. He hasn't come back yet," Bakhit told him.

Nafisa Fouda came out when she heard the noise. The soldiers cast lascivious glances at her obvious charms, so she pulled her black headscarf over her face and stepped back to take cover behind the door. The Egyptian looked down and quietly asked God to protect him from temptation.

"There aren't any men in the house," Nafisa answered from behind the door.

"This Sudanese man," the man said, pointing at Bakhit, "is he one of the dervishes from the Nujoumi group?"

"Yes, he is. My husband captured him a week ago."

"The government has given orders that all the dervishes are to be brought together and moved to the Cataracts prison. You can't keep him here."

She tried to object but the Egyptian man ignored her. The soldiers grabbed Bakhit. The dates fell out of his hand and spilled on the ground. They tied him up with a rope, with his hands behind his back. The old woman came out shouting. "Damn you! You're taking away the slave we won," she said.

The soldiers dragged him off away. He stumbled several times and fell on his face. They picked him up roughly and he had to spit the dust out of his mouth. He pleaded with the Egyptian man to let him go but the soldiers hit him. They put him in a pen with a group of other prisoners. He recognized one of the Jaalin that he had traveled with. He looked at the man with eyes that spoke of weakness and sorrow.

He tried to remember the man's name but he couldn't. He went up to him and greeted him. The man ignored him. Bakhit went off and kept to himself.

Some officials came into the pen and wrote their names in a large ledger. They asked each one which tribe he was from. Bakhit was trembling.

"Sudanese," he said.

"What kind of Sudanese?"

He didn't know how to answer. He couldn't remember where the slavers had brought him from. He only knew himself as a slave in Khartoum. He remembered with difficulty some of the language of the faraway mountains. He used to speak it perfectly but it had melted away.

"From Omdurman," he said softly.

The clerk shook his head and said, "Slave." He wrote it down quickly and went on to the next prisoner.

Bakhit cleared his throat to get rid of the bitter taste. He had been a worker in Omdurman Market. He had been a fighter in God's cause. But after all that he was just a slave that could not go free.

He had no clear memory of the day they caught him in the mountains in the west. Just vague, haunting memories of the slave traders attacking the village. He ran away with his mother and climbed up the rocks. He remembered that he had brothers. Maybe three of them, older than he, and a baby sister who didn't have a name yet. He was terrified. His mother was shouting in the mountain language: "Run away, Shakta, don't stop."

Was Shakta his old name or was it the name of one of his brothers? He couldn't remember exactly. The last thing he saw was his mother falling to the ground and dropping his sister. His little legs hadn't taken him very far when they caught him.

His European master loved the fact that he was black and ugly. When he was alone with him he admired the coarseness of his features. When Bakhit was on top of him, he shouted, "You're my Negro love, you're my ugly slave!"

Bakhit hurt him out of anger and the European man was delighted. Buthayna, the daughter of his Turkish master, Abdüllatif Effendi, liked his blackness. She said that his sperm was rotten worms.

His eyes filled with tears. He succumbed to sadness. He wasn't worried about the morrow because all evil was the same.

5

Theodora carried out her promise and set about teaching him English.

He was an enthusiastic pupil.

"This is English," she told him. "The best-known language in the world. The whole civilized world speaks it."

He wasn't interested in the language but he liked that she was happy to see him learning.

She would come to Idris al-Nubawi's vegetable stall in the market in the afternoon. She opened her notebook, which was full of writing and bits of paper. Bakhit looked and saw squiggles that he couldn't make out. He didn't know that his name covered all the pages. He wanted to learn good English so that he could read what she had written. He confided that to her and she laughed.

"There is some writing in Arabic, but after the fall of Khartoum I started writing in English," she said.

He looked at the page she had opened in front of him. "Why?" he asked. "Why the change after the conquest of Khartoum?"

"Bakhit, the dervishes don't trust people like me," she said. "They might try to read what I've written one day. The people who are good at English are my people, Europeans. They won't hand me over."

He repeated English words after her. She laughed as he struggled with the words. He frowned and said, "You have trouble pronouncing Arabic words too."

"Oh, my black brother, Arabic is a difficult language, but English is easy."

He said the words after her and remembered what they meant. He spelled out the letters in awe. Then she broke off the lesson and said, "I'm going. Younis is waiting for me at the tomb of the Mahdi. He says it's something important."

His heart writhed. "Hawa!" he said.

She looked at him with a smile, innocently. Can't you see how I feel, he said to himself. Can't you feel the heat of my love?

"What does Younis want?"

Her face clouded over in anger. Her eyes were stormy. "What's it to you?" she said. "Why do you ask?" He quickly backed off. In a panic he held back all the words that were on the tip of his tongue. "Nothing. Just curious," he said instead.

She showed him no mercy, and went on the offensive as he mumbled his denial. "It's not curiosity. You're harassing me. Whenever I mention Younis's name I can see the anger in your eyes. You get upset whenever you find out I've met him."

You can see all this, but you can't see that I'm dying on the threshold of the temple that is you.

"Nothing's upsetting me," he said. "Why would I be angry if you mentioned him? I'm just curious."

"You're lying."

She stood up angrily. She left him holding her notebook and walked off. He ran after her with the notebook and called her back. She snatched it from his hands without a word. She looked at him in fury and went on her way.

Bakhit went back meekly to Idris's stall. He sat down under it, his mind distracted. Idris leaned toward him. "What's up with the Christian woman, storming off like that?" he asked.

Painfully, Bakhit told him what had happened.

Idris laughed. "You're blind," he said.

Bakhit looked at him in puzzlement.

"May God cut my head off if that jihadi guy didn't take her off to some secluded spot," said Idris.

"Damn you!" Bakhit shot back. "You're crazy."

Idris laughed noisily. Bakhit's heart raced. His spirits sank. Was it possible that Idris was right?

He picked up his sadness and ran off. In his imagination he saw her in Younis's arms. Her body was like the day he saw her bathing, with the water running over her, as naked as a wild rose, as white as the milk of bulbuls. Her chestnut hair was wet and stuck to her neck and her cheeks. She had a neck as long as a gazelle's and breasts like the fruits of the baobab tree, and Younis was holding her.

Bakhit screamed in the street.

6

The specter of Theodora was a costly jewel that he held in his arms as he sought precious sleep.

When he was awake, he saw her in dreadful daydreams. He embraced her and smelled her musky scent. He writhed in pain. He thought about the time she had come back from meeting Younis. After going to the Mahdi's tomb, where had they gone? He roamed the streets imagining. From the Mahdi's tomb there was a narrow street that ended at the Jihadiya barracks. He remembered her touching Younis's arm with her hand. He looked at his feet and tried to bury the memory. He thought of Theodora as drops of rain, innocent, untainted by contact with the world. But she was stupid and didn't recognize evil when she saw it. Her lips haunted him. He knew they had never been touched.

She was as beautiful as Omdurman. But she crushed him as Khartoum had crushed him.

He was on fire with desire, torn to pieces by his own anger. He sought sleep because the painful dreams roared inside him. He longed for her as a dervish longs for Paradise.

He cursed his friend Idris and his tears flowed.

7

Youssef Effendi bit into the sugarcane and sucked it with pleasure. His mouth dripping with juice, he said, "Love is the curse of man, my Sudanese friend, but the comfort of woman."

Bakhit Mandil laughed in admiration. He chewed on his own stick of sugarcane and nodded.

"My cousin Nafisa is the love of my life. But nothing will ever satisfy her. She's happy that I love her. But I . . ." He spat out the sugarcane and banged the stick on his chest. "I'm sitting here with you eating sugarcane until she calms down and accepts me. Women are crazy, my Sudanese friend."

Ever since Youssef Effendi caught up with him in the stockade and paid the soldiers a ransom for his release, Bakhit had liked his master. He felt indebted to him. He had saved him from the clutches of the government and taken him back to his house. Youssef Effendi laughed when he saw Bakhit look back in alarm when they were on their way home.

"Don't worry, my Sudanese friend," he said. "Bribes work like magic with soldiers. No one will ever bother you again."

When they reached the house the old woman screamed. She was never happy with anything.

"You idiot!" she said. "The soldiers saved you the trouble of looking after him and then you go off looking for him. Why have you brought the slave back here?"

Nafisa frowned and moved away without a word. She didn't speak much, but you could tell from her shadow on the ground that she was annoyed. She lived in the house as if she were in prison.

She went about her work grudgingly. She didn't answer her husband till he had called several times. Only rarely did she look at him. Her mother, Wasifa Salama, never stopped talking. She complained the whole night long and shouted all day.

The day Youssef Effendi brought Bakhit back he asked Nafisa to make them some food. "Bring us something to eat. The Sudanese guy has had the fright of his life," he said, ignoring the old lady.

"We don't have anything to eat," Nafisa muttered.

Youssef Effendi went to the kitchen himself and came back with a covered dish. He didn't ask her if he could. "That's the remains of my lunch!" the old woman shouted. "Are you going to feed it to the slave?"

"Really, my dear, I'm hungry too," he said.

"And what have I done to deserve having you eat my food?" she said.

He ignored her and gestured to Bakhit to follow him outside. They sat down under the palm tree and ate the food.

"She's short-tempered but kind," he said apologetically.

By the time they were eating sugarcane again four months later, Bakhit had discovered that the only kind person there was his master, Youssef Effendi. The man escaped from his wife ignoring him and from her mother's sharp tongue by sitting and talking with him. He read poetry to him and laughed when he saw how ignorant he was.

"The poet said: 'If my head was nicked by the sword, then my head would fly off and quickly fall in her direction.' I love her but I'm not in a hurry to have her love me. Her aversion to me will disappear with time. Patience is the lover's best ally against rejection."

"How long have you been married?" asked Bakhit.

"Three years. She's my cousin. My uncle gave her to me in marriage and then died. She didn't like him sending her to me here. She loves Cairo. This exile is killing the two of us. That's why I forgive her. Her aversion to me will diminish. I know that."

Youssef Effendi loved his wife, and poetry was his consolation. His house was full of books. He had crates in which dozens of them were piled up. Bakhit read some of the titles on the covers. *The Meadows of Gold*, a history book. *The Methodology of Egyptian Minds* and *The Insights of Tawfik al-Galil*, both by Rifa'a al-Tahtawi. *Encyclopedia of Witty Constructs* by Ahmad Faris al-Shidyaq.

When Youssef Effendi came out at night to wake Bakhit up, Bakhit knew his wife had rejected and abused him. Bakhit fought off his drowsiness and sat with his master.

"Let's discuss poetry, my Sudanese friend," said the Egyptian.

"I don't memorize poetry," said Bakhit. "I just memorize the Quran."

"Amazing," said Youssef Effendi sadly. "That's good. But it won't do for tonight."

Then he came up with an idea and beamed. "Never mind," he said. "I'll recite a poem and you say the first word

233

that comes into your head that starts with the last letter in the line of the poem. That way we can have fun."

Nothing that happened to Youssef Effendi made him angry. He was easily satisfied. He told Bakhit about his wife's dislike for him as if he were telling a joke. He would come out of the house to escape her wrath without any bitterness.

"'If your heart softened toward me and showed mercy, I would no longer endure the pain of passion.' That's *n*, my Sudanese friend."

Bakhit hesitated and then said, "Nizam."

"Then that would be *m*. How about that line from the Muallaqa of Imrul Qays: 'Men's games cease with their youth, but my heart does not cease to love her.' So take an *r*."

"Rapist," Bakhit said without thinking.

Youssef Effendi was taken aback. He looked at Bakhit in surprise and laughed. "Rapist? Okay. So that's a *t*. 'Those by whose partings and meetings I distracted the designs of fate and forgot the day when I returned.' A line from 'Majnoun Leila,' the poem about the man driven mad by his love for Leila."

"So what letter is that?"

"*D*, Bakhit."

Youssef Effendi was relaxed and seemed happy with the poetry. He looked like a man sitting with a friend, not with his slave.

"*D*? Okay, death," said Bakhit.

"That's a bit gloomy, Bakhit. Say something else."

"Distress."

Youssef Effendi laughed. "That's not very nice either, but never mind. So that would be *s*."

He mumbled as he tried to remember. Then he said, "From 'Majnoun' as well: 'Some say that for a woman such as Leila a man would kill himself, even if you were wrapped in despair over Leila.' So that's an *a*, Bakhit."

234

Bored, Bakhit didn't say anything. He didn't understand the game and he wasn't interested. Youssef Effendi prodded him. "I don't know," Bakhit replied.

He thought of saying "army," but he had no desire to take part in this nonsense that he didn't understand and the words he chose at random put him in a bad mood.

Youssef Effendi tried hard to tempt him, but it was no use. Bakhit was profoundly unenthusiastic. The Egyptian sighed in exasperation; then his restless mind drove him to pursue their conversation.

"Have you heard of this Majnoun who the poem is about?" he asked.

"He's a madman from your country?"

Youssef Effendi laughed. "No, he's an ancient Arab poet. He fell in love with his cousin but his uncle disapproved and wouldn't let them marry."

He told Bakhit the story of Qays. He told it with passion. When he reached the part where Leila dies, his voice quavered as he recited the lines that Majnoun composed over her grave: "O grave of Leila, if we had seen you, then women of all kinds, Arabs and non-Arabs, would have lamented you. O grave of Leila, they have honored her place that is yours and as long as we live she will bring us blessings. And, O grave of Leila, Leila is a stranger in your land, without a friend or a cousin." His tears glistened by the light of the stars. "That's what love is, Bakhit," said Youssef Effendi. "That's what love is: to become a dervish to the one you love."

Bakhit nodded and thought about sleeping. He had a hard day ahead of him. Youssef Effendi expected him to fetch water from the canal half a mile away. But Youssef Effendi did not tire of repeating "That's what love is."

Fifteen

WHEN TAJEDDIN THE MOROCCAN ABANDONED his silence, he took Bakhit's hand and took him out to the courtyard.

They watched the birds landing on the ground to look for seeds that had been forgotten. The guards were strutting around among the prisoners. The shackles on their legs made life miserable. In fact, misery was all around them. The sad sparrows picked up the seeds of despair and flew away.

"You were asking me about peace of mind for good Muslims," said Tajeddin.

"I am the prisoner of my sorrows," said Bakhit.

Tajeddin was thin, with dark-brown skin. He had mad eyes partly covered by bushy eyebrows. His beard was as white as the clouds and he buried his fingers in it, combing it in silence. Prisoners walking by, bantered with him.

"Hey, Jesus! Hey, Spirit of God!" said one.

Bakhit told them off.

"That's peace of mind, Bakhit," said the old man.

He pulled his fingers out of his beard and pointed at them. "They're content in their sadness. What happens to them doesn't do them any harm. Do you think I'm happy that God has given me the task of conveying His message?"

"Are you a prophet?" asked Bakhit.

Tajeddin looked at him and frowned. "You idiot!" he said. "The signs of the Hour are these." He counted them

237

out on his fingers. "It grows darker. God sends the Mahdi. Then my time comes."

Bakhit nodded. He thought of taking Tajeddin to Touma. His words could be tested in front of a flirtatious woman, or between her legs. Bakhit had gone through his test. Touma had never aroused him. Hawa was stronger inside him than any other woman. Would Tajeddin's prophetic vocation withstand that test? His master, Youssef Effendi, had once said to him, "Love is the strongest of the fundamental forces."

Youssef Effendi believed in his love, but he didn't have peace of mind.

"Have you seen the sparrows?" asked Tajeddin.

Bakhit looked where Tajeddin was pointing at. He knew the sparrows, and she knew them too. He had been giving her sparrows to make her forget Younis's bird.

"What about them, Hajji?"

"Those are the lowliest birds there are. They're a plague. They land on the ground every day to steal the things that people have dropped. And people catch them. Children play with them. The birds are happy with whatever they find. They have found peace of mind and they believe in it. Do you believe in your situation, you jackass?"

"Are you advising me to accept being in prison?"

"Is being in prison the end of the path?"

"I can't see the path."

"You fool, how can a blind man be afraid of the dark?"

He thought about the old man's words. Did peace of mind for him lie in his ordeal? Hawa was his ordeal. Or was she the path? Or was the path his peace of mind? He didn't understand.

"Tell me something I can understand," he said.

"Ask me about peace of mind and you'll understand."

He saw her face filling the heavens.

"I want her."

"Then go to her if you're telling the truth."

"So I should kill myself?"

"That's one way. Or you could submit to God and believe in the path that lies at your feet. Do you think I'm happy that God has given me the task of conveying the message?"

"What path is this, that doesn't let me know what tomorrow will bring?" asked Bakhit.

Tajeddin reached out and put his hand on Bakhit's chest. "The stupid birds come out every day. All they know is they're going out to forage and to stay alive, but they don't know what's going to happen to them."

"Are you advising me to be stupid?"

"I'm advising you to have faith."

"But I'm sad."

"You're sad because you're not content."

Bakhit heard the clanking of chains behind him. He turned and saw Father Johann approaching. Johann always reminded him of Theodora.

"I'm not content because I don't understand," said Bakhit.

Tajeddin tapped him gently on the head. "You're looking for peace of mind, not to understand," he said.

Father Johann came up to them and smiled at Bakhit. "Is the old man playing with your mind?" he said with a laugh.

"You Christian," Tajeddin replied. "Prophets speak to people's hearts."

"That's true," Johann said gravely. "So do you know what language the heart of our poor friend understands?"

Tajeddin bristled and his brown face glowered. "Is that the kind of question you'd put to a prophet?" he said.

Bakhit left them to argue. Father Johann was joking pleasantly, while Tajeddin was defensive and tense. Bakhit went into the cell, dragging his chains behind him. He had to take short steps. The shackles were digging into his leg, but they no longer hurt. Am I comfortable in the shackles? he wondered uncertainly.

2

Omdurman angered Hassan al-Jerifawi.

What had come over people? What had become of the Mahdi's cause?

Hassan wandered around a city that had lost its way. The streets were whispering about Othman Sheikheddin, the son of the Khalifa. They said that the Khalifa was preparing him as his successor. Would the Khalifa overrule the decree of the Mahdi, peace be upon him? The Mahdi had named four men to succeed him in turn. The first was the Khalifa Abdallah, who had the same status as the caliph Abu Bakr al-Siddiq, and then there was the Khalifa Ali Wad Hilw, the equivalent of the caliph Omar al-Farouq. As the equivalent of the caliph Othman ibn Affan, the Mahdi had named the Libyan leader Mohamed al-Mahdi al-Senussi, who didn't even believe in the Mahdi at the time, but the Mahdi had promised that he would inevitably come around. The fourth in line was the Mahdi's nephew, the Khalifa Sharif, whom the Mahdi had brought up as a boy and married to his daughter. Was the Khalifa Abdallah going to change the Mahdi's will?

At home, people talked about Othman Sheikheddin's parties, at which beer was drunk and singing girls appeared. People coming from the borders said he was receiving mail from Egypt, including Turkish books and foreign newspapers.

People still believed, as Hassan knew they had in the past. The commanders were hoarding valuables. Their close associates were plotting against each other. In the market cheating was rife, and the gallows were in constant use. Every morning boys collected from the riverbank the bodies of babies that their mothers had disposed of to avoid the shame of illegitimacy.

What has come over you, Omdurman? Hassan wondered. Was it for this that we swore allegiance to the Mahdi, peace be upon him?

The night they entered Khartoum, the Mahdi stood up and said: "Swear allegiance to me on pain of death."

What has come over us? Has our faith rotted away?

The Mahdi said to us: "This world is the abode of those who have no abode, and it is the prison of believers. The Afterlife is better. It lasts longer and it is the abode of the godly. So fear God and work for the day when you will return to God."

Hassan walked through the streets of the city and couldn't see any of the things for which they had sworn allegiance to the Mahdi.

He remembered Fatma, the love of his life, and he couldn't think why he had left her. His faith was troubling him. What he saw pained him.

In confusion he headed to the home of Ibrahim Wad al-Shawwak. A slave with a limp met him at the door. He asked for his friend Abdel-Gayoum.

"My master, Othman Sheikheddin, summoned him so he went off there," the slave said.

Hassan asked after Sheikh Ibrahim.

"He's in the men's reception room," said the slave.

He walked along the wall of the house, wrapped in sadness. "Anyone in this city who hasn't been consumed by sadness has no soul," he said to himself. He turned left, stopped at the door to the men's reception room, and called Sheikh Ibrahim. The sheikh came out, smiling as usual. He embraced him and Hassan kissed his head. At social gatherings around the city Hassan had heard disturbing things about the sheikh. But Hassan was one of the Mahdi's soldiers and the sheikh was a close associate of the Khalifa, so he couldn't believe what he had heard. He showed affection and esteem for him, because he knew better than anyone the good work Sheikh Ibrahim had done when the Mahdi was besieging Khartoum.

"Welcome, my honorable friend!" Sheikh Ibrahim exclaimed as he led him in.

He showed him into his reception room. Hassan sat cross-legged on an embroidered green cushion and rested his feet on the fine carpets. Sheikh Ibrahim called his slaves to bring some food. Hassan said he wouldn't be eating. Sheikh Ibrahim looked at him quizzically.

"It's anxiety," Hassan explained. "The anxiety, dear sheikh, means I'm not in the mood to eat."

"My boy, has something happened to weaken your faith?"

Hassan thought about it in silence. Had his faith weakened? This anxiety. All this pain.

"I don't know, my sheikh," he said.

He aired his misgivings. He talked about his anxiety. His pain. His sadness. His uncertainty. He wept and his tears ran as he told his story.

"What if the Mahdi were to see us today?" he said in anguish.

Sheikh Ibrahim's eyes flashed. He stood up from his seat. He walked around the room tensely. He turned to Hassan and looked at him as if he were trying to read his mind.

"My boy," he said. "The Devil is playing with your heart. This city is the creation of the Mahdi, peace be upon him. He built it under God's caring eye. Have you forgotten the day he preached to us in Khartoum? The day he forbade us from living in the homes of those who had fallen into evil ways. He told us to cross the river to this place. To this sacred spot, Omdurman. This piece of land that the infidels had not tainted. God chose it to receive the Mahdi's body. Didn't you know that God created the Mahdi out of the light in the heart of the Prophet? What ground could be purer and more sacred than ground that has received the Mahdi, peace be upon him?"

The sheikh came up to him, sat down beside him, and put his hand on Hassan's shoulder. "The Khalifa is following in the footsteps of the Mahdi," he continued hypnotically. "Are the rumors the only thing you notice in the city? Can't you see the mosques packed with believers? Can't you see the people that the Khalifa has compelled to memorize the Quran?"

Hassan nodded pensively.

"These rumors!" Sheikh Ibrahim continued. "The things you're complaining about are rumors. The infidels have spies among us, my boy. They're the ones who are spreading these reports. They make up stories. They say untrue things about the faithful. Don't believe everything that's said. Listen to God's advice: '*Why is it that when you believers, men and women, heard it, you didn't think well of each other and say, "It's obviously untrue?"*' Do you have better counsel than the word of God, my son?"

"God forbid, sir."

Sheikh Ibrahim smiled and looked into Hassan's eyes. "I have the cure for your ailment, my son," he said. "The Devil found his way to you when you abandoned jihad. When was the last campaign you took part in?"

"I came back from the Abyssinian campaign in the seventh year. But I went to Suakin twice with Commander Othman Digna to fight."

"How long ago was that? Five years?"

"Maybe three."

Sheikh Ibrahim looked shocked. "That's too much, my son. Faith gets rusty. And the sword gets rusty. That's what's wrong with you. If you go back to jihad you'll see things differently. Have you signed up for Commander Mahmoud Wad Ahmad's campaign?"

"No, I haven't."

"That's a shame, my boy," said the sheikh. "A great shame. The infidels are advancing. They are close to Dongola. That's why their many spies are spreading rumors. Every day some infidel escapes from the city to join them. The infidels are escaping whenever the chance arises. I had an infidel servant I had raised as if she were my daughter. Then she ran away. That was some years ago, five or six. At that time an infidel or two would run away every few months. What do you say I sign you up for Commander Mahmoud's army? You could go off with him to fight the infidels. You could fight and raise the banners of God."

"I fear my guilt might prevent me enjoying jihad, dear sheikh," Hassan said sadly.

"Those are the ravings of the Devil, my boy. I assure you that when you hear the Ansar shouting 'In God's cause!' and see God's swords glinting in the sky, you'll forget all these worries and fight. Don't you miss the pleasure of jihad?"

"I miss the pleasures of faith, dear sheikh," said Hassan.

"So go, my son, with God's blessings. When you go this time you'll find your faith," said Ibrahim.

Hassan nodded obediently.

Sheikh Ibrahim laughed loudly and said, "Shake off this sadness, because now you know how to cure it. In a few days you'll be a mujahid fighter again, my boy. Congratulations."

3

Bakhit put his finger at random on a line in Theodora's notebook. "What does this mean?" he asked.

"Try to read it," she answered.

He tried to make out the foreign letters she had taught him. He pronounced the phrase with difficulty, then looked up at her. "I've got it," he said, happy as a child.

Her face beamed. "Read it," she said.

"Man is a lonely being. Even when there are noisy people around him, his only companion on the path of his suffering is himself."

"That's me, Bakhit," she said.

4

It was the night of the twenty-seventh day of the month of Rajab, the night of the Prophet's ascent to heaven from Jerusalem. The angels descended on the mosque of the Mahdi to attend to the faithful. The congregation was chanting the Mahdi's special liturgy. The beating of drums shook the darkness. The Ansar were calling, "Allah! Allah! Allah!" and Taher Jibril was carrying his charge as he rode his horse surreptitiously through the city streets. He asked for a grave-digger and they recommended a slave called Bakhit Mandil.

He asked after Bakhit and was told that he was at a friend's house in the Abu Seid district. He went on, his heart weighed down by its burden. He had no choice but to obey, because a true believer doesn't raise doubts. He stole through the dark streets, pursued by the pounding of the drums. He stood outside the house and could hear the sound of revelers inside.

"Greetings! Is there anyone at home?" he called out angrily.

Idris al-Nubawi came out, drunk on home-brewed beer. In disapproval Hassan said a quick prayer, and then asked for the gravedigger by the name of Bakhit. The thin black slave emerged from the thick darkness. He was drunk and unsteady on his feet.

Hassan didn't notice his face. He never imagined the man would kill him seven years and a few months later. If he had known he would kill him he would have looked at him more closely on that day. But Hassan had no idea who Bakhit was, and he had the weight of his charge to distract him.

When Bakhit left him for dead, gushing blood, he didn't regret it. He had hated him since the moment he saw his vast frame. He hated the money he had paid to him. He saw it as filth that tainted him. He had seen Hassan before he met Naim—the guide and son of al-Hajj Taha—later that night toward dawn. By then Bakhit was even drunker. Naim looked at him and asked him who he was.

"Leave him. He's suffering," said Idris al-Nubawi.

But Naim wanted to talk to get it off his chest. He blurted out the story of Theodora, giving Bakhit the news.

Oh darkness of the world, shout out,
Oh devils of the earth, go on the rampage,
To be buried by his hands rather than someone else's?
Was it in his heart that he should plant the ax?
Fires burned inside him. Was it your strong beer, Idris? Or was it anger for your sake, Hawa?

He was devastated by the news he heard, and Naim was just chatting away regardless.

When he hadn't known, he was happy in his suffering. Why did he ever have to find out?

With his hands rather than someone else's?

Oh, the blood that had stained him unawares.

As he was cutting into Taher's fingers, Bakhit asked him: "Who told the details to Abdel-Gayoum?"

"I don't know. I didn't ask. I'm a soldier who's given orders and obeys."

As Hassan was feeding him, a day short of Musallamiya, Bakhit told Hassan al-Jerifawi the story. Hassan didn't say a word. But Hassan thought, "Wasn't it our downfall that, when we were given orders, we did what we were told?"

God confound him! If he had disobeyed, he would have survived.

5

If he had disobeyed, he would have survived.

If he had disobeyed, he would have survived.

The horses galloped into Metemma. Fire swept through the houses. Women were screaming. Men rushed toward death, which received them with a welcome.

The city was torn apart. Allahu akbar. White smoke.

Kill the infidels. They have betrayed Islam. Kill the dogs.

He shouted, raised his spear, and rushed on.

6

Wednesday, June 4, 1884
The Egyptian traders have hidden grain. Prices have doubled. Fadl al-Aziz says that the shopping allowance is no longer enough to buy anything, and Father Pavlos doesn't know what to do about it.

The city is reeling from hunger. The siege is getting tighter and the local people can't find enough to eat. Gordon has refused to expel the families of people who support the dervishes. Supplies are inadequate but Gordon is giving out grain to Sudanese families who are known to have relatives fighting on the western side of the river and besieging Khartoum.

The consuls and prominent Europeans and Egyptians formed a delegation that met Gordon and spoke to him about this. If these people were expelled from the city it would be possible to save the supplies for government supporters who deserve to have them.

Tuesday, July 1, 1884
Gordon Pasha has obtained a fatwa from the Muslim scholars in the city allowing Muslims not to fast in Ramadan because of the war.

Wednesday, September 3, 1884
I heard a big noise in the street. I looked out of the window and couldn't see anything. I went downstairs and found one of the maids on the ground floor. I asked her what was happening. She said that the pasha, meaning Gordon, had ordered that the dependents of people who support the dervishes be expelled from the city. They are to cross the river and go to the enemy camp on the western bank.

Friday, October 10, 1884
News has spread that Gordon has despaired of writing to the dervishes and that he sent their commander, al-Nujoumi, a letter yesterday, Thursday, breaking off negotiations with him.

7
In his last year Bakhit grew close to Tajeddin the Moroccan.

He became his inseparable companion. Tajeddin's madness brought comfort to Bakhit's heart. From him he learned to pray regularly and he even became enthusiastic about praying. He stood in front of his Lord to ask Him for peace of mind and seek forgiveness for whatever misdeeds he might commit. The years of imprisonment wore him down. He grew used to it and began to take on board the idea that he was bound to stay in prison forever. When he spoke to others, he claimed he was going to leave prison and take revenge. But inside himself he became reconciled to life in prison.

He was held captive in the Sayir prison. That was his excuse for not taking revenge. He knew that peace of mind lay in resignation to his fate, and that freedom lay at the heart of bondage. Man was most free when he was a truly a slave.

He attended to Tajeddin like a slave to his master. As a disciple to his prophet.

"You're almost like Saint Paul the Apostle," Father Johann teased him.

Merisila visited him, bringing him life. He felt a responsibility toward her. She told him that Niamat al-Sater had died and that she herself had moved to her mother's old house. She was maturing day by day. A shiny black grape hanging on the vine of misery. He asked her if she had a man in her life. She laughed.

"There's not a man in Omdurman whose temperament I don't know," she said. "There's not a man in Omdurman whose ability and strength I don't know. But they don't deserve Merisila."

"What strange things you say!"

She shrugged with indifference. "They're all full of themselves," she said. "They think they're studs. Stupid goats."

"Are you looking for love?" he asked.

She looked at him disapprovingly. "You and your crazy white talk!" she said. "What's love? A woman wants one man, someone she can rely on, someone who satisfies her so that she doesn't need anyone else. But the love you cry over is just one of those white people's fantasies that you dream up with them. Those fantasies have been your ruin, haven't they?"

"Love, Merisila, is like a sting in the heart. But it also gives joy. Like you, I was surprised when Youssef Effendi used to tell me about it. But when I felt it I realized how pleasant it was."

She pursed her lips. "Bullshit!" she said.

He laughed at her language.

He told her how Youssef Effendi loved his wife Nafisa Fouda. How his wife tormented him. How Youssef Effendi took comfort if one day his wife let slip a smile. It was as if the sun had come out after a long period of cloudy weather. The nights Youssef Effendi spent trying to win his wife over. How he hated his sinister mother-in-law, Wasifa Salama, but he sought her approval in the hope that it would please his beloved. As he told the story, Merisila watched indignantly. She looked irritated. Her heart seethed with an intensity that she didn't understand.

She looked at his coarse features, his chubby fingers, the wrinkled folds of skin on his knuckles, the smell of suffering and oppression that he gave off. His big sad eyes that looked as if he had just finished a lifetime of crying. But he also seemed to have more pride than some of the commanders and leaders she had known. The ones who would run after a nubile Abyssinian girl that they happened to catch sight of in the street, and then crawled to Merisila, their eyes burning with desire and seeking a way to meet the girl. She offered them her services, arranged trysts, provided them with advice. Then she locked them up in her house and waited outside, calculating her profits. When, sooner or later, they finished and came out, the men looked like docile, insignificant creatures. They had spent their seed, and thrown away their prestige and authority too. They came out breathless and stumbling, and they only wanted to escape. But she saw Bakhit Mandil as a legend. He was prone to strange emotions and sometimes appeared to be docile, but the more submissive he was to his love the more he seemed incandescent in his virility.

The last time she visited him in prison, nineteen days before the city fell, she had wanted to be able to touch his arm. He was talking about Hawa. He was going over the painful memory of Younis and threatening revenge. As she listened, she had to resist an overwhelming desire to touch him. By a miracle she managed to restrain herself.

As she was leaving that time, Tajeddin saw her. "What's the story?" he asked Bakhit.

"She says the infidels are advancing," said Bakhit. "The Ansar will meet them outside Omdurman."

"What's the story of the girl?"

"The girl? She's Merisila. She's been coming here for years."

Tajeddin watched her disappear behind the walls before he resumed. "I have known her for years. But she wasn't like that many years ago." Then, before Bakhit had a chance to ask him what he meant, he added: "Come on, it's time for prayers."

8

Bakhit read what Theodora had written in her notebook.

> Don't let the passing days make you sad. That suffering is over and salvation is nigh. I don't understand those who fear death. What do people have against salvation?

He was thinking about her. About her sadness and suffering. Did they save her from her suffering?

Even so, he would kill Naim Wad Hajj Taha the guide that night.

Sixteen

1

DISASTER STRUCK HIS MASTER, Youssef Effendi Said, in a way he wasn't expecting.

Bakhit could see the waters gathering, giving warning of a flood. But he was still inexperienced and didn't trust his own judgment. He just watched in silence. He didn't know whether he should trust his nascent instincts or not. His master, Youssef Effendi, looked weak and fragile and unable to handle news of the kind he would bring him. So he took shelter in silence and continued to observe.

Their neighbor, Fawzi Amin, was a swarthy man. He always wore a squat, funny-looking fez. He was stout and well built, but he had the face of a newborn baby. He had a mustache that was soaked in oil and he laughed like an innocent child. When Bakhit met him on the road, Fawzi embraced him and said, "Hello, hello, my Sudanese friend."

He insisted on inviting Bakhit to eat at his house but Bakhit was evasive. Fawzi Amin dropped in on Youssef Effendi's house every few days. He stood at the door and sent his greetings. Bakhit noticed how Nafisa smiled at him. He could see the excitement in her face, which flushed when she heard Fawzi's voice. When Fawzi visited her husband, she rushed to the kitchen to make strong black tea. She had a spring in her step and looked as hale and hearty as a plant that had just been watered. Fawzi drank the tea with relish and praised it loudly. Youssef Effendi beamed.

"Thank you very much," he said.

"This tea is fit for a sultan," he said in a loud voice. "You're a lucky man, Youssef Effendi."

When he was gone, Youssef Effendi made nice to his wife by saying how their neighbor had praised her handiwork. "Bless you and well done," he said. "Fawzi loved the tea."

She pursed her lips and went off unimpressed.

Her old mother praised Fawzi. Bakhit heard her saying, "He's a generous man. He doesn't keep his money to himself. His house lacks for nothing. Whenever he goes out visiting people at home, he always has a present to give."

Fawzi Amin bought the old woman some cloth and Bakhit carried it over. He gave Bakhit a message to go with it: "He said he had brought some new Indian material that only you deserve to wear."

When Youssef Effendi saw how happy Wasifa Salama was with the gift, he hurried off to Fawzi Amin for more of it. Fawzi swore he wouldn't take money for it and loaded him up with as much as he wanted as a gift, with many smiles and kind words. Overjoyed, Youssef Effendi took the cloth back home but the older woman met him with a scowl and took it from him grudgingly.

When her husband was away, Nafisa seemed cheerful and radiant. She flounced around happily, singing, "Come around, my love. If you don't come to me, I'll come to you, and if the sea is too deep, you can climb up my heart to reach me."

There was something brewing in the air. Bakhit thought he could see tragedy approaching. It was sniffing at his master's arms and legs and was about to bite him. But he had his doubts.

At night his master would come to him carrying some food or cold tea. He sat down and told him sad stories about Arab lovers and their poetry. He asked him about Sudan, the Mahdi, and the dervishes. He was amazed at how they hated civilization and loved death.

"My Sudanese friend," he said, "I'll never understand you as long as I live."

"And I'll never understand what you say about love, sir, as long as I live," Bakhit replied. After a year in the same household, Bakhit spoke to Youssef with great familiarity.

Youssef Effendi smiled. "Don't speak too soon," he said. "Everyone is bound to fall in love."

2

A crisis was approaching.

One day Bakhit went home before his master, and Nafisa came in after him, out of breath. Her eyes were flashing and she was breathing rapidly. When she saw him she looked at him threateningly but didn't say anything. She threw off her gown and rushed to her mother.

They whispered to each other and laughed. When Youssef Effendi came in they fell silent.

In Bakhit's mind the name Fawzi Amin had a powerful impact, but he didn't know why.

He was watching the storm approach from the crest of the dam.

His heart told him that the horror was imminent. But he didn't speak out because he wasn't sure that he knew.

3

Once when Theodora hadn't come by for a long time, Bakhit decided to do something crazy.

"I'll tell her I've gone mad and I want to give back something that she left with me," he said to Idris al-Nubawi.

Idris brushed the flies off his vegetables.

"That would be childish. She wouldn't believe you," he said.

"It doesn't matter. I want to see her."

"Ask her lame friend about her."

"I'm not looking for news of her!" he exclaimed in frustration. "I want to *see* her."

"What can I tell you?" said Idris fatalistically. "You're crazy about her. Off you go. Soon I'll see you hanging from the gallows in the market."

Bakhit left the market and headed to the bank of the Nile. He set up his trap on the ground and covered it with some soil. He hid some way off and waited. After a while some sparrows landed to forage. One of them was careless and the trap snapped shut on it. Bakhit came out of his hiding place and the other birds flew away. He held the bird gently in the palm of his hand.

He walked through the city streets, anxious it might be too obvious he was in love. He stared at the ground in case the passersby saw Theodora in his big eyes. When he reached the house of Sheikh Ibrahim Wad al-Shawwak he didn't linger at the door. He plucked up his courage and went into the servants' quarters. The women looked at him in surprise. They flashed furtive smiles and spread out around the large courtyard. He stood there speechless, unsure what to say. Should he call Sabah al-Kheir or should he ask for Hawa? He froze to the spot and felt the sweat on his forehead and under his armpits. But God took pity on him when he saw her coming out of the gate between the servants' courtyard and the courtyard of the main house. With her eyes lowered, she was walking alongside Abdel-Gayoum, Sheikh Ibrahim's son. He was walking with a swagger and talking with her. His eyes were fawning over her, touching her. As he spoke to her, his smile was as vicious as that of a rat gnawing on a piece of bread. And she, the love of his life, was smiling too. She wasn't speaking. She was walking alongside Abdel-Gayoum, listening to what he was saying and smiling. She had an aura that was magical and playful. When Abdel-Gayoum turned to go back she looked up and saw Bakhit.

He was burning with anger, but at the same time he loved the happiness of seeing her. He was deeply conflicted. But she smiled. She hurried toward him as the other servants looked on surreptitiously.

"Bakhit, thank God you've come," she said.

But he didn't say anything. He offered her a sad look. He left his sadness in her tender hand and turned to go. Without a word. He couldn't find words harsh enough to reflect his state of mind. When he left the house he remembered that he hadn't given her the sparrow he was holding in his hand. He opened his fist and the bird flew away with a flutter.

He walked off with his anger. In a feeble voice, his desire for her told him to linger. But he didn't look back. She watched him go with an anger that outdid his anger. She was irate with him to the point of hating him. And when he did finally look back, her reaction betrayed the fact that she really did care for him. She was about to call him back to appease him, but he slipped away before she could speak. Two days later, when she met him at Idris al-Nubawi's stall, he was still speechless and she was hesitant. She smiled at him flirtatiously.

"What's up with you?" she asked.

He didn't reply. He looked at her in search of answers to the questions that had kept him awake for the past two days. She didn't look angry that Abdel-Gayoum had been so friendly toward her. She wasn't as annoyed as he might have expected. He could have killed Abdel-Gayoum then and there if he had seen any sign that she was rejecting his attentions. But she looked happy. Happy? Was she really happy? If she wasn't happy, then why was she smiling?

"I was embarrassed," she said. "I don't know how to stop him harassing me. I wasn't giving my consent, Bakhit," she said.

"I didn't ask you for an explanation," he mumbled.

"But I owe you one. And you owe me an apology. You insulted me."

He was shocked. "I insulted you?" he shouted angrily.

Her wonderful face looked upset. "You walked off rudely and left me. I was looking forward to seeing you."

Looking forward to seeing you.

Looking forward to seeing you.

He shuddered at the phrase. He stammered. His mouth was full of words and they spilled out, all mixed up and with no clear meaning.

She knitted her brow and said, "You're very dear to me. But you offended me with what you did. The maids were making snide remarks all night about how stupid you are."

He found the words to apologize and they poured out of him in the heat of the moment. She acted coy and showed her pain at what he had done. Then she forgave him. She beamed in delight and Idris al-Nubawi watched him angrily. When she laughed at Bakhit, he jumped to his feet.

"Where are you off to?" she asked.

"I'm going to catch you another sparrow," he said enthusiastically.

4

Bakhit stood in the empty house, unsure what had happened.

Where were Nafisa Fouda and the old woman, Wasifa Salama? The house looked as if it had been abandoned. The furniture was out of place. The sheets and the pots and pans were missing. The rooms that were always closed were now open, like eyes bulging in surprise. The strong wind was slamming the windows open and shut.

There was some Indian cloth thrown on the floor as if it had been forgotten in the rush to escape. He went into one of the rooms and found a woman's pink jelaba and some cheap gold-colored bracelets.

He searched the house carefully and found many things that had been left behind. He gathered them and put them on the wooden bench in the sitting room. Then he went out and crouched near the door. He kept an eye on the end of the street, waiting for his master to come. He couldn't help thinking about Fawzi Amin. The house had been abandoned because of Fawzi Amin. The water had reached the crest of the dam and had then spilled over, sweeping everything away. Youssef's wife and her mother had run off with their ingratiating neighbor. Was that what love was?

He had known women in the brothels in Omdurman. He had known the bodies of black women and Abyssinian women. He had experienced desire and lust, but he hadn't experienced the love that Youssef Effendi Said raved on about. To be on fire because of one woman. To suffer because you want just one word from her. To be on fire while waiting for her to look at you just once, and then she leaves you. She turns her back and plunges into the void. He was angry and upset that his master had been betrayed. This wasn't what his master had been waiting for so patiently.

Bakhit saw Youssef Effendi appear at the end of the street, carried along by his ignorance. He even seemed to have a smile on his lips.

Youssef Effendi approached the house. He was biding his time as far as his wife's unfriendliness was concerned. His hope never flagged that he would come home one day and find Nafisa greeting him with love and a smiling face, but today he was coming back to be greeted by something he hadn't expected.

5

What Bakhit had gained from his last adventure was that it allowed him to slip into the servants' quarters and visit Theodora from time to time.

They no longer met only at Idris's stall in the vegetable market. He started visiting her in the house in secret. He waited for darkness to fall, then sneaked in. He knocked on the window of her room, then slipped back out. She joined him and went for a walk with him under cover of darkness. They chatted cheerfully. They looked at each other but could hardly see in the dark. He could smell the musk she wore. She told him little disconnected anecdotes about her mistress, Hassaniya Faraj. He spoke in a nonstop flood about his work in the market, the houses he had been to, and the jihadiya fighters he had met, and gave her news about the beleaguered government.

Sometimes she sat with him in the courtyard, confident that the other servants were fast asleep. She laid her courage on the ground and invited him to sit with her, with their backs against the wall of her room. They looked at the sky and chatted. He recited the lines of poetry he could remember from "Majnun Leila" that Youssef Effendi had recited on similar nights. She told him about the stars. She pointed to the constellations of the zodiac. With her finger she traced the shapes on the black sky.

"Can you see that star?" he asked. "I'll go up on the roof, then fly to it. I'll grab it and steal a ray of moonlight and make you an anklet you can wear around your leg."

She laughed, then pretended to be angry. "Only one star?" she said.

"The whole sky."

"No, you only said one star. You're mean."

He asked her about the sparrows he had given her. Where had they gone? She smiled and didn't answer. He looked up to the window of her room. He imagined it full of sparrows flying around inside.

He told her about the first time he saw her passing in front of him in that same courtyard. The day her old mistress died, Nuwwar Bint al-Hajj Qasim.

He smelled the musk. The smell filled the whole universe. He looked up to see what it was. His most beautiful dream. She was walking in the yard, with an intriguing hint of sadness on her face. She looked at him without seeking him. But his heart felt hot, as if he had a fever. She passed by like a vision.

*

She laughed at his story and shook her head in amazement.

Five days after he saw her in the courtyard of Sheikh Ibrahim's house, he met her by chance in the market.

Never in his life had he known such days. His mind was obsessed with the white woman he had seen fleetingly. Whenever he walked down the street he wondered whether she might be there, looking at him from a distance. He walked upright, with his back straight, to look stronger than he really was. He heard people talking and wondered what her voice would sound like. The image of her filled his days. He was in a stupor, unable to understand what had hit him. What was this feeling? After three days obsessed with images of her he threw himself on his bed and prepared for sleep by addressing her in resignation. "I've put a saddle on my dreams for you, so come on," he told her.

When she came to ride his dream, he had to admit he had finally succumbed to the heresy that Youssef Effendi Said had so often spoken about.

On the fourth morning after seeing her for the first time, when he woke up with his longing, he said to himself in amazement, "O Mahdi! I'm turning into a white man."

But he didn't turn into a white man, and he never achieved Youssef Effendi's level of indifference toward rejection and confidence in the hope of union with the woman he loved.

His world was turned upside down. The ground was now sky and the sky was now earth. He was tethered to the tent peg of the unknown. Like Joseph in the Quran, the wolf did not eat him; nor did he fly off into space.

He was consuming himself. But when she looked at him he gave her a smile of contentment. He burned and burned. But he didn't dare to keep his distance, nor did he venture to move closer.

"Why do you trample on my chest so cruelly?" he asked her.

Younis Wad Jaber appeared and she rushed to him, leaving Bakhit as a pile of ash.

They whispered to each other. She reached out and touched Younis's arm. Her eyes shone. Her chestnut hair slipped out from under her headscarf. Then she walked on with him, leaving Bakhit Mandil under the vegetable stall.

"Sheikh Ibrahim is complaining that his money's being stolen," Sabah al-Kheir said one evening. "He's punished some of the women servants."

Idris al-Nubawi took a swig of his beer. "It's obvious," he said. "She's stealing money from her master to spend on Younis Wad Jaber."

Bakhit looked at her walking, preoccupied with Younis. He could almost hear her voice singing merrily: "Come around, my love. If you don't come to me, I'll come to you, and if the sea is too deep, you can climb up my heart to reach me."

But, he said to himself, maybe she. . . .

6

Until the day he died there were two things Bakhit Mandil would never forget: the surprise when he saw Theodora walking past in the courtyard of Sheikh Ibrahim Wad al-Shawwak's house, and the surprise when he opened his eyes and saw Cairo. When his master, Youssef Effendi Said, wanted to take him across the bridge between Cairo and Giza, Bakhit looked terrified. He stepped back in horror when he saw the water running under the bridge. The army barracks was behind him. The guards, Sudanese like him, looked at him and laughed. Youssef Effendi tried to tempt him but he emphatically refused. He would not cross the river. Youssef Effendi took him back to the Abdeen district. He sat him down at a coffee shop. He asked the waiter to look after him and hurried off to pursue his mission.

They had come to Cairo to follow up news that Youssef Effendi had picked up over the previous two months. He had mobilized all his acquaintances to find news of Nafisa and Fawzi Amin. He had pestered senior civil servants. He had asked for favors without knowing how he could ever repay them.

He had paid bribes that threatened to bankrupt him. But all he could think about was how to find them. When he was close to despair he learned that Fawzi Amin was living in Giza with his wife and her mother. As soon as he read the telegram that brought him the news, he shouted to Bakhit, "Get your stuff ready. We're going to Cairo."

Traveling in exile. From one homesickness to another. But the farther north he went the less familiar was the world he saw. The world changed and he came across a life he didn't know and had never heard of.

When he sat down in the coffee shop he exchanged looks with the other customers. He was shaking nervously in his chair and they looked at him with contempt. He saw how busy everyone was and watched in amazement. His eyes were popping out of his head as if he were trying to take in everything to understand it.

"Coffee, tea, or sahlab?" the waiter asked.

He hesitated, then ordered a coffee. It was forbidden in his country. The muftis had issued fatwas that it was haram. But his curiosity overrode any other consideration.

Curiosity was what drove him in the thirty-six days he stayed in Cairo after Youssef Effendi set him free. He followed his curiosity wherever it led. Out of curiosity he smoked hashish, drank bouza, tried to learn stick dancing, and listened to slave girls singing. Then, when he stumbled by chance upon Sheikh Abdel-Rahman al-Abbadi the camel trader, his curiosity had exhausted him. He didn't hesitate to beg the trader to take him back to his country. Abbadi wasn't interested in his stories. He asked him for money. He still had the money that Youssef Effendi had left him as a gift—about four pounds. The trader took it grudgingly and gave Bakhit a place in a caravan that was going to make its way into Sudan.

As he came into Sawarda swaying on a camel, Bakhit remembered the moment when Youssef Effendi had turned his back on him for the last time and walked away. "Love is my path," he said. "I won't go back till I've found her."

"None of the information we've received has helped us find her, sir," said Bakhit. "Let's leave her and go back."

"Bakhit! You still don't know what love is. When you find out you'll follow it to your death, my good Sudanese friend."

He gave Bakhit a large amount of money, embraced him, and then turned away and went off to look for his runaway wife. He left Bakhit to be free and to ask in puzzlement, "What is love?"

He knew the answer when he saw her walking through the courtyard of Sheikh Ibrahim's house. That was the second surprise in his life. After that, Bakhit began to think that maybe Youssef Effendi had a point.

7

The month of Rajab was a dark, sad month.

He hardly saw Theodora. She and Younis Wad Jaber seemed to be inseparable. Bakhit went to her master's house and stood at a distance, watching. He caught sight of Younis waiting on the waste ground. Then she came out to meet him and went for a walk with him and they disappeared into the darkness. Inevitably Bakhit was anxious and suspicious.

Idris al-Nubawi laughed at Bakhit's naivety. Bakhit got drunk on beer and the world spun around him.

"You've lost her. Forget it, my friend," said Idris.

But when she had a hurried meeting with him, she made him as happy as ever and his heart no longer had outbursts of anger.

"Hawa!"

She looked at him distractedly. Her face showed signs of hesitation and suffering.

"You're not helping me, Bakhit."

"Tell me what you want."

"I just don't want you to be a burden. Please."

"You're hiding something."

She didn't respond. She looked away, mysterious tears in her eyes.

"Is it Younis?" he asked hesitantly.

She started and looked at him angrily. "What about him? Why are so obsessed with him? You're stupid."

He was at a loss. He didn't know what to say.

"You don't understand!" she exclaimed.

Idris al-Nubawi didn't pity him. He gave him news about things Bakhit hadn't seen and explained to him things that Bakhit was too cowardly to confront.

On the night of the twenty-sixth of Rajab the city was preparing for the celebration of the Prophet Mohamed's ascent to heaven. The children in the streets looked unusually excited. The women were walking down the side of the streets in droves. Wealthy and powerful people were celebrating with banquets open to all. Riffraff such as Bakhit smuggled in beer in preparation for celebrating the Prophet's night journey to Jerusalem.

"I'll meet you tonight," Theodora told him at noon.

He looked at her uncertainly.

"Tonight," she repeated. "Come to the house."

There was something about her eyes. After all the secrets they had shared, Bakhit knew that something was up.

"You're changing."

"Bakhit! Stop fretting and asking questions, please. Don't spoil life when we don't know how long or short it will be. Come to the house, without any questions."

He was about to ask, but she beat him to it. "Don't ask me about Younis, please. Just come to the house," she said.

She could see the hesitation in his face. She took out her notebook and handed it to him.

"Have this."

"What is it?"

"It's my notebook, you know the one. I want you to take it. It might reassure you. Read what you can of it and bring it with you when you come tonight."

She left him and went out. He didn't know what a struggle it had been for her to say to him what she had said. He would later read the last thing she had written in her notebook: "Bakhit deserves this from me. I don't care what the Lord said and I'm not afraid of anything."

But he didn't understand. He obeyed her, but he didn't understand.

It was the night of the twenty-sixth of Rajab.

Their last meeting.

8

This damned country.

The land of blood and tears. She had lived here for years of degradation as if she hadn't once been a normal human. She had been in despair so long that enslavement had almost taken control of her thinking.

She hated every speck of dust in this ugly city. She hated the black faces covered in scars and beards. They were so thin, with their flashing eyes and their lousy faith in a crazy impostor. They dreamed night and day of going back to the civilized world. They asked her about Cairo, Alexandria, the sea, and the treasures of the khedive's palace. When Sheikh Ibrahim's friends gathered in the evening, she could hear them chatting loudly about how they desired the women of the world. The talk of the town was that the Khalifa had written to the queen of England inviting her to convert to Islam and telling her that, if she did, he promised to marry her to his military commander, Younis Wad al-Dakim. They were primitives, barbarians. Death on the gallows in the marketplace was so commonplace that only children bothered to watch.

And her heart, that stupid thing that rebelled against her, was drawn in desperation to a daydreaming slave. She hated the way he loved her, the way he fussed over her. She didn't understand why she was drawn to him. Why did he appear in her dreams? Her heart, which had been corrupted by Omdurman, skipped a beat when she saw him. But she maintained her coldness and her aloofness. She was the Lord's envoy to the land of sheep, and saints aren't meant to fall in love with their sheep.

Bakhit gave her a sparrow and that made her happy. But when the burst of childish excitement had passed she came to her senses. She hid from the servants in the house and squeezed the sparrow angrily in her fist, but found she had killed it. Then she rushed to her room in tears. "You've gone mad!" she shouted at herself.

But Younis Wad Jaber saved her from going mad. Whenever she saw him in the market she saw salvation shining in the darkness of her own uncertainty.

Younis Wad Jaber didn't hide from her the fact that he admired her, even if she did put on airs and pretend not to notice. Younis had experience and connections, as she knew from her epic journey from Suakin to Khartoum, when she was an Abbasid princess in the *Thousand and One Nights*. It was Younis who was going to smuggle her, who was the gate to her hopes.

She deceived him and he allowed himself to be deceived. When she asked him to help her escape he didn't hesitate. Money wasn't a problem. But it was a problem finding people who could be trusted, in a city where secrets were sold to all sides. Nevertheless, he reassured her. He would find someone who would take her to Dongola, where she could meet up with the Egyptian army. They would need a guide and someone to provide camels. Younis would be her guardian angel. He would protect her and take her to safety.

It was the Lord who had sent her Younis Wad Jaber.

On the night of the twenty-sixth of Rajab, her last night in Omdurman, she decided to reward Bakhit's love.

All she could leave him was a memento. Saints aren't meant to fall in love with their sheep.

If it hadn't been for Bakhit she wouldn't have survived the last year. Alone without her friend Hortensia. Desperate and fearful that she would weaken in the face of Abdel-Gayoum's attempts to seduce her. Her spirit had been so hardened by slavery that she had almost forgotten who she was. Bakhit had protected her with his love. He deserved a last souvenir from her.

She couldn't tell him straight that she was leaving. She knew that people in love could do stupid things and she was worried that her heart might also do something mad.

She was worried about Bakhit's fantasies.

I'll ask your master for your hand. We can live together in my house. You'll never be a maid again. I'll work and bring you everything you want. We'll have our own yard. I'll buy a ewe for milk. You can raise pigeons. We'll have children. Three. Four, including a girl as pretty as her mother. I want to have children the same color as me but with eyes as beautiful as yours.

She didn't want black children who believed in a dead dervish who dreamed of invading the world. She didn't belong here. This wasn't her city or her world. Nothing held her here other than this stupid love that had become annoyingly familiar.

She would escape. Go back to her world. The Alexandrian air and the whisper of its loving sea. This was the last night before her escape. When she reached her own world she would forget all this. She would live again. Perhaps she would go to Greece. Or move to London and have her memoirs published. She would live a new life. Perhaps she would get married. Her husband wouldn't be a black slave. And she wouldn't live in a yard raising pigeons.

The years of torment had passed. The next day, when the city was busy with the celebrations, she would escape with Younis and the caravan he had arranged.

Farewell, torment.

The next day she would escape and take the diadem.

9

Blessed is the man that endures temptation: for when he is tried, he shall receive the crown of life, which the Lord has promised to those that love him.

James 1:12

Seventeen

1

EVENTS HAPPENED AT A BREATHLESS PACE.

Events are like waves that cover the tracks of previous waves with malicious pleasure. Bakhit Mandil couldn't keep up with what was happening.

People were beating drums and blowing onbeia trumpets day and night. Anxiety gnawed at the city, chewing the prison and those inside it. Prayers were neglected. It was forbidden to go out. Rumors wailed in the streets. All they could hear was the shouting and the noise of bare feet running across all over the city.

Who was chasing who?

The prison was full of Jihadiya soldiers who had deserted. There were more prisoners than chains to hold them, so some of the new prisoners were lucky enough to have their legs free. In the daytime, when the city was being shelled, the guards shoved them, terrified, into the cells with stone walls. Bakhit found himself being herded by a guard with a whip into a cell with Rifaat Effendi al-Salamouni and dozens of other frightened people. The guards piled them up on top of each other and locked the doors. Someone screamed when the heavy wooden door cracked his skull. He died the next day. The cell had no ventilation and was stifling. The air was so heavy that it weighed them down. The smell was disgusting. It was like a rathole infested with the plague.

The prison shook with the boom of a shell. They could smell the blood. They heard voices shouting that the women's prison had been hit. Rifaat Effendi called out to Bakhit in the darkness.

"We're going to die here, Bakhit!" he said.

Whenever a shell fell they thought it was going to bring down the stone walls on their heads. Then they heard the news: "The dome has been destroyed. The Mahdi's tomb has been destroyed."

The prison trembled. The infidels were destroying the sacred dome.

After that they heard nothing from the guards. The guards ran away and left them to their fate. In their prison, they lost track of the days. They couldn't tell if it was day or night. They could smell gunpowder and smoke. Night and day were the same. Death laughed aloud outside. Within the prison walls it amused itself by taking some of them off by suffocation.

The shells boomed. The cell shook. The ceiling spilled dust on top of them. "Oh Mahdi, save us poor souls!" they shouted.

But the guns didn't fall silent, and the Mahdi didn't save his dome.

The city fell and the invaders opened the prison. The prisoners emerged, unable to believe they had survived.

Someone clapped Bakhit on the shoulder and shouted, "At last! Freedom, Bakhit!"

Bakhit escaped the celebrations of his colleagues and slipped into the crowds in the street, looking for Merisila's house. It was the only place where he knew he would find safety.

A few days later the invaders disinterred the sacred body of the Mahdi. They burned it and scattered the ashes in the Nile.

2

When Bakhit left Omdurman he knew where to find his six targets.

He left Merisila standing behind him, breathing heavily because of the love she was hiding. In his heart were the remains of a longing to visit Theodora's grave and an anger he had planted there seven years earlier—an anger that was now ripe and ready to harvest.

Sheikh Ibrahim Wad al-Shawwak. Abdel-Gayoum, Sheikh Ibrahim's son. Naim Wad al-Hajj Taha. Younis Wad Jaber. Taher Jibril and Mousa al-Kalas.

The one closest to hand was Naim Wad al-Hajj Taha, the guide. He was staying with some members of his Bedouin clan a few hours south of Omdurman. Bakhit tried to reach them before midday but failed. He spent the day waiting in hiding and saddled his horse at sunset.

He had hoped that Younis Wad Jaber would be first. But the reports that Merisila brought him made that difficult to achieve. "Naim would be a good start," he said to himself.

He spent the day in the shadow of his horse. His brow was covered in sweat and he was panting from determination to carry out his plan. He reached out to touch the bulge her notebook made in the saddlebag.

"Don't fall in love," she had written in Arabic in the notebook. "If you want to emerge safe don't owe anything or be owed anything." And then in English: "Days to go. I hate everything in this city. It may be hard for the civilized reader to understand this hatred. But I would say that my years in the city of the self-styled Mahdi have greatly changed my heart. These monsters can be treated only with the hatred and savagery that they deserve. But that doesn't mean there aren't any puzzling exceptions. Bakhit Mandil is one of these exceptions. Bakhit Mandil is an exception. Bakhit Mandil is the only exception."

He was puzzled by long passages written in Greek. Written in a nervous, tense hand. There was much crossing-out and underlining for emphasis.

On the night of the twenty-sixth of Rajab he had gone to Idris al-Nubawi's place to read the notebook.

He grew rather careless and started to drink beer as he read:

Bakhit Mandil isn't like this city. If any of these memoirs were to be published in a book, it would have to mention Bakhit Mandil. He was different. He was an example that the Western reader would be surprised to discover. Western literature ought to write about his changing ideas on love. He was like a lover from one of Shakespeare's plays who had landed inadvertently in this savage country. If only he hadn't been black. If only he hadn't been a dervish slave. The worst mistake is to become attached to anyone in any way. I don't want to become like Bakhit.

Why did she want him to read this?

Was she telling him how confused she was about him? To what extent did she see him not as someone in love, but as a slave who didn't deserve to be more than an object of curiosity? Wasn't Younis Wad Jaber black like him? Why did she write "Younis is my hope"?

Was she really mad?

When she left, Idris asked him, "What's wrong with her?"

Bakhit shrugged in confusion. "I don't know, Idris. She's mad," he said.

Idris laughed. "All white people are mad," he said.

Bakhit looked at the crowd into which she had disappeared. "But I'm madly in love with her," he said.

Was he still madly in love with her?

He had some more to drink. The alcohol was making his head heavy as he read.

When he slipped into the Bedouin encampment looking for Naim Wad al-Hajj Taha he was shaking from the weight of the memories. Darkness enveloped the place as he walked warily between the matting enclosures.

His first kill. The ecstasy of seeing the face of his rival in the throes of death. The last thing left of them was that terror and incomprehension.

I'm killing them for your sake.

To satisfy the longing for you that is inside me.

When the sword fell on Naim's chest he caught a glimpse of her in the fear in the man's startled eyes.

She was crying.

But Bakhit stabbed Naim one more time.

3

The noise of the drunks in Idris al-Nubawi's house annoyed Bakhit.

Someone came in and shouted, "Have you heard the news?"

The drinkers, tipsy with beer, were shouting at each other.

"No Mahdism and no Turkish state," said the newcomer.

There were loud guffaws of laughter in the house. It was a mud-brick room fifteen cubits wide and the revelers were piled on top of each other. It had a thatched roof, and whenever the wind blew against it their hearts froze for fear of a raid by the patrols. Bakhit looked at the people around him. He knew five or six of them who had been with him on the Nujoumi campaign in Egypt. Another man had fought the Abyssinians in the army of al-Zaki Tammal. They were old soldiers whom time had forgotten and who had ended up in Idris's house, drinking beer and cursing the Mahdist movement. Is there any truth in this world? Bakhit wondered.

On the night the rockets exploded in the sky over Khartoum the Ansar attacked the city. Turks were killed in the streets and in their houses. The horses of the Mahdi's companions roamed the city and there was much screaming and wailing. Bakhit Mandil heard a horrible noise and came down off the roof of the house to investigate. His master, Abdüllatif Effendi Mazhar, had been slaughtered on the steps. He was lying on his back. The wind was blowing his jelaba, baring his stout thighs. There was a leather sandal on one of his feet. Blood was dripping from his nose.

Where was Buthayna with her pink breasts and that ugly thing like a septic wound between her legs? They must have taken her off to some place where dozens of dervishes were giving her what she wanted.

Blood in the name of God. Blood for the sake of God. Blood, oh Mahdi.

Then, from the heart of death, life arose. Life emerged from among the corpses of Khartoum, crossed the river to the west bank, and settled in Omdurman. The Mahdi's sacred patch of land. Bakhit moved there in the crush of people crossing, following the Lord of Creation, the Mahdi. The city of faith. The abode of Islam, since true Islam did not exist anywhere else in the world at that time.

O Mahdi of Allah. Fire has broken out in your realm. Who will put it out?

He flicked through the notebook and read. He heard someone asking him about the book he was holding. But he didn't answer.

Time passed. He had to meet her in the house of her master, Ibrahim Wad al-Shawwak, as she had requested. But he was engrossed in her notebook. He felt let down and pained. It was the only time he had decided to be angry. The only time he had felt that he couldn't bear to see her.

He took a tattered piece of paper from the middle of the notebook and read:

From the true Muslim who longs for God and who trusts what his Lord has in store for him, Muhammed al-Mahdi ibn Abdallah, to his honored and revered friends and to people of knowledge—that is, army chief Farajallah and his friend Abdel-Nabi and the great and small who have joined them.

Know and be certain, my friends, that I hold this position only by virtue of people's prayers to God and because of their

274

great good fortune and because they have high rank in Paradise and because they have eschewed base and transient pleasures that would do them harm and give rise to long-term regrets.

Oh Mahdi, loving what is ephemeral has brought me sorrows.

You see me only as a black slave who doesn't deserve to be loved by the civilized white woman.

Oh Mahdi, what has befallen us? Oh Mahdi, what has befallen me?

I am her dervish.

But that night the dervish was carried away by anger.

The memories dragged him into a dark pit.

She had told him to meet her in her master's house and not to ask questions. But he wasn't going to join her.

He decided to wallow in his obstinacy, so he lost out.

If only he had known.

4

Bakhit Mandil isn't like this city. If any of these memoirs were to be published in a book, it would have to mention Bakhit Mandil. He was different. An example that the Western reader would be surprised to discover. Western literature ought to write about his changing ideas on love. He was like a lover from one of Shakespeare's plays who had landed inadvertently in this savage country. If only he hadn't been black. If only he hadn't been a dervish slave.

5

Monday, February 22, 1892

Everything has been prepared. Younis told me we'll escape on Friday night. Everyone will be at a Muslim celebration. He told me a plan that seemed rather insubstantial. But he was confident and said it had worked with many others.

6

He killed them one after another.

God made it easy for him and guided his sword. They just seemed to drop dead, and no one noticed amid all the waves of vengeance. Mahdism was defeated and those with grievances had come to take their belated revenge.

Slaves who had been subjugated. Poor people who had had enough of begging. Hot-blooded nomads who demanded blood for blood.

Everyone was killing for their own reasons. He was killing for her sake. He pursued them in Soba, in al-Kamlin, in Rifa'a, in al-Musallamiya and Abu Haraz. Naim Wad Taha, the treacherous guide. Abdel-Gayoum, the son of Ibrahim Wad al-Shawwak, who had sent them after her. He went on to seek out Ibrahim Wad al-Shawwak, who stood and watched as they killed her in front of him. Mousa al-Kalas, the caravan leader. Taher Jibril, who chased her and brought her back. None of them deserved to live. How could they live when she had died?

Everyone who had betrayed her or had done her harm deserved to die. All of them had to pay the price.

Naim, Abdel-Gayoum, Mousa, Sheikh Ibrahim, and Taher were dead. There was only Younis left.

But now Bakhit had fallen into captivity.

One night Hassan al-Jerifawi was sitting with Bakhit and he asked him about the killings. Bakhit told him the story.

He was drunk at dawn the next day, after coming back from the Taher Jibril mission, drowning his sorrows in beer, when Naim Wad Taha came into Idris al-Nubawi's house. Naim was flush with money, as usual whenever he went on a trip. He earned money from caravans trading to Suakin in the east or Dongola in the north and maybe, rarely, to Fazogli. He earned twice as much from the illicit caravans that smuggled travelers or goods. The more dangerous it was, the more money there was to be made. Naim stood in the middle of the room and called Idris. "I'll take care of a sheep for the drinkers today," he said.

The drunk people cheered, because they could now be sure they'd have plenty of meat to go with the beer. Several of them hurried off to take part in the slaughtering. Naim sat down proudly and was brought a special mug of beer. He took a sip and belched. He was asked about his trip but he just smiled mysteriously. But he was not able to sustain his air of mystery when the beer started to creep up on him. As he grew more intoxicated the story leaked out of him.

"The infidel woman who wanted to escape is now lying dead, a corpse," he said.

He guffawed.

"She thought we were traitors. Would we betray the Mahdi and Islam for a few piasters and riyals?" he asked.

Bakhit looked up and listened. There were names and details he didn't understand. Then Naim laughed and said, "What's with this slave not joining in?"

Bakhit Mandil looked at him in astonishment. As Naim told his story, the world's devils were screaming in Bakhit's head, and all hell was breaking loose.

"Tell me," said Bakhit, "was there a man with you with a big frame, a flat nose, and a mustache that hung down over his mouth?"

"That would be Taher Jibril, one of the Mulazmin," replied Naim. "He's the man who was sent to us."

When was the last trump sounded?

The last thing Bakhit remembered was that when he came back to his senses there was no one around him. The drunk men had gone, leaving him in a stupor. So he picked up a sword and went out into the streets of Omdurman screaming.

They've killed her. Woe betide them.

He screamed revenge until, in his drunkenness, he passed out in the hands of a police patrol.

Eighteen

1

THEODORA GATHERED HER FEW MEAGER possessions and waited. There was nothing left for her in this country. There was just her notebook and her meeting with Bakhit. All she was taking with her was a bag with some odd clothes, her notebook, and her memories of Bakhit. Two hours after dinner she heard the crunch of gravel at the gate to the servants' courtyard. She slipped out cautiously. Bakhit hadn't come yet. She found Younis waiting for her, crouching in the dark, his face covered with a piece of cloth.

"Off we go," he said.

She looked around her in the expectation that the person she was waiting for would emerge from the darkness.

"Let's wait awhile," she said anxiously. "I'm still waiting for something."

"There's no time," Younis said irritably. "The men are waiting for us. If you don't want us to be caught and killed we have to go now."

He took her by the arm and pulled her after him.

"Do you have the money?" he asked.

She put out her hand and offered him the money she had saved.

Where's Bakhit? she wondered. Why hasn't he shown up yet? She couldn't leave without seeing him.

My God! How reckless she felt now that it was time to part. She wanted to see Bakhit, to throw herself into his arms.

She would hug him. She would press her lips to his ears and whisper many things to him. She would hold his black hand tightly. But where was he?

Younis didn't give her time to wait. He pulled her behind him roughly. She was terrified at what she had decided to undertake. How had she ever thought of doing this? What kind of life was she escaping to? A life in which there was no Bakhit Mandil. Would she never see his eyes with their wild love again? Where else could she live? The black slave with his crazy love. I don't want to leave. I don't want to leave.

The streets were dark and still except for the sound of the Sufi celebration in the distance. But they were full of memories. She tried to find her way through the mass of memories but there were just too many of them.

From which country inhabited by angels do you come?

"You're very dear to me," he told her.

She heard words of love in languages she had never imagined that she would understand. She smiled to herself.

"And you're very dear to me, as a brother. And we are all children of the Lord, born of suffering, Bakhit."

"Take me to the river. I want to see the sunset."

"I want to have children the same color as me but with eyes as beautiful as yours."

Before she left he said to her, "Tell me that happiness is possible, Hawa." A frightened child seeking reassurance.

"I can't give you any good news," she said gloomily. "You'll have to put up with sadness for the rest of your life. You'll have to put up with sadness as long as you love me. I know myself better than you do, and the worst may be yet to come."

Was all this an illusion? Was she running away from all this? Who said that Omdurman was gloomy and unpleasant? Omdurman was splendid with love. The ground evoked friendship and the houses spoke of love. What other place on earth was like Omdurman?

"Younis, I don't want to leave," she whispered anxiously.

But he didn't stop. He kept pulling her along.

North of the Muslimaniya quarter she found the caravan waiting for her. They were hidden in the dark. Rabie Wad Taha the guide and Mousa al-Kalas were there. There were four camels that were as guardedly silent as their owners.

"On you get," said one of the men.

"We don't have any time," said another.

She looked back. Where was he? Does a man in love break his promise?

Oh Bakhit, appear. Oh Bakhit, appear.

But he didn't appear and the camel took her up to the sky. The animal growled and she swayed from side to side. She clung to the saddle and took a deep breath.

The journey was about to begin. The escape from Omdurman. The escape from years of captivity. Return to civilization and the civilized world. Far from the land of the dervishes and death. Return to a country that wasn't ruled by blood.

She would go back to Alexandria, where she had her friend the sea and tender memories. But her heart was drawn to this place.

When the caravan was about to set off in flight she heard the sound of people approaching. Could it be Bakhit? she wondered.

But a rough voice shouted at them. "Stop right there, you infidels!" it said.

2

When Hassan al-Jerifawi ordered the caravan to set up camp before going into al-Musallamiya his subordinates grumbled.

One of them said, "The trip only takes a few hours, so why do you want to spend the night here?"

"Don't argue," Hassan replied.

They whispered to each other skeptically, but found they had no option but to obey. They unsaddled the horses and tethered the animals close to the Nile. They spread out to forage for firewood. Having a fire in the open is more important for deterring devils than for keeping warm. They set up camp near the water and laid out their bedding in a circle with Bakhit in the center.

Hassan was still hesitant. The more Bakhit told him the more questions he wanted to ask. The closer they were to al-Musallamiya the more apprehensive he became.

It hurts when someone who used to believe starts to have doubts. For two years Hassan had trained himself to forget. But memories are stubborn and he couldn't stop dreaming about the girl in the blue flannel gown, his beloved Fatma.

The day he believed in the Mahdist movement he knew the end of the world was nigh. He would invade other countries as a conqueror so that people would embrace Islam in droves. The Mahdi's justice would cover the world. The Light would shine and fill the world. The Mahdi, peace be upon him, had promised to conquer Mecca, Syria, and the land of the Turks. The infidels would die and Islam would spread.

He believed that Islam meant justice and bounty. Islam was the opposite of what the Turks had to offer, which was injustice, oppression, and murder. But under Mahdist rule he had tasted blood and seen death at close quarters. Why would people reject justice? Why did justice lead to injustice? Things were no longer clear. The Mahdist movement was undoubtedly right. How could he deny the Mahdi's mission when it was a mission from God? But how could a mission from God promote killing? Under Turkish rule he had been an aggrieved believer. And when God opened his heart to the Mahdist movement, he became an oppressor who had doubts. Where was the truth? If he had met Bakhit as he was ten years earlier he would have killed him without a moment's hesitation. Bakhit Mandil was a criminal. A murderer. He was someone who was liable to the divinely ordained punishment that involved the amputation of a hand and a foot on the opposite sides of his body to set an example to other outlaws. But the years of blood had sullied everything. The truth was no longer clear.

If we were right, why did we treat people unjustly and kill people, and why were we defeated? If we were wrong, then why were we more devout and God-fearing than the Turks and the Egyptians?

Aren't they infidels? Aren't we believers?

Isn't Bakhit Mandil a murderer?

Or do you think he's just unlucky? He murdered people and we murdered people. He killed because of love. And we killed for the Mahdi's sake.

There's blood on his sword, and there's blood on my sword.

Hassan stepped toward his prisoner, who lay in a heap on the ground. Bakhit raised his head and looked at him. In Bakhit's eyes there was a peace of mind, a contentment. He was like a worshipper at the gates of Paradise.

"Aren't you frightened?" Hassan asked him.

"A lover isn't afraid to meet the one he loves."

"You're going to die in a state of sin."

"I'll die having failed to kill Younis Wad Jaber, but if she forgives me that will more than compensate for my failure."

"Do you think a woman can count for anything compared with God?"

"But isn't God just love?"

Hassan al-Jerifawi had once reveled in love, but in God's cause he had descended into hatred. Was it God's cause or

283

was it a delusion? His only fault was to believe in the Mahdi that God had sent to humanity.

He gripped Bakhit's shoulder and helped him to his feet. As his skeptical companions looked on, he pulled him behind him. He made him sit down near the river, and then sat down nearby.

"They caught your girlfriend when she was about to escape. Then what happened?" Hassan asked.

"They betrayed her."

"All of them?"

"All of them."

"How do you know that?"

"God has messengers, and some of them are murderers," said Bakhit.

He remembered how, back at Idris's place, Naim Wad Taha the guide had chatted cheerfully about the mission he had accomplished. He told his story proudly and Bakhit listened in amazement. They had grabbed her as she was screaming. Taher Jibril, who had been with Bakhit a few hours earlier and had crossed over to Khartoum with him, had slapped her, and she had fallen on the ground.

"You infidel!" he had shouted at her.

She had screamed for help. But they just stood there watching. Taher and those who were with him carried her back to her master. They left her to her master and his men with smiles on their faces. No one helped her. She was begging. She reached out toward Younis Wad Jaber. But he was busy with his tooth stick, which he stuck in his mouth to rub his teeth. As they disappeared into the dark, Younis said to them, "Off you go. Farewell. A messenger from Abdel-Gayoum Wad al-Shawwak will bring you your reward."

"And of all possible people in the world it was you that Taher Jibril came to find?" said Hassan.

"That was my fault, and it's unforgivable. I buried her myself without knowing it."

Months passed as he searched. He went into towns and ran
away from villages. Soldiers pursued him and he almost succumbed to death from a vicious disease. But he didn't flag.
He was like a sleuthhound on the trail of the killers. He made
use of Merisila's information, the Omdurman gossip that she
gathered for him.

When she passed on what she had gleaned about the
whereabouts of his six targets Bakhit heard the voice of destiny saying, "Arise."

His black body stirred into action. He loomed over Merisila when he stood up. He could see Theodora's chestnut hair
in the sky, adorning the horizon. Before he left he only had
one last visit to make—to Theodora's grave.

"I'll come with you," Merisila told him.

"I'd rather be alone with her," said Bakhit.

But Merisila shook her head stubbornly and he gave in.
Just after sunset they slipped through the lush darkness to
the bank of the Nile. They crossed to Khartoum. The city
was still half dead, although some of the invading soldiers
were camped there. They walked among scary ruins. Merisila
was full of sympathy. Her gait as she walked was like that of
a pigeon pecking. But Bakhit missed the chains of his love.
He was unconscious, like a dervish at a ritual Sufi dance. His
heart beat to the name of Hawa like the drum at the dance.

He remembered walking behind Taher Jibril in this place
seven years earlier. There were two other men with them, carrying the wrapped body. Taher Jibril was trying to tell him
something about a maid who had died of natural causes in
her master's house. But Bakhit wasn't interested in the expla-
nations. It was just a job from which he would earn some
money to go back to Idris al-Nubawi's house, drink more beer,
and get drunker and angrier, and sadder and sadder. And
when they stopped at the spot that Taher had chosen amid the
ruins of Khartoum, Bakhit had bent down to slip the leather

notebook and the bag that held the few things he cared about under the remains of a wall. Taher watched him inquisitively.

"My life's treasures," Bakhit said.

Taher laughed nervously. "Who's going to steal your bag, slave?" he said. "Come on, get to work."

He widened the grave with his hands. As he lowered the body into the grave he could smell the musk flooding the world. When he began to pour the soil back on top he could hear the ruins wail. He started to lose consciousness with the soil that trickled into the spaces between the corpse and the walls of the cavity. The world spun and Bakhit almost collapsed.

"You're drunk, you dog!" Taher shouted.

He pulled himself together but didn't reply. His heart was howling. The world went hazy and he almost fainted. Taher Jibril's companions carried him on the way back.

"Don't expect to get paid in full," said Taher. "We had to help you."

He was interested only in going back to more drinking. He had left his bag there by her sacred grave. They left him outside Idris's house and the streets gobbled them up. He staggered in and asked for more to drink. A few hours later, when Naim Wad Taha came in, the smell of musk still lingered around him. But Bakhit didn't even notice the smell.

Of all people, he had helped Taher Jibril. He had thrust her into a hole in a ground and poured soil onto her pretty face. They made him do it.

He could see their ghosts around him as he followed Merisila through the ruins. When he was close to her grave he could see them all gathered around the grave. As he stood on top of the trench that held his beloved, he felt dizzy and unsteady on his feet.

3

The men threw Theodora at the feet of Ibrahim Wad al-Shawwak.

They gathered around her like predators. She wasn't aware of anything. Her body was covered in blood. She was frightened. She was lamenting that she was alone and weak. "Have mercy," she whispered.

Sheikh Ibrahim kicked her.

"How dare you dream of running away, you infidel!" he shouted.

His foot dug into her flesh. Abdel-Gayoum put his foot on her hand and pressed, crushing the bones.

The sound of song billowed through the night air from afar. It was the night of the Rajab celebrations. The angels brought peace down to those on earth. Her body shuddered with the pain. Her face was covered with dust. Her dress was torn. Her chestnut hair had wrapped itself around her face and her neck. The pain was unbearable.

"By the Lord Jesus!" she screamed.

She was waiting for a deliverance that didn't come. A kick landed on her jaw, and she realized there could be no relief or deliverance. This life was all suffering and faith would not save you.

One of her eyes was gouged out. She wailed with a choked sound.

Crown of thorns. Via dolorosa.

She was filled with pain. She screamed. She implored someone to have mercy on her. The blows rained down on her once again. Her breathing stopped and her screams were held back for a moment. The pain was excruciating and she shuddered. But they wrapped her in a woolen rug and tied her up.

The blows rained down on her again and she groaned. Eternal darkness enveloped her.

As she lost consciousness she tried to scream "Save me, Bakhit!" but she couldn't speak and Bakhit did not come. The rug wrapped tightly around her jerked several times, then was still. Taher Jibril gave it a last kick and everyone fell silent.

Sheikh Ibrahim Wad al-Shawwak was the first to speak. "Everything happens by God's command, things past and things to come," he said. "Bury her far away. We don't want any scandals on this holy night."

4

Hassan al-Jerifawi remembered leaving Omdurman on the campaign led by Commander Mahmoud Wad Ahmad.

That was toward the end of the time when his heart was full of faith. God's soldiers were heading north to meet the infidels at Dongola.

Hassan hadn't seen the Turkish-Egyptian invasion of his country sixty years earlier. They had destroyed the kingdom of Sennar and suppressed the true faith. They made the faithful who worshipped God worship the government. They repressed the sheikhs who were learned in Islam. They abandoned the Maliki school of Islam, followed by the imam of Madina, the city of the Prophet, in favor of their own school. They introduced strange customs and turned Islam into something alien. They encouraged corruption and coffee drinking, and they imported slave girls.

But God had honored Hassan by giving him a chance to swear allegiance to the Mahdi. The saying of the Mahdi—that the least of his companions was better than the followers of the Prophet himself—was true in the case of Hassan.

But the Mahdist state had damaged his faith. When the Ansar were fighting the infidels in Qadeer, Aba, El Obeid, and Shikan, the angels were fighting with them, walking among them, talking to them, and giving them consolation. They promised them victory and domination over Khartoum, Cairo, Damascus, and Mecca.

But when they gained possession of Khartoum, the angels spread their wings, rose to heaven, and disappeared.

Perhaps we didn't deserve the victory that God had granted us.

Some faith remained deep inside him. He honed it as he sharpened his sword and went out to meet the infidels.

He would fight against falsehood. There was no question about that. None of God's people disagreed that the Turks were infidels and that it was a duty to fight them.

The Ansar sat around the fire at night, murmuring the Quran to themselves. Their faces were pale from exhaustion and the light of faith. Inside they seethed with hatred for infidels and the corrupt. They were driven by their wish to rule the world, as God had promised. *God has promised those of you who believe and do righteous deeds that He will ensure you inherit power on earth, as He has done to others in the past, that He will empower for you the religion that He has approved for you, and that He will do away with your old fear and replace it with a sense of security, since you worship me and do not worship any others. After this, all those who do not believe are iniquitous.*

The earth was God's earth, and they were God's soldiers.

But Mahmoud Wad Ahmad's army stopped at the town of Metemma.

Hassan and the rest of the army were shocked that the people of Metemma had abandoned Islam and turned apostate. They had prevented the Ansar army from staying in their town. Hassan heard the mujahideen saying that the sheikh of the Jaalin tribe in the town had sent messengers to the infidels asking for assistance and announcing that they disowned allegiance to the Mahdi's successor.

Commander Mahmoud had asked the Jaalin to vacate their houses and cross the river to the other side so that the army could quarter in the town. The Ansar were tired and needed some rest and some food. But the people of Metemma refused and disobeyed, and the wrath of God descended on them.

The Ansar raised their spears and attacked the town.

"In God's cause!" Hassan al-Jerifawi shouted from his horse.

The horses galloped though the streets of the town. People were screaming and some of the houses were on fire.

The whistle of bullets and the wailing of the bereaved. Blood coated the walls. Death swaggered down the narrow lanes. The apostates perished, or most of them, and the women of Metemma threw themselves into the Nile to drown and avoid the dishonor of enslavement.

A young girl was running. She was wearing a blue flannel dress that reached her calves.

Hassan's horse caught up with her. It neighed as it stepped on the girl's shadow. He embedded his spear in her back, then lifted her up on the tip. For a moment she fluttered like a deathly banner. Then he tossed her behind him and galloped on.

He left her corpse in the street but he couldn't really put her behind him.

He could no longer sleep. Whenever he closed his eyes, she came to him.

"Please, where's my mother?" she said.

Her eyes were running with blood. Her hair was disheveled. Her lips were cracked by death. Hassan could no longer see Khidr, the prophet of God.

Hassan questioned his faith. "Oh Mahdi of God! Why have you become like the Turks?" he said to himself.

And the little girl kept coming to him and asking, "Is my mother looking for me? Is she crying?"

5

Ordeals come from God, and good health comes from God. Commandments emanate from God and prohibitions are to be obeyed as a way of venerating God.

al-Hallaj

6

The man who came back from Metemma may not have been the same person who went off to fight there.

It was the same body and the same face. The scars that adorned his body from the Mahdi's campaigns were still in place. And the head injury that Hassouna inflicted on him at school with the wooden board was just as it had been. But his spirit felt enchained. Guilt at the deeds he had perpetrated ate at his heart. When he reached home one noontime and threw his bags down against the wall, he was staggering under the spiritual weight. Falling over himself, he walked to his bed and collapsed.

His mud-brick room was dark, with hardly any sunlight. On the floor there was a palm-frond mat he used for praying, with a tin jug next to it. On a low table there were slips of paper with the Mahdi's ritual prayer and sections of the Quran on them.

He closed his eyes and rested his chin on his chest. He saw the girl come into the room, full of reproach for him.

"Leave me alone. Don't come back again," he said.

"But please, where's my mother?" she said.

He choked on his guilt.

He didn't know what had happened to him. It wasn't the first time he had fought. He had waged jihad in God's cause in Gallabat, Bahr al-Ghazal, Senkat, El Obeid, and Khartoum. He had the blood of hundreds of unbelievers on his sword. He used to delight in victory. Inflicting death and destruction was his fondest wish. He had worshipped God with blood for many years. He had reserved his affections for true believers, as God had commanded him to do. Toward his comrades he was submissive and obedient, while against unbelievers he waged relentless war. But on that day he wondered who he had killed.

That old Ethiopian man in Gallabat. He wondered whether his brown-skinned daughters had been able to recover his body and bury him as they wailed? Had anyone mourned him? Had anyone slapped their cheeks and wailed? How did the Amhara mourn their dead? The Shilluk warrior in Bahr al-Ghazal who was as black as the heart of an infidel—did his little fledglings in Gondokoro know that Hassan al-Jerifawi had killed their father? Shame on you, Hassan, for all the women you have widowed.

Shame on you, Hassan, for the people you have left bereaved.

Shame on you, Hassan, for all the people you have saddened or orphaned.

He cried out and slapped his own face. He rolled out of bed and buried his face in the dust. He punched and kicked the ground with his hands and feet.

"What a waste, Hassan! God's curse be upon you, Hassan!"

7

Hassan was on the run.

On the run from himself. He abandoned his faith and his commitment to jihad, the banners stained by the sacred truth, and wandered aimlessly.

His feet drew him back to the school of his master, Sheikh Salman Wad Hamad al-Duwaihi, and to Fatma, the apple of his eye.

The sheikh had died years earlier.

While Hassan was waging jihad against the Abyssinians in the east of the country he met someone who had been with him in the school and who told him that Sheikh Salman had ascended into heaven.

"The day he died his soul recited the Quran to God the Lord of Might three times," his friend said. "Then God Almighty said to him, 'Choose whatever place you like as your abode in Heaven.'"

Some months after his death, mujahideen carrying the banners of the Mahdi destroyed the school and killed some of his pupils and disciples who refused to abandon Sufism and believe in the Mahdi. They took away others of them bound in chains to make them reconsider their heretical beliefs.

The books on Islamic law and Sufism were burned. Sheikh Salman's copy of *Khalil's Mukhtasar* was thrown into the Dinder River.

His feet were burning to get back to those traces that had been obliterated. But his heart was uncomfortable with faith.

No one knew where his beloved Fatma had gone.

It was she who had pushed him to follow the way of God.

"I wouldn't stand between you and God's command," she had said.

He was running away from himself.

He bared his soul to Sheikh Ibrahim Wad al-Shawwak, the mentor who had recommended jihad to him.

"I'm tired of bloodshed, Sheikh," he told him.

"Faith is a test, my son."

"But too much faith is about to lead me to disbelief."

Sheikh Ibrahim was startled. "God forbid, and the Mahdi too!"

Hassan appealed to the sheikh's better nature. "I no longer want jihad, Sheikh."

Sheikh Ibrahim looked the distressed young man up and down. "How about going into business instead? The Prophet favored trade."

And the Mahdi said that merchants were the dogs of the world. But Hassan didn't have the luxury of choosing.

"Save me from myself through worldly things. Save me from faith through worldly things," Hassan said.

"My son, there's no escaping yourself."

But Hassan did escape. He plunged into his new work as an agent in Sheikh Ibrahim's businesses. Jihad no longer bothered him, except when it came to selling grain to the army. And the foreign invasion didn't interest him, except when it came to helping his master prepare to escape.

"Let the infidels come or go," he said. "I don't care now. I'll still make a living from trade, as long as God wants me to."

He no longer had dreams about the prophet Khidr but he did have dreams about Abdel-Rahman bin Awf, the wealthy companion of the Prophet Mohamed, and how he had to enter heaven crawling.

When he and Sheikh Ibrahim escaped from Omdurman, a few hours before the city fell and the Egyptian army came in, he was hoping never to come back to the spot—the land that had once been full of faith and then ended up ravaged by it.

He settled down in al-Musallamiya and was haunted by dreams of marrying again. But in his heart Fatma was stronger than the knot of faith that he had abandoned, so he kept waiting; waiting for nothing in particular.

8

Bakhit Mandil listened to Hassan talking about himself and his dreams. He could see tears glistening in Hassan's eyes. He tried to move his body and the chains clanked. Hassan clicked his tongue, warning him that his colleagues might hear the noise.

"But the Mahdist movement was all good," said Bakhit.

"But what was the Mahdist movement if not our faith?" said Hassan. "If the faith died, the movement died too."

"Isn't love faith?"

"Did you love the Mahdi?"

Bakhit thought awhile. "I love Hawa," he said finally.

"One day, on a day whose time has not yet come," said Hassan, "those of us who survive will sit down to ask ourselves how we escaped all this faith, and we'll be surprised that we didn't perish under the piles of certainty that rained down on top of us."

"I didn't escape."

They fell silent. Hassan al-Jerifawi looked at the ground at his feet. The red dust. And the sound of the river wearing away the bank nearby.

"I'm tired, Bakhit."

Bakhit caught sight of the light in the distance.

She's coming. She had come again to flirt with his desire. How he missed her!

"Me too, but when were we not tired?" said Bakhit.

"What's it like to kill for revenge, Bakhit?"

"It's life, like love . . . maybe more pleasant."

Hassan looked at him. He looked where Bakhit was looking, but he couldn't see anything.

"If I took you into al-Musallamiya, you'd be a dead man," Hassan said dejectedly.

The smell of her wrapped itself around him. She was standing behind Hassan with her eternal light. He could smell the musk. In her eyes he could see her enduring sadness.

Then he remembered that he had already died, when she died. He had blood on his hands and she was in his heart.

"Can I make a last request?"

Hassan suddenly remembered his old dream of the prophet Khidr leading him by the hand in a Sufi procession. Khidr made him stop at the Nile and showed him some red soil in his fist.

"Are you certain you're going to die?" asked Hassan.

"I've been dead for years," said Bakhit. "But there's a debt I have to repay. So if you'll accept my request, then please send my regards to a woman in Omdurman called Merisila. Tell her how I was killed. Tell her I fulfilled my debt to Hawa as far as I could, but Younis was saved by Him who saved his namesake, Younis, or Jonah, from the whale."

"Younis!"

"Just tell her that and she'll understand. Just as I now know that Hawa protected him from me. I now know that everything I did for her was nothing in comparison with her happiness at receiving the first sparrow he gave her, so she protected him from me. He was at my mercy and he didn't die. I tracked down all my enemies and left him till last, although my feud was really with him and no one else. And now I'm breaking off my journey under duress. Let him remain alive, with everything he has done, both good and evil."

"I will."

"And my notebook. If you can bury it with me, then do so."

"Don't you want to escape?"

"What I've done is enough. I'm like you and more. I'm tired. Now I only want to meet her."

As Bakhit spoke he was looking at her. On her face there was a pain that was unmistakable. She was standing behind Hassan with her hands hanging by her sides. She was unable to speak. Everything he had tried was in vain. All his love was in vain. But he didn't have it in him to renounce her.

At the moment when you understand everything, you know it's the moment of death. Like the transcendental vision that sweeps a drowning man as he gasps his last breath. At the moment of death comes the truth. There are no longer any delusions, no hopes to confuse you. You see everything as it is, not as you would like it to be.

Hassan al-Jerifawi rose. He brushed the red soil from his cloak.

"Tomorrow we'll take you into al-Musallamiya and let God decide your fate," he said.

Bakhit moved away, exhausted, and she advanced toward him. She stood in front of him.

"I asked you to live, Bakhit, but you refused," she said.

"I couldn't do it, Hawa."

"Your only mistake was me. If it wasn't for me, you would have lived another life," she said.

"I've lived many lives, Hawa. More than I can bear. Maybe I haven't lived very long, but I've lived a lot. And I never found a life that was sweeter than the one that was you. If only you had loved me. But I don't blame you. In one of the lives I have lived I learned that love is like fate. You have no control over it."

She said nothing, but looked at him sadly. Her light filled the world. Even the stars could smell her scent.

I'm coming, Hawa.

At last.

Maybe I know now what I didn't know before. Maybe I'm justifying to myself my tiredness and my impatience for the end.

But I don't care. I'm tired.

In a few hours they will hang me on their gallows. Only the noose stands between me and meeting you.

Don't be sad. Once we meet we will never be parted again.

I'm on my way. At last.

9

Longing diminishes through being together, and if it does persist in spite of being together it is because imagining the possibility of separation prolongs it. Many a wretch has asked for relief from the pain, but we have always told them that not all difficulties in life can be relieved. This is merely one of the characteristics of love, for love is a malady that is buried deep in our hearts.

Ibn Arabi

Selected Hoopoe Titles

No Knives in the Kitchens of this City
by Khaled Khalifa, translated by Leri Price

Otared
by Mohammad Rabie, translated by Robin Moger

Time of White Horses
by Ibrahim Nasrallah, translated by Nancy Roberts

✱

hoopoe is an imprint for engaged, open-minded readers hungry for outstanding fiction that challenges headlines, re-imagines histories, and celebrates original storytelling.

Through elegant paperback and digital editions, **hoopoe** champions bold, contemporary writers from across the Middle East alongside some of the finest, groundbreaking authors of earlier generations.

At hoopoefiction.com, curious and adventurous readers from around the world will find new writing, interviews, and criticism from our authors, translators, and editors.